MW00990154

A Forced Marriage with an Unbridled Lady

A Clean Regency Romance Novel

Emily Barnet

Table of Contents

Chapter 1

The wind whistled through Hannah's honey-blonde hair, driving icily into her face as she rode. She clung to the reins, heart pounding and soul soaring with exhilaration. Screaming with joy as she galloped across the field on Sapphire's back, she barely noticed that her spine ached or that her face was cold in the icy spring air. She laughed as they leapt over the fence and thumped down into the field beyond.

"Go, Sapphire!" she called out, her voice high and bright. "Go, go!"

Sapphire must have heard her joy because she set back her ears and then thundered forward, increasing speed from a canter to a gallop. Hannah shut her blue eyes for a moment, terrified and elated as they pounded up the path.

"Easy, girl. Easy, there."

The feeling of fear wore off instantly and she leaned back a little, adjusting her weight in the saddle as she'd learned when she was just four and riding her first pony. As she had hoped, Sapphire felt the shift in her weight and slowed a bit, moving first to a canter and then into a trot. Hannah looked around, starting to notice her surroundings again. Before her, dense green woodland whispered, and on either side, they were surrounded by green grass, edged with a sturdy fence. They were high up in Farmer Atwood's field, two or three miles from her home at Grassdale Estate. She noted the dense woodland up ahead and felt a shiver.

"We should go back."

It wasn't just the inhospitable look of the woods; it was the thought of being late and displeasing Mother. Mother was already upset because she had stormed off to go riding, and it didn't do any good to anger her any further.

Sapphire turned, ears swiveling, and Hannah smiled. Her horse was listening to her. They had been companions since Sapphire was just a year old, the best gift and the closest friend a sixteen-year-old girl like Hannah could have imagined. Now, three years later, Sapphire was a beautiful young mare and Hannah, at nineteen, was withering under growing expectations thrust on her by her mother.

You must make a good catch at this Season, Mother always said. *We're relying on you to raise this family's status.*

Her mind went back to breakfast that morning, when she'd argued with Mother.

"You don't even make an effort to be an educated young lady! Why! You don't even read the *Gazette*. How will you make conversation with anyone?"

Hannah had made a face. Her mother meant the *Ladies' Gazette*, and having read it once was all Hannah needed to tell her she wasn't interested. If educated young ladies liked reading about fashion advice and housekeeping, they could keep it. She would rather read about riding.

"Mother," she complained. "We go to balls to dance. Not to talk about fashion."

"Yes! And you don't dance enough. Your dance card should be full by the start of the evening. You're not making an effort, like I said."

"Mother..." Hannah bit her lip in frustration.

"And don't make faces! It's most unseemly. What do you think? That educated young ladies grimace?"

"Please," Hannah whispered. "I can't bear much more of this." Every time they sat anywhere Mother would start. She'd been doing this constantly since the announcement a week ago that they would spend the Season at the townhouse in London.

"Your mother is concerned for you," Edward said thinly. His long, smooth face barely looked up from the newspaper.

"Is *that* why she wants me to be a fine lady?" Hannah challenged her brother. "Because of concern? Nothing to do with raising the status of the family?"

"I'm reading the paper. I don't want to get involved in this." He glared at her. "And don't talk back."

"*What*?" Hannah exclaimed. Edward was only older than her by four years—he had no right to talk to her like that. She felt her cheeks redden with indignation, but Mama shouted first.

"Don't raise your voice! How can you be a lady if you shout?"

"I'm not a lady," Hannah murmured, the two of them wearing her down to the point of tears. "And I beg to be excused."

She pushed back her chair and strode from the room,

keeping her back straight and dignified. She could hear her mother and Edward yelling after her, but she didn't turn around. She hurried to her bedroom and changed into her riding clothes, then ran to Sapphire's stall in the stable.

She sighed, tucking a strand of dark blonde hair back from her face where it escaped its confines. All she had ever wanted to do was ride.

She looked around. Their family was vastly wealthy: Papa had purchased landholdings to rival those of many noblemen, and their house, Grassdale, was the most beautiful place she could imagine, recently redecorated entirely by a leading architect. But still, her mother seemed discontented. A title was what Mother craved. Papa had made vast wealth in his lifetime, but he was ordinary Mr. Darlington; an industrialist, striking it rich with innovations and factories. Mother longed to be like the people they mingled with at Almack's Assembly in London—noble and rich, instead of just rich.

Hannah looked down sadly at her hands where she held the reins. Her fingernails were torn from tacking up and grooming her horse, a little dirt streaked on her skin from where she'd touched the fresh-oiled tack in the stable. She had freckles on her pert nose and sometimes in summer she was even a little sun-darkened. She was no lady, and she had no wish to be. Papa had known that. He had understood that all that mattered to her was riding.

"We should go back," she told Sapphire sadly. "But let's take the long road. We don't have to rush." The rebellious thought made her grin.

She heard her horse make a huff of assent and she felt her spirits lift. She had always believed Sapphire understood every word, and the longer they associated, the more convinced she was that Sapphire really did—or she had to, since now she was setting her feet towards the path.

Hannah looked around as they rode, her head filled with wild plans to escape.

"Maybe we should just ride to London, just you and me," she told Sapphire with a small smile.

She would turn up at an inn with Sapphire, disguised as a boy, and rent lodgings with her allowance. She would try to find work as a tutor and save enough money to buy them somewhere to stay.

Her heart twisted with the knowledge that she couldn't really do it. The roads were far too dangerous. Even if she disguised herself as a man, they might not reach London, and there the chances of her getting employment were slim.

Mayhap I can pretend I'm sick.

It was another wild plan, but this one seemed more rational. Margaret, the daughter of the local apothecary in Oakwood village, could help her. Margaret knew so much about illness and cures that she could come up with some convincing pretense for Hannah to escape the trip to London. She hadn't seen her in a long time, and she felt a twist of guilt in her chest. She ought to drop in and visit her.

"Come on, then," she murmured gently to Sapphire.

She leaned forward, increasing their speed. They would have to hurry. Mother would already be enraged because Hannah was missing morning tea and defying her was all very well, but it would mean that she would need a strong stomach to put up with the yells and shouts.

"Whoa! No!" Hannah screamed as something flapped in the woods.

Sapphire reared up and then bolted.

Sapphire was a wonderful horse, spirited and lively, but she was prone to spooking, especially if she saw something move suddenly. Hannah gritted her teeth, trying to hang on. Her hands sweating, she shut her eyes for a moment. They raced on.

"Sapphire! Stop. Please, stop."

Sapphire's muscles bunched with running. She didn't seem to be tiring—she seemed, rather, to be becoming more afraid. Hannah gritted her teeth. Her dark thoughts had likely troubled her horse, making her skittish. She screamed aloud as Sapphire reared.

"No!"

Hannah fell backwards and landed with a solid thump on the ground. Her vision faded for a moment as pain shot up her spine. She lay there, too tired, sore and frightened to move.

She heard footsteps and she managed to open her eyes just as Sapphire bent down to shove at her with her nose. Hannah gazed up at her, love flooding her heart as the horse shoved at her again, her brown eyes wide in confusion.

"Shh, Sapphire. It's all right," Hannah told her gently. She felt a stab of warmth and guilt in her heart—Sapphire was obviously concerned, thinking she'd killed Hannah. She managed to make herself sit up and Sapphire huffed a small neigh that seemed to indicate she was relieved. Hannah smiled at her, even as pain thudded through her head, making her dizzy. She wasn't angry with Sapphire—she had done what horses do.

Slowly, painfully, she managed to stand up, looking down at her dress sorrowfully. She was covered in dirt. The brown velvet of her riding-dress was caked with mud on the back and front, and she had mud smeared on her hands.

Imagine going to London like this.

She had to grin at a thought that was so bizarre, and then she started laughing. The sound startled Sapphire, who huffed in surprise and Hannah stroked her nose gently.

"Come on, you dear," she said gently. "Let's visit Margaret."

Mayhap her friend had clothes to borrow, or at least water to wash her dirty face and hands.

The village appeared slowly as they walked—the church spire first, then the cluster of little houses as they descended lower. There were only twenty or thirty houses in Oakwood, and a church, bakery, and apothecary's shop. The roofs of the cottages were thatched, the walls whitewashed. Apple trees grew in some of the gardens, the buds white and beautiful against the dark wood. Hannah walked up the cobbled street, breathing in the scent of rain, hay, wood-smoke and damp earth that was the smell of the village. The apothecary's shop was in the center of town, and they arrived at teatime exactly—nobody was in the village square, and they walked past silently, glad to avoid critical gazes.

Cottages with pretty gardens lined cobbled streets, the fragrance of blossom in the air. When they reached the shop she knocked firmly at the door, holding her breath, nervously. She heard footsteps, and the door opened, revealing Margaret's father, Mr. Blackwood, a short, solid man with broad shoulders and a big grin. He raised a brow at them in surprise, then chuckled.

"Miss Darlington!" He greeted her warmly. "Come in! We've not seen you in the shop for months. I'll see where Margaret is, if you like. I'm sure she'll have already heard your horse and be running to the door. She's always so pleased by your visits."

Hannah thanked him and waited for her friend to arrive, her eyes moving, intrigued, across the garden. Tall foxgloves grew at the back, their pink-tinged blooms beautiful and showy. Closer to the gate, rosemary bloomed, and lavender scented the air, its blossom drawing bees that buzzed lazily about the garden. Little plants of thyme grew in one flowerbed, the strong, clean scent piercing in the cold morning dew. Hannah let her gaze wander, identifying the many plants that she recognized. Margaret had been a good tutor.

Hannah looked up as she heard Margaret call out to her.

"Hannah! You're here! How grand!"

Hannah held her close, smelling the scent of exotic herbs that seemed to cling to her from work, no matter what else she did.

"How wonderful to see you," she said softly, stepping back to gaze at her. Margaret grinned impishly, her heart-shaped face flooded with warmth. Hannah grinned back.

"I was busy preparing the Gum Arabic for one of Father's pastes," Margaret explained, dusting hands that were covered in white dust.

"Can I see what you're making?" she asked with interest, following Margaret into the shop. Margaret laughed.

"Of course! You can help, too, if you have time." She glanced at Hannah and her bright smile shifted into a frown of concern. "You seem troubled."

"I must hurry," Hannah answered, though she felt sure that her tension was plain to see. "I did want to ask you a favour," she added as they went through to the workroom. She breathed in the familiar scent of spice and incense and wished that she could stay there all day and help Margaret in her work.

"Anything! Of course, you only have to ask," Margaret answered at once. "What happened to your hands?" Her voice was aghast as she looked down at Hannah's bleeding palm in the brighter light of the little workroom.

"I fell off my horse," Hannah confided. Margaret knew she was an excellent rider and so she did not feel embarrassed to say it. "I cut my hands. And I also got dirty," she added, glancing down at her velvet gown, torn and dirtied as it was.

"Let me see to your hands," Margaret stated at once,

reaching for a small linen towel, which she dipped into a bowl of water on a high wooden table. "And you can brush the dirt off that dress...I'm sure it'll clean up nicely. I've got a shawl you can borrow to hide the tear until you ride home," she added swiftly, noticing the tear in the neck which made the gown a little more low-cut than it ought to be. Hannah smiled.

"Thank you, Margaret," she breathed thankfully as her friend washed her hand with the damp towel. The relief from the stinging ache of the scratches was considerable.

"No trouble," Margaret answered at once. "Now, I have an ointment to put on those. You must take a pot of it with you. And then I'll go up and find that shawl. You don't need to worry about anyone in the village seeing—they're all either having tea or out working in the fields."

"Thank you," Hannah repeated appreciatively.

Margaret rubbed a greenish paste that smelled of pine into her hands, then handed her the little container of it to put in her purse and went upstairs, returning with the shawl of brown linen.

"Thank you so much Margaret. Do I look all right?" Hannah asked swiftly as she brushed her dress with the clothes-brush Margaret brought for her, then wrapped the shawl around her.

"Of course," Margaret said gently. "I told you that velvet would clean up," she added with a smile. "Though you won't be wearing that in London—I suppose it's all balls and parties in the city." Her eyes were bright and shining.

Hannah bit her lip. "Yes. Though they'll be no fun at all without you."

Margaret smiled. "You'll have all manner of fun. And there are far more handsome men in London than here."

"Margaret!" Hannah giggled. Margaret always lifted her spirits.

"It's true," her friend said with a laugh. "I'm sure you'll meet dozens of them. And dance every night. And maybe even ride sometimes."

Hannah smiled fondly at her. Her friend was just trying to cheer her up, she knew. Margaret knew how she felt about London and balls. And eligible men. "I hope I can ride. But I'll look shameful for London," she added, lifting her hand to her cheek where the scratch was.

"It's just a bit of dirt," Margaret said, touching the shoulder of her gown where a bit of mud still clung. "No-one can reproach you for that."

Hannah felt a pain in her chest. Margaret was so sweet—it would never even occur to her to think that someone could be angry with their daughter for a scratch on their cheek. She took her hand in her own. "I appreciate it, truly I do. I hope I can call on you as soon as we return from London."

"I look forward to seeing you," Margaret replied fondly.

Hannah mounted up, feeling awkward with the shawl knotted around her shoulders. She lifted a hand from the reins to wave to Margaret, and then turned her horse in the drive, riding to the gate she'd opened earlier. She jumped down to close it, even as Margaret ran up to do so, waving to her fondly.

As she rode back towards the manor, her mood shifted from delight to fear. She knew Mother would be furious when she saw the dirt and the scratch, even though she'd done her best to hide it. As soon as she rode near the stables, she started planning the best route for sneaking back up to her room, but she saw her brother's wife, Philipa, standing in the drive.

"Hannah! You're late!" Philipa reproached her instantly, her thin, pretty face tense and angry. "You almost missed tea. Where, may I ask, have you been?"

"I was riding," Hannah said swiftly, slipping out of the saddle and standing close to Sapphire, her place of safety.

"You were out riding by yourself? Unaccompanied? That's most unseemly," Philipa replied, though her voice wasn't even raised, now, just frankly disinterested. "And you'll get sunburned, too." She sniffed in distaste.

"I went up to the farmland. Not the village," Hannah explained. That was partly true. "So, nobody would see me." She didn't add that there was no sun to burn her, but an incredulous look at Philipa must have conveyed her meaning.

"Oh." Philipa sniffed again. "Well, it's *still* unseemly. Most unnatural pastime for a girl. You lack proficiency in both sewing and playing the pianoforte, yet you choose to spend your days frolicking about like a hoyden." She turned around and walked back towards the house. "Your mother wondered where you were."

"I'll come in a moment," Hannah told her quickly, ignoring the insult, and darted into the stable. "I just have to groom Sapphire quickly."

"Can't you let the groom do that?" Philipa demanded. "You spend too much time in the stables. People will think you're a hoyden."

Hannah glared at Philipa, but she was already returning towards the house, her blonde hair in its elegant chignon pale against the green of the estate around them.

Hannah led Sapphire into her stall and removed her saddle and bridle, then pressed her face against her horse's neck and cried. She hadn't shown it in front of Philipa, but her words had cut deep into her heart.

"Why can't they just accept me for who I am?" she asked Sapphire quietly. A soft neigh was her answer, and a nuzzle at Hannah's neck that made her cry. Sapphire accepted her utterly. And that was enough. It had to be.

She winced and reached for the brush and combed Sapphire's mane, wishing for the thousandth time that she could stay in the countryside and not travel with the family to London the next day.

Chapter 2

The wind buffeted Maxwell's face when he stopped on the ridge. He stared out over the distant cliffs, narrowing his dark eyes and breathing deeply, drawing air into his lungs. The unfamiliar scent of grass and wet earth smelt strange, and he wrinkled his long, elegant nose. He'd only been on the ship for three days, yet already it seemed a real change to be on land once again. His legs ached, and his head spun with the sudden transition from the shifting deck to firm ground again.

One good thing about being an earl, he thought thankfully, *is being able to afford good passage on a decent boat.*

It seemed the only good thing, given that he'd inherited the title so recently. It was that sudden inheritance that had him speeding across the countryside in the late evening, heading from Dover to Carronwood Manor. He stared ahead, running a hand briefly over his dark hair, a habit when he was thinking.

"How do you feel about riding on?" He called out to Gavin, his companion and cousin, who rode a little ahead. Gavin turned, making a disgruntled face, his chestnut hair bright in the late afternoon sunshine.

"I feel like lying down in that field and sleeping until a hundred years pass." Gavin told him with a grin. "But if you insist, we can ride onward. I suppose it's better to find somewhere to sleep that isn't a field."

"You might say so," Maxwell answered, his thin lips twisting into a grin. "Fields are not the best place to lay one's head. You're liable to wake up without boots on at the very least nowadays." The crime along the London road had increased and the thought of an attack by footpads or other brigands was constantly present in his mind.

"They can have them. You have any idea how bad these boots of mine smell?" Gavin asked.

"Yes."

They both laughed.

Carronwood, Maxwell's estate, was three days' ride east from London. Maxwell looked around; brow lowered in confusion. He'd been in Spain for three years, and England was at once alien and familiar. The English weather was still cool and refreshing, and the grass was still emerald green on the coast, the high cliffs still imposing and beautiful. The people at once seemed friendly and familiar and maddening for their familiarity. England was just the same as it was.

He had changed.

When he had left England three years earlier, he was twenty-two, and he had lived in a different world. He had been young and reckless, and Father was living.

Now, he was five-and-twenty, and he had seen much of the world, and Father had passed away. The world was not as it had been, and Maxwell felt out of place in the familiar scene.

Gavin had surpassed him, Maxwell falling behind as he pondered. Leaning forward, Maxwell urged his steed to quicken its pace, clicking his tongue in encouragement. His tall, dark stallion bunched his legs to increase the pace and they cantered across the grass, drawing up alongside Gavin.

His head pounded, confusion and dizziness pressing in equally. The shock of the news of Father's passing had numbed him, and he'd slept deeply on the ship; it was only now that they were in England that he was starting to feel more than a dull ache inside.

Gavin had slowed, stopping to admire the view. Maxwell cantered ahead, and Gavin hurried to catch him. In Spain, during their stay, they had raced often; both of them taking delight in equestrian sports. It was, after all, why they were there.

Maxwell was pursuing his dream of becoming an expert horse-breeder. Gavin was there because he, too, had an interest and because they'd been friends all their lives, since they were just three.

"I'll get you!" Gavin yelled teasingly, catching up on Maxwell's left-hand side.

"That's all very well. But you haven't yet," Maxwell replied jokingly.

Maxwell's black thoroughbred strode easily ahead, with Gavin's smaller, half-Arab stallion bunching his muscles and racing to meet the challenge. The two gentlemen sped over the landscape, coat-tails flying. Maxwell's thick dark hair was almost the color of his mount, while Gavin's was a richer, darker red than that of his fiery stallion. They raced across the landscape, two shadows moving swiftly over the grass in the darkening evening.

Maxwell looked around as fields and trees flashed past, gripping with his knees as he'd learned when he was a child. He had always loved riding, but horses themselves—their power and grace—had captured his spirit.

And just as I decided to start a horse farm, I had to become the earl.

He shrugged. He was not going to let that be negative, even though it might feel so. There were definite benefits to owning the estate and land, and having inherited money meant that, at least in theory, he could begin farming horses in England. Whether he would actually be able to do it or whether the pressure of society and his duties would render that unlikely, he didn't know.

"There's that farm where they make good bread," Gavin commented as a low building with a sun-bleached thatched roof came into view ahead of them. "You are sure that you think we should continue down the road?"

"I think we should stop at the other inn," Maxwell agreed. He was determined to make the journey as swiftly as possible. Mama had a sickly constitution, and news of Father's passing might have worsened it. He needed to reach her.

I haven't been a good son, Maxwell thought sadly.

He recalled his mother—pale and thin, her eyes red from tears as she waved to him—and guilt twisted in his heart. He needed to reach her as fast as he could, and that meant riding the ten miles this afternoon, even if he would much rather have stopped to sleep.

It wasn't my choice to leave then, he reminded himself sadly. *I had to.*

"Are you going to go to London this year?" Gavin called out as they rode side-by-side.

Maxwell turned to give him a confused frown. "No. Why should I?" he asked neutrally.

"Well, London has what the countryside hasn't. Lots of girls." Gavin grinned.

Maxwell glared at him. "Gavin, you know I've no interest in the soulless bartering-market that is the London Season." He felt his heart twist.

14

Father had tried to force him into a loveless match—it was one of the reasons he'd left England. It was, in fact, what prompted his departure a year before he'd planned it. He'd hoped to attend Cambridge for another year and complete his law studies. But Father's insistence had led him to flee, all thoughts of the law forgotten.

He shuddered. The last thing he wanted was to show his face in London at the time of year when dowagers would be hunting for eligible suitors for their debutante relatives.

He rode on in silence.

"Sorry, old chap." Gavin sounded like he felt guilty.

"No trouble," Maxwell said formally. He drew a breath. Gavin was who he was. He had a different outlook on life to Maxwell, who was more serious and contemplative.

He smiled at Gavin and Gavin grinned back. In a second, Gavin was cantering off again and Maxwell leaned forward, letting Nightfire do the job of racing to catch him.

They caught up quickly.

He leaned back in the saddle, allowing Nightfire's pace to slow, and they settled into a walk as Gavin drew up alongside. He appreciated Sunshine, Gavin's horse, as much as his own. They had both come with them from Spain and were eager for exercise after three days on the ship. By the time they reached the inn, the horses would be exhausted, using the excess energy too fast, but he couldn't wait. He had to reach Mama.

He shut his dark eyes, trying not to think of her, especially not of how ill she could be.

"Gavin...I owe you two pounds," he commented as they rode ahead.

"You do?"

"Yes. I bet that we'd both be sick on the journey over, and we weren't."

"I was," Gavin argued, then grinned. "But, since you owe me two pounds, I'll forget that."

Maxwell laughed. "Very well. I'll pay for our stay at the inn. Then we can consider the debt cleared."

"Maxwell...you can't do that," Gavin protested, but Maxwell inclined his head.

"I want to," he said firmly.

"Well, I'm not about to refuse staying there without the inconvenience of having to pay."

They chuckled.

The landscape changed, becoming wilder with longer grass and more trees and hills. The distance stretched and Maxwell felt his spine jarring and his vision blurring.

I really am tired.

He felt himself falling asleep in the saddle, his legs gripping the horse and his hands tightening on the reins without him needing to think, even as he swayed, and his head drooped forward to his chest. "What...?" he murmured, shaking himself. He opened his eyes, looking around. The sky was darker now, the sunshine low on the horizon and the early blue of dusk tinging the edges. They must have been riding for three hours. He recognized the countryside. They were almost at the White Crown. "Just a few minutes before we can get to bed," he commented, riding beside Gavin, who grinned.

"I'm asleep, as I said. This is all some figment of my fevered imaginings."

They were both laughing as they rode into the inn yard.

Maxwell dismounted lithely and winced as he landed on his booted feet.

"Look at me," Gavin chuckled, slipping out of the saddle and catching onto the gatepost to steady himself as he almost fell, his legs still wobbly from the recent sea-journey. "Anyone is going to think we stopped off at the brewery and drank their stock before riding here."

"We don't smell like it," Maxwell said, breathing in. "We smell like we've been marching in the tropics for days." He felt awkwardly aware of his sweat-stained clothing. Gavin laughed.

"I suppose you're right."

"Let's go in," Maxwell answered, his feet sore and swollen from the long time in the saddle. "Perhaps they have hot water."

"A bath. Heavenly."

Maxwell was laughing as they staggered up the few stairs to the door, paying the groom on their way in to take very good care of their horses.

"We'd like two of your best rooms, please, and a meal tonight and tomorrow," Maxwell requested briskly as the innkeeper came into the entrance-way. "And care for our horses. Oh, yes. And a bath if you can provide that." He added. He took out his wallet. One positive thing was that he now had money to spend lavishly, and right now their needs were not complicated. Food, a bath, and the best accommodation they could get.

The innkeeper wrote their names into the book and widened his gaze at the coin Maxwell passed him.

"Thank you, my lord."

Maxwell inclined his head politely and accepted the keys he was passed in turn, then he glanced at the stairs. It seemed darker here, with less sunshine compared to Spain. It was springtime here, but in Spain it already felt more like summertime. He stepped up the staircase, which was dark with the onset of evening, barely awake enough to climb.

"Must be these ones," Maxwell murmured on reaching the second floor. The innkeeper had given them two keys for rooms there. There were only two doors on the second floor. The inn was not particularly large—there were three floors, four including the uppermost one in the roof-space. Each floor had two or three rooms, and he guessed the inn could host no more than fifteen guests at any time.

He was about to open the door when he heard two female voices, one of them raised in annoyance.

"And the best rooms already taken! I will *not* stand for it. I might not be titled, but our family is one of the wealthiest in London."

Another woman answered, voice high and indignant as she agreed. "Quite so. Most shocking. Most shocking."

Maxwell winced. Gavin and he himself had taken the best rooms, clearly cheating these ladies of their desired accommodation. They might be angry, but that was how inns worked—they could only provide the first customers with the best. He felt a little guilty, but reminded himself that he didn't exactly have a choice. There were only two good rooms, and they had them.

The woman was speaking again, getting closer.

"And the way that innkeeper spoke to me! I...oh."

The woman's voice paused as she stopped on the landing, and Maxwell blinked as he found himself face-to-face with two

17

ladies and a tall man with a long, disinterested face. He could just make out a fourth head of blonde hair behind the women, but whoever it was—woman or boy—he couldn't see; they were too short to appear over the heads of the people in front.

"We need to pass," the younger woman—slim, with pale blonde hair and hazel eyes—demanded. Her voice was hard and haughty.

"Madam, this landing is very small," Maxwell stated politely. "If you give me a moment, I will open my door and go in, and then you may all pass more easily." He took out his key and inserted it in the lock.

"The nerve! Arguing with us," the older woman began. She was also slim, with golden hair that was tightly ringleted about her face, the top of it covered with the briefest of widow's caps. Her eyes were blue and angry as she glared at him.

Maxwell wanted to protest—he had not argued. But one look at the woman's cold stare told him to get away fast. He unlocked the door and stepped into the room.

He chuckled to himself as Gavin retreated swiftly, shutting the door on the party of people who marched past angrily.

He sat down on his bed, exhausted. He'd been travelling for so long. He allowed himself to rest for a moment, then tensed again. He had forgotten to ask the stable hand to check Nightfire's front leg where he had strained the tendon. He had to go down to the stables to remind him, or see to it himself.

"I hope that bath is ready when I return," he muttered. He buttoned his riding-coat and marched out. The horses were the one thing that mattered in this changed world, besides his Mama. He stumbled down towards the stables to check on Nightfire, already swaying and drowsy and longing for a nice warm bed where he could fall asleep.

Chapter 3

The distant sound of people talking and laughing in the taproom filled Hannah's ears as she tiptoed into the hallway of the inn. Her head was pounding with an ache like a band tightening around her brain. The coach trip to the White Crown had lasted but six hours, but it had worn on her nerves to the point that, if she didn't escape outdoors, she feared that she would lose her wits. Mother hadn't stopped reprimanding her all the way from the house.

Her ruined riding-dress and the scratches on her face and hands were mentioned, as was the fact that she had chosen a white dress to wear for the coach-trip—utterly foolish, Mother said, since it would be travel-stained when they arrived at the inn, and what if someone saw?

Nothing Hannah did was right, from the way she drank her tea to the way she sat in the coach, and the pain of being constantly criticized was like an ache in her heart.

Hannah tiptoed onwards down the dark, winding wooden stairs, sneaking past Mother's room to the entrance. Her head pounded and her heart raced with confusion and fear. She reached the foot of the stairs and leaned back against the wall; head spinning, fingers gripping the door handle for a moment so that she could stay standing. The headache got worse as she recalled the constant reprimanding she'd received from Mother.

I can't be that bad.

If she was to believe her mother, she was the worst creature that ever walked the earth—inconsiderate, cruel, foolish, headstrong and thoughtless. She felt her soul cringe with shame as she remembered the words that her mother had spat at her. Each word made her feel ashamed of herself. Philipa agreed with Mother on everything, as usual, and Edward didn't say anything, but he didn't defend her; just sat there looking annoyed and staring out of the coach window as if they were all a great bother to him.

Footsteps sounded in the hallway behind her, and Hannah shoved the door open in haste and fear. Mother's constant criticism made her feel as though anybody who saw her would hate her on sight. The cold air outdoors hit her, and she leaned back against the front of the building for a moment, taking a breath of cold air. Outside, the sky was low and dark with rain-clouds. The air smelled damp and the dirt path was muddy. She gazed down at her boots, which were white like the dress, and stepped sideways to walk where there was paving, rather than risking walking through the mud. She didn't want to do anything else that would earn Mother's ire.

She stopped again at the gate of the inn yard. The inn was built on slightly higher ground than the surrounding countryside, and she could see out over fields and farms, across to distant woodland. She felt her head pound as she stood there, squinting out at the trees and the rainy landscape, and wished that Margaret was there to offer her some remedy.

And not just medicine for the headache, she thought sadly. *Margaret is always at least kind.*

She shuddered with cold. She'd walked out of the inn without even thinking of her cloak. She shuddered, drawing a breath of cold, fresh air, but as she breathed in, she smelled a familiar smell.

The smell of a stable.

Something sparkled inside her; some light she had thought that Mother had entirely extinguished, and just for a moment, she remembered that she wasn't unlovable. Sapphire, at least, loved her. Sapphire was stabled at Grassdale Manor, but the coach-horses were in the inn stable, four beautiful gray ones, and Hannah decided to go and find them.

It would do her good to spend time with them.

She hurried across the yard, careful to avoid stepping in the mud in her white boots. The door to the stables was opposite her; a dark opening in the long, low stone building with a high, sloped roof. The smell of horses—a warm mix of sweat and hay—reached her as she ducked inside.

"Shh. Easy," she murmured, hearing the neighing of a horse as soon as she entered. The horses didn't sound panicked, and she felt her lips lift. Probably whoever fed them came in at this time each day.

She looked around, her eyes adjusting to the gloom inside, and spotted a black horse with a white blaze on his brow. He was looking at her with a mix of annoyance and boredom, his nostrils flaring a little as he caught her scent. She liked the look of him instantly.

"Sorry, old chap," she murmured, holding out her hand so he could sniff it. "I didn't bring any food for you. I'm sure whoever feeds you will be along any moment."

The horse laid back his ears as she talked, and she stood very still. She was not afraid of horses, but she knew stallions could be flighty and the chances of him biting her were not impossible.

"Easy, old fellow," she said gently, though the horse didn't look particularly old; he was quite young, not more than four years old, if the fine coat and the sparkle in his eye were anything to judge from. Her eyes became more accustomed to the darkness, and she stared at the stallion, impressed by his beauty. He had a small, fine-boned face and the slight flare of his nostrils suggested an Arab lineage, though he was too big to be pure Arab.

"Whoa," she said softly as he snaked his head forward, but he hadn't meant to bite; rather, he was sniffing her palm. She felt the softness of his nose, a velvet-soft touch on her hand and her own tears fell on her cheek. He didn't think she was disgraceful or disgusting. He accepted her.

"You're so lovely. Look at you," she murmured as he smelled her hand, then lifted his head to look at her. She could see from the set of his ears that he had relaxed, and she smiled warmly.

He huffed again.

"Aren't you a fine fellow?" she asked, feeling more confident. The sound of footsteps on stone made her turn sharply around, but she saw nobody. She shivered, thinking it was Edward coming to find her, but nobody appeared and she ignored it, lifting her hand to scratch the horse's nose.

"Hey, boy. You're a fine fellow, aren't you?" she said softly, reaching to stroke him. As she did, she heard something from the doorway.

"What do you think you're doing? That's my horse!"

Hannah jerked her hand away instantly, pure terror rippling through her. She tried to think of some way to explain she meant no harm, but words wouldn't come. Her vision darkened as the ache in her head pressed in, blinding her. She stumbled and slipped, shrieking in alarm as she plummeted to the floor.

The floor was dirty, just hard-packed earth, and her only thought as she reached out desperately to stop herself falling was that her dress would be filthy, and Mother would never stop shouting at her.

She felt strong arms tighten around her just before she fell full-length on the muddy stable floor.

Hannah cried out in alarm, tense with fear and surprise.

She was held tight to a man's chest. His arms were firm around her, and she could feel his soft shirt against her face. His body was warm, his arms strong, and the chest against which she was held felt muscled through the thin fabric of his shirt. She could smell a strong smell of leather and a musk-like scent that she couldn't identify but that made her senses swoon. She gazed up at the man.

He was taller than her by a head, and he had a thin face with prominent cheekbones, a long nose, and a fine, firm chin. It was a stern, thin-lipped face, with chiseled edges and firm lines, and she wouldn't normally have found such a face handsome, but when she looked into his brown eyes, she almost gasped and had to admit silently that they were the most beautiful eyes she'd ever seen. They were very dark and seemed almost wary like the eyes of a startled creature. They were fringed with thick lashes and bracketed with slight wrinkles from the sunshine. She felt her heart thump as she stared up into them. She wasn't frightened anymore.

"You fell," the man murmured. His brow lowering. He didn't look angry but concerned.

"Yes. You caught me," Hannah whispered back.

She bit her lip, wishing she could think of something eloquent to say, some way to explain how grateful she was that she hadn't landed in the dirt and got stained with mud. She couldn't imagine what might be an appropriate answer, and she was still thinking about it, when she heard a yell from the doorway and the man tensed. Hannah felt her head pound with sheer terror as she recognized the voice.

"What are you doing? That's my daughter you're holding there! Unhand her at once, you scoundrel!"

Chapter 4

The sound of the woman's voice, strident and enraged, rang out like a slap, and Maxwell stood very still. He recognized the voice at once...it was the woman on the landing who he'd seen just minutes ago. His attention returned to the young woman he held in his arms, who was abruptly tense, letting out a little cry of fear. The sound touched his heart, and he whirled around angrily to face the person who had shouted.

"Your accusations offend me," he said crisply. "And also dishonour the lady. She fell. I caught her. I will release her as soon as she is steady on her feet. She seems feverish," he added, feeling the young woman shiver in his arms.

He looked down at her, his heart stopping as he did. She was beautiful, hair the color of honey framing her neat, heart-shaped face, freckles dusting her pert nose. A small scratch or scar crossed her cheek—not marring it, but somehow adding to her prettiness. She was lovely, enough to make him catch his breath. Even if she had not been, he couldn't have borne hearing a person so insulted. He opened his mouth to tell the older woman so, but she began to harangue him freshly.

"My daughter is quite well!" the woman shouted angrily. "You are a meddling scoundrel, and you are dishonouring her. Step away this minute! Or I will call for the Watch to have you arrested. Filthy, lowdown fellow."

Maxwell had been about to respond, to say that the Watch would have nothing to see besides a young woman terrified out of her wits, but the last comment made him almost laugh.

Lowdown? I'm descended from one of the oldest noble lines in England.

He pushed his pride aside and stared hard at the woman. He was known for his intimidating stare, and he relied on it now to make the woman be quiet and, ideally, to go away. In his arms, the younger woman gave a frightened murmur. He disentangled her gently from his grasp, holding her arm steady so that she might regain her balance. As soon as the poor young lady stood a little away from him, the older woman rounded on her in fury.

"Hannah! What do you think you're doing? Colluding with

some smelly peasant in an inn yard? Disgusting!" the woman spat the words at her daughter. "Who do you think you are? How can you?"

The young woman covered her face with her hands. Maxwell heard her sobbing, and his rage became white-hot. One thing Maxwell could not abide was the tyranny of rowdies. His own father had been oppressive and cruel, and he couldn't stand by and see another person so harangued.

"This young woman has done nothing," Maxwell explained stiffly. "I caught her. She was about to fall. Nothing further happened. I swear as God is my witness that this is so." He swallowed hard. He was neither religious nor irreligious, and the swearing was uncomfortable, but he'd do anything to make her stop tormenting the young lady.

"You dare to swear?" The woman challenged.

Maxwell took a step back, thinking of going inside to fetch the innkeeper and requesting him to take his horrible customer indoors, but as he did so, he heard footsteps.

"What's going on here? I say, Maxwell. Are you all right?" Gavin demanded.

Maxwell tensed as the woman turned on Gavin.

"You ask if *he's* all right?" she shrilled. "What about me? I'm a lady in distress! Can't you see that? This filthy friend of yours has just dishonoured my daughter! I recognise you," she added, squinting at them. "You're the filthy peasants who obstructed us on the staircase. I shall have you barred from here."

"*What*?" Gavin laughed. He sounded incredulous. "My dear lady. I am sorry you're distressed. But this is the Earl of Carronwood you speak with."

Maxwell felt his jaw clench, his spine stiffening. He shot Gavin a hard look, warning him not to say more. He didn't want her to know that. The woman might become avaricious at the sound of a title, and she might demand monetary recompense. He could well afford the money; he didn't want to get involved with such awkward happenings, however. He tried to warn Gavin with an imploring look.

"The Earl of..." The woman asked. She turned to stare at Maxwell. "He doesn't look like an earl. He's covered in mud," she added with a sniff.

24

Gavin laughed. "I can explain that, madam. We have just arrived in England. We've been travelling for a long time. We need a set of fresh clothes. But I assure you, we mean no harm. I can vouch for my friend here...he's a good man." He beamed at Maxwell, who tensed again.

"Is he?" the woman asked, and Maxwell could almost see the thoughts racing behind her hard, sharp-eyed gaze. He cleared his throat to speak, but before he could say anything, the woman began again. "Oh, Lord Carronwood! I do apologise. I am sorry. My silly tongue got away with me." She let out a soft laugh. "I am Mrs. Darlington, and this is my daughter Hannah," she added with a small smile.

Maxwell tensed. "I need no apology, ma'am," he said swiftly. He tried to escape, stepping towards the door, but he almost walked into a man who had just arrived. He recognized him as the same tall, disinterested-looking man he'd seen earlier on the stairs with the woman. He must be her son, he thought, glancing at the older woman swiftly, as their oval faces were similar in shape, and he had her long, fine nose and well-formed mouth. His eyes were as cold as his mother's, and he raised a brow at Maxwell.

"What's happening, Mama?" he demanded angrily. "Is this scoundrel bothering you?"

"He touched your sister," the woman explained swiftly. "I think you'll wish to duel with him for that?"

"Mama..." The man made a sour face. "Are you sure that would be needed?" He looked dismissively at his sister.

"Of course!" His mother told him firmly. "Now mayhap you should go inside, Edward. I don't want this fellow and you to argue right now." She looked firmly at her son, as if warning him. He shrugged.

"I'll go and organise dinner. Philipa is hungry." He stalked to the door.

"Of course, son. Now you go upstairs. We'll settle this ourselves," she added, smiling brightly at Maxwell.

Maxwell looked at Gavin. He wished he felt angry with Gavin, but he could not...his friend had done nothing besides tell the woman who he was. He couldn't expect Gavin to guess that he didn't want her told.

"Maybe we can all go into the inn and get warm," Gavin

began brightly, but the woman interrupted him.

"Lord Carronwood," she said smoothly, addressing Maxwell formally. "I thank you for forgiving my earlier assumption. But you must understand, my lord, that you have compromised my daughter. You have put her reputation in jeopardy."

"I..." Maxwell started explaining that her reputation couldn't be harmed by something only the horses saw, but the woman spoke across him.

"You will need to agree to marry her. It's the only way. Or duel my son—who is a feared duelist."

"What?" Maxwell demanded. This was sheer madness. He had embraced the young woman, Hannah, it was true, but it had been a few seconds only, and the only living person to witness the embrace had been her own mother. There was no compromise of her reputation.

"You will need to marry her. It's the only way to save her reputation," the woman said tightly. "Or would you prefer her to be sent to Ireland as a nun?" she demanded cruelly.

"No, Mother..." the girl whispered, and Maxwell felt his heart twist.

"This is madness," he began, but the woman shook her head.

"My son will fight you. And he will win. And even if he doesn't, the scandal will harm your reputation. Think about it." She tilted her head to the side. "Or do you think the Prince Regent would overlook a duel? You know he banned duels. You think he'll let one slip past him?"

"No," Maxwell said at once.

The young woman started to sob. He felt as though someone was stabbing him, each sob racking his soul. He glared at the older woman, his face a picture of confusion and frustration.

Gavin cleared his throat. "My lady, I can vouch for my cousin. He would never have compromised the young lady's reputation. Of that, I am sure."

"He did! He already did that. Do you think I am crazy, that I *imagined* seeing him embrace her?" She rounded on Gavin, who threw out a hand.

"No! Of course, I don't." He looked helplessly at his cousin, and Maxwell swallowed.

"I want time."

Maxwell's voice was loud and firm and both Gavin and the woman fell quiet.

"I cannot decide what to do on the spot," he continued. "All I want is to give me tonight to decide and I will give you my answer in the morning."

"But my lord! My daughter..." she clamoured.

"We will speak in the morning," Maxwell replied, surprised at the flinty tone of his voice. She gazed up at him, eyes wide.

"Of course, my lord."

Maxwell glanced again at the young woman, who had stopped crying, but was staring out of the stable door, her long honey-blonde hair coming loose from its neat chignon. The look on her face was pitiable; her eyes huge, her mouth tight. She was working hard to suppress her sobs, and he longed to embrace her in truth. She looked like she needed a friendly embrace. He knew nothing about her, but he could see she was hurt and that was enough to make him feel sorrow for her.

"Gavin?" he said swiftly, trying to make a plan that would help all of them. "Will you please escort this woman and her daughter into the inn? I need to tend to Nightfire." His horse was watching over the stall door. Maxwell swallowed. Maybe it was cowardly of him to hide out in the stables a while and let Gavin escort her, but he knew he could not stay in the company of that awful woman a second more. And Gavin could do him a favor—it would help Maxwell to feel less angry with him.

Gavin glared at him. Maxwell almost chuckled, despite how serious the situation was. His friend's long, slim face was a picture of fear and Maxwell felt a little less angry as he watched Gavin stammer to the women and lead them into the inn.

When they had all departed, the stable fell abruptly silent.

"What should I do?" Maxwell murmured as he tended to Nightfire's leg, using the liniment from his saddlebag. He rubbed his horse's leg and brushed him down, then walked slowly and exhausted out of the stable. He could not come to a decision, or even imagine how to do so.

His mother would want him to accept this craziness, he knew that. Mama was gentle and good-natured, the kindest person he knew, and she would see the young woman and pity her.

27

But it's my life, he wanted to scream. How hard had he fought for his independence?

He rested his head in his hands. In so many ways, this terrible madness made sense. The girl was from a wealthy family—he seemed to remember a well-moneyed industrialist called Darlington, and to judge from Mrs. Darlington's manner, this must be the same family. Young Miss Darlington seemed respectable, and she was certainly pretty. He was a new earl and people would expect him to settle down.

His dream was to have a horse farm. And if he was disgraced for dueling, that dream became less likely.

He sat with his eyes shut, pain twisting his heart. He had not imagined having to make a quick, cold decision about this. Father had already tried to force him into a loveless match and that was why he'd run overseas. Now here he was, facing the same choice again, but with Mama so ill, running was not a possible remedy. Running away, even from an illegal duel, would take that dream of a horse-farm from his grasp as well.

I have to do it, he decided sadly.

He stood from the bed to go and find the woman and her son and to tell them he had decided.

Chapter 5

The sound of raised voices, muffled but still discernible, set Hannah's stomach lurching, her heart racing, as she sat on the bed in the cool, dusty inn bedroom. The voices were Mother's voice, and Edward's, in the next room.

"Edward. You have to. I tell you, it's the only...."

"Hush, Mama. The innkeeper himself might hear with you shouting."

"Don't you understand anything? This is urgent."

Hannah gripped the coverlet, her fingers white-knuckled in fear. The incident in the stables that Mother was shouting about had been no incident—the man had merely helped her. She'd tried to explain it half a dozen times, but her mother had just shouted her down. Edward had threatened her, shaking a fist. She'd retreated to her room to think.

I have to do something.

She barely believed the crazy suggestion her mother had made to Lord Carronwood or whatever he was called, and she prayed silently that Edward or Philipa had talked her out of what was obvious madness. She couldn't marry a man whose name she didn't know, who she'd seen once in a stable for five minutes only, and who had once caught her when she fell. He had literally said one sentence to her. That was the total of their knowledge of one another.

Admittedly, he had caught her, and he seemed to be kind. But she was no tender young lady, and she didn't need his care.

She stood up, hearing Mother complaining at Edward, and she couldn't hear exactly what she was saying, only the strong tone. She considered getting up and walking to the next room to listen by the door, but the thought of Edward or Mother opening it was more than enough to keep her where she was. She didn't want them to insult her again. She wanted a plan to escape.

Ride.

Her heart lifted. She could find a horse, or take one—ideally the earl's horse, since it was the earl's fault, in a sense, though he meant no ill-will—and escape to the countryside. With any luck, she could follow the road to Grassdale, where she could find

Margaret and elicit her help. Escaping was the only plan.

She stood up, walking to the door. Her mind was set. Even if it killed her, it would be better to risk escaping than to allow a woman obsessed with only one thing, nobility, and her brother who wanted only for everyone to give him peace and quiet, to decide for her.

She stepped out into the hallway, listening for voices but the room was silent opposite. Mother appeared from across the corridor.

"Hannah. Come here. We need to tell you something."

"Mother, *please*," Hannah whispered, feeling fear flood through her. She couldn't face Mother, Edward and Philipa all screaming at once. She looked around wildly, wanting to run to the stairs, but Edward appeared behind her mother, and she rooted to the spot in fear.

"Hannah," he said, and he sounded tired and annoyed, as always, not angry as he had been just a few minutes before. "Come inside a moment. You need to listen to what we have to say."

Hannah said nothing.

Her mother made a noise in her throat, a disapproving noise as if even Hannah's quietude was an attempt to defy her. Hannah shot her a look but walked into the room behind Edward. She felt numb, her brain unable to think of anything, even to help her escape. She looked around the room wildly. The fire burned low in the grate. The sky was dark beyond the casement. Philipa was blessedly not there. Mother shut the door and stood in front of it.

"Hannah," she said lightly. "We have good news. Your reputation has been saved by the gallant Earl. He has said he will make you respectable again."

Hannah stared at her, stumbling backwards.

"You mean..."

"He will wed you, Hannah," Edward explained. He looked oddly calm. "He said he will agree to do it in just a week's time. That way, the scandal is reduced."

"What?" Hannah shouted. Fear had subsided, replaced with absolute disbelief. They really thought this was good? She gaped at them, terrified.

"Hush," her mother demanded. "Hannah. Raised voices are unseemly. You're to be a countess. You must learn to behave properly."

"I will never be a countess," Hannah stated, and she was surprised by the fact that she was no longer silent. Angry words hissed through her lips, tight and fueled with rage. "I will never be a countess because I will never agree to this plan. I will die on the road to Grassdale before I let you force me into this. You and your schemes will get nowhere."

"Hannah!" Her mother sounded shocked. "How dare you! The insult! Schemes, you say! How can you speak to me like this! Edward! How can you let her speak to me in this way?" She turned to her son, who coughed.

"Hannah, stop talking like that to your mother. We are doing what is best for you. You must accept this solution."

"What solution?" Hannah shouted, and angry tears poured down her face. "You are solving a nonexistent problem! I did nothing. The earl, also, only tried to help me! You're all crazy." She was crying now, her hands covering her face. Anger mixed with horror and made her sob wildly, her face messy with tears, her breath heaving.

"Hannah! I am not crazy!" Mother shouted. Behind Mother, Edward cleared his throat.

"All of you, hold your tongues! This is madness. Mother, stop shouting. Hannah! Accept your mother's decision and go back to your room."

Hannah looked at him. Her anger was cold now. He acted as though he could order her about, but he was her brother, not Papa. He might have stepped up to replace Papa as head of the house, but he was just a few years her senior and he could not order her around.

"You are all mad," she whispered, and turned around in the doorway, walking to her room. Her back was stiff, pride holding her head up and back. She went into her room and sank down onto the floor by the tiny fireplace and rolled up, hugging her knees to her.

God, she prayed silently in her mind. *Help me. Guide me.*

She shut her eyes. She could hear the fire's comforting sound and she breathed in, trying to find calm. She tried to reach out in her mind to Papa. He would know what to do. If he lived, she would not suffer like this.

These people do not care about me, she said inwardly. *They*

31

care for nobody, not even, really, for themselves.

All Mother wanted was a title. All Edward wanted was to sit and read the newspaper without anyone disturbing him. What Philipa wanted was unclear—maybe it was material wealth. None of them were truly happy; none of them truly cared for anything. She was different: She cared for riding. It was a joy to her, her inner light. Mother and Edward and Philipa had no light. They were moving about emptily, following society and its mores like puppets, with Society pulling on the strings.

The flames danced as she stared into them. They wavered and moved, making pictures in her mind. She could see herself, riding across the fields on her beloved horse. She saw stables, and the newborn horses she loved so much. The estate in springtime came next into her vision, and the housekeeper, Mrs. Church, singing with her little children, playing in the kitchen when they came to visit her at the manor. Life was beautiful. It was a priceless gift, and she could not throw it away with some crazy plan to escape.

I need to see what will happen.

She felt stronger, as though the fire had warmed more than her body. A light was kindled inside her and she no longer felt like running blindly out of the inn and throwing herself on the moors. She wanted to find out what would happen.

"Why should I let them do this?" she whispered into the empty room.

This was her mother's wild plan—to secure a title by using every event. But why give up a life of joy and freedom for the ambitions of someone like Mother, who didn't like her?

She stood up and went to the window. It was dark outside, the sky bright with silver stars. They hung there, huge in the darkness, bright like flames burning in the deep black. When she looked up at the stars, she thought of Papa, up there watching over her.

"Papa," she whispered, crying. "I need you. Please, help me to know what to do."

A memory flashed into her mind. Papa, when she was little, holding her steady at the bedroom window, teaching her some of the constellations. She could make out the Bear, and where the North Star was. She stared up, seeing how it flickered like a light to guide her. Somehow, the North Star was like Papa—solid and anchoring, always there guiding her. She watched it, her heart full of love and aching for him to be there.

In the scene she remembered, Papa had come to her room to comfort her after she'd argued with Mother. She recalled his words as if he spoke them in her ear again.

A decision that is right for you, and a decision someone else might approve of, are often two different things, he said gently. *Make your decisions based on what you know; not to win approval.*

As an adult in the inn window, Hannah drew in a breath.

It's hard, Papa, she told him silently. *This isn't my choice. I just want to know if I should do it anyway.*

She stood where she was by the window, reaching out to Papa in her thoughts.

What do you want? Papa asked in her memory. *Your heart knows. Wait, and watch, and look with your heart, not with fear and anger.*

As she watched, she saw a movement across the sky. A star moved. She had seen shooting stars, and in itself it was not surprising, but now she gazed at it, her heart almost stopping. It shot slowly across the starry blueness, moving in the direction of the Winged Horse constellation. She stopped breathing.

"Papa," she whispered. Tears ran down her face, soaking her neck. "Thank you!"

It was her answer. If she waited to see what would happen, there was hope. Horses were there in the future she was promised, she already knew that—Lord Carlisle had a horse, and probably many more—and where there were horses, she could find happiness. She should wait. She was alive, and the story could move on, shifting and changing from a path under the shadowing trees into a path of light.

"Thank you," she whispered.

She went and sat down on the bed; her choice made. She would stay and wait and see what would happen next. The future was not certain, and so much was possible, and part of her—a curious and irrepressible part—wanted to know what might happen.

Chapter 6

The view from the townhouse was always gloomy, and the sight of drizzling rain falling on the leaves outside did nothing to make it more cheerful. Hannah stared out of the window and tried to forget about what was happening, focusing on the rain-soaked lawn and the tiny patch of the flower garden that she could see from her bedroom.

In a few hours, she'd be going to the private chapel of one of Mother's acquaintances, to be married.

She tried valiantly to stay calm. Part of her felt as though she was almost asleep, as though she was dreaming and none of this was really about to happen.

"Miss?" Betty, her lady's maid, called from the wardrobe room next door. "I have the wreath for your hair. Should I arrange it for you now?"

"Yes, Betty," Hannah replied softly. "Do as you feel is right."

She couldn't find a single ounce of excitement—all her emotions were blanketed with the dull, aching horror. No matter how much part of her was curious to see what would happen, over the remaining four days of the journey to London, even that much interest had been snuffed out. Mother had not ceased in talking about Lord Carronwood, about how she was sure he had a fine estate and coaches with a coat of arms, and a place at Court. She felt nauseated every time her mother gloried in their newfound link to nobility.

My life is not for you to elevate yourselves with.

She could think of nothing except those dark, cold eyes of the earl and his distant manner. She was going to another home, where she would know nobody, and where nothing was known about her.

Lord Carronwood doesn't even know my name.

Mother had said it once, but how likely was he to remember?

A defiant thought entered her head. He probably didn't even care what she was called. If he was horrid enough to play along with Mother in this, she had no sympathy for him. She was going to ignore him as much as possible.

I don't have to talk to him. I can just nod and mumble.

The idea made a flicker of warmth dance in her confused mind.

She looked up as she heard footsteps entering the room.

"Miss Darlington?" Betty asked softly. "I can help you dress now, if you like. I found the stockings I was looking for."

"Of course." She felt absolutely nothing. "As you see fit, Betty."

She went behind the screens in the corner to change her clothes. Mother had ordered everything new from the seamstress, and Hannah couldn't imagine how it had all been made at such short notice—a new undershirt, a new dress and a veil—but she could only imagine a small army of seamstresses working long hours to get it done within the five days Mama required. She'd sent a rider ahead to London with the order, and it had all been made by the time they arrived.

"Almost done with the buttons, milady," Betty murmured as she fastened the buttons behind Hannah. She refused to wear stays at any time.

"Thank you, Betty," she told her softly when she had completed them.

"Oh, no, milady! No need to thank me! You look so lovely! Come and see in the looking-glass. You look so fine!"

She studied the reflection as though she really was looking at somebody else. The dress was truly beautiful, made of pure white silk that hung down to her toes, the ends of her silk dancing shoes showing underneath it. It had a high waist, as was fashionable, banded with a thick white ribbon, and the sleeves were slight puffs of silk over her upper arms. Hannah was not particularly tall, and she felt very small in the dress, and when she studied her face, she was shocked by the blank sorrow in her blue eyes.

"Come, now, milady. I'll arrange your hair. There's a fine garland to put in it. Pearls and orange-blossom. Fine good luck for your special day, those are."

Hannah swallowed hard. Betty was clearly aware of how sad she was and was trying to cheer her up. She appreciated it, but it just served to make her feel sadder—she knew she was supposed to be happy, and the fact that it wasn't possible made it worse.

"Thank you, Betty," she murmured.

She went and sat at the dressing-table, studying her reflection as it became even less like herself. Betty arranged her hair in an elaborate chignon that framed her face with tight golden-blonde curls, and she wore gold earrings that she'd never worn before. Around her neck was a gold chain with a pearl pendant, and in her hair, Betty set a wreath of orange-blossom, held in place with pearl-ended pins, and with a thin, filmy veil arranged to hang from the wreath.

"Thank you, Betty," she murmured as she stood up from the chair. Betty stood back, smiling admiringly at her, and Hannah stiffened, suppressing the urge to run.

"You look lovely, milady," Betty told her gently.

"Thank you," Hannah said tightly. She turned and walked to the door, wishing that the words didn't twist like a knife in a wound. She walked down the hallway silently, terror starting to cut through the dull emptiness of earlier in the ringing, hollow silence around her.

It's all right. All right. No trouble. Safe. You're safe.

She repeated words as though she was gentling her mare and took a breath, knowing that it wasn't true—she wasn't safe, and it wasn't all right. But she had to try and be calm or she'd run away before she reached the coach.

The only thought that kept her standing was the thought that she could ignore Lord Carronwood if she wanted. She had the power to do that, at least.

"Hannah! Why, my daughter! Look how fine you look!" Mother greeted her at the foot of the stairs, voice as sweet as honey. "Come on...we don't want to be late. I wonder if the Earl is there in his embellished coach."

"Mother..." Hannah began, but she knew she couldn't argue with her.

"Sister! Come on. We've got to get to Lady Arundel's." Edward was already waiting by the coach. Hannah took his hand, not even looking at him, and stepped in.

Hannah stared at the buildings as they passed. They rolled on for a time that she couldn't have said was long or short, and she blinked in surprise as they slowed. They had reached Lady Arundel's manor on the edge of town.

"Here we are! Oh, this is such a grand day. I'm overcome,"

Mother murmured.

Hannah swallowed hard, feeling her stomach twist painfully. She didn't look at Mother but waited for the coachman to help her out of the coach. Her feet jarred on the stone-paved path.

Edward took Hannah's hand. She winced. He would walk her down the aisle. It was right that Papa wasn't walking her into the chapel. If he had been, this farce wouldn't happen.

She blinked, looking around, distracting herself from her sadnesses. The chapel was small—just space for perhaps a dozen people, if they packed in tightly, and an altar surmounted with a cross. The altar was decorated with flowers and the parson stood there, and across from him, his back to the chapel, stood the tall, loose-limbed figure of the earl.

Hannah stared at him through the thin veil. She felt determined to dislike him. He wore a black jacket and black trousers and he struck her as a sorrowful sort of person, the way he stood there seeming almost depressed. He turned to see them when she came in, and his brown-eyed gaze made her heartbeat become abruptly faster. He was looking at her intently and she felt her cheeks flush red.

What's wrong with him? she thought crossly. *Why does he have to stare at me like that?*

She looked at her toes, the flush in her cheeks warming and spreading through her body. It was almost annoying, this effect he had on her heart and body. She swallowed hard, making herself look up from watching the floor.

The parson beamed at both of them reassuringly. He cleared his throat and began the words of the ceremony. It was happening. She couldn't run away now.

She tried to listen to the words, hoping that the lilting tone of the parson would calm her, but her breathing was tense, and her chest hurt, and she couldn't calm herself. She could hear the words, but made little sense. All she was aware of was the earl.

"...and do you, Hannah Margery Darlington, take thee Maxwell Alfred Dartford Carlisle to be your husband?"

Hannah cleared her throat, still thinking about the fact that at least she knew what he was called now.

"I do," she said automatically.

She tensed. She'd said it. Those words changed her world,

and she'd said them herself almost unthinkingly.

"And do you, Maxwell Alfred Dartford Carlisle, take thee Hannah Margery Darlington to be your wife?" The parson beamed at them. Hannah wished she could feel his innocent pleasure.

"I do."

Despite her horror, his voice was deep and gentle, and it calmed her.

He must be good with horses, she thought distantly. He has a good voice for it.

Hannah strained to listen, but the parson's words flooded past her whirling mind. A sentence jumped out at her, startling her into staring.

"You may kiss."

Shock mingled with intense curiosity and fear as the earl, very gently, lifted the veil from over her face.

She blinked, surprised by the sudden brightness. His brown eyes gazed into hers and in that moment, despite being determined to hate him, she felt safe.

He leaned forward and gently, so gently, pressed his lips to hers. His hands grasped hers and his lips touched hers like a whisper. They were hard and firm, but warm, and her heartbeat raced. Heat flooded through her and then he was straightening up and turning to face the assembled group behind them.

Hannah blinked in confusion. She had not felt repelled or shocked by his touch, as she had expected. Instead, it had warmed her, and she had found herself wishing for a moment that he had not stood up so soon.

Their guests—just Mother, Edward and Philipa, Lord and Lady Arundel and the earl's tall, chestnut-haired friend whose name she couldn't remember—started to murmur.

"Congratulations," Mother gushed. "How wonderful! How very wonderful."

Hannah wished that they could hurry and get out of the church, as having Edward smile and Philipa grin and her mother's honeyed tones in her ear, was too much. She knew that they were not being honest. She felt Maxwell tense too, and for a moment she wondered if he was aware of the same feeling of falseness that she was. He took her hand, very gently, and they walked out of the chapel into the light. The coach was waiting and Hannah felt her heart soften a little as Maxwell helped her up into it. They settled down and the coachman shut the doors and then they were heading into London, where they would set off for the three-day journey east to his home.

Chapter 7

The countryside moved slowly past, the rattle and jolt of the coach barely noticeable after two hours within it. Maxwell stared out of the window, trying to distract himself from staring at the woman who sat opposite him. She wasn't just "a woman" now...she was his wife.

She sat opposite him staring out of the other window; her face turned away. Her profile was extremely pretty—a slight, pert nose, rounded forehead framed with her thick, curly hair, and an endearing, determined chin. The dress in white silk suited her well. She looked truly lovely. He couldn't help being curious about her and he found that he wanted to talk, and turned over a half-dozen topics in his mind. The silence was deafening him after pretending to sleep for an hour so as not to disturb her.

"Good rain we're having," he murmured.

"Mm."

He shut his eyes for a moment. Could she not reply at more length than that? Ever since London, she'd replied monosyllabically to whatever topic he talked on. It was enough to drive him mad.

Maybe it's my own silly fault, he told himself angrily. *Maybe she just has no interest in anything I've said so far.*

He tried the next topic.

"Two more days until we reach Carronwood." His voice was tense with a forced brightness.

"Good."

Swearing inwardly, Maxwell tried the third topic he'd thought of. "We didn't have so many guests at the chapel," he noted mildly.

"No."

Maxwell tried to hide his incredulity. If she replied with a monosyllabic response once more, he was going to go mad.

I'm not exactly happy, too, he wanted to tell her. *For Heaven's sakes, can't you also try? I'm making a real effort here.*

He cleared his throat again, struggling to hide his hurt and annoyance. "Would you like to stop after a few hours?" He asked. "Or should we keep going until we need to change horses?" They would stop to change horses at three o' clock, after the midday meal.

In answer, Hannah gazed at him as if he'd spoken some foreign and unknown tongue. "If you think we need to change horses, we can stop." Her voice was mild, her gaze wary as though she expected him to argue. He drew a breath.

"We're going to stop and change horses, of course," he replied impatiently. "But I inquired as to whether you would like to stop first, before we do." He glared at her. She couldn't be so slow-witted that she'd not understood him.

"You can decide," she said flippantly.

Maxwell felt his head start to throb, a headache threatening him as it always did when he was in a bad mood. "We'll go on until three o' clock and change horses at Rochester," he snapped.

They would stay in Rochester that night and travel onwards the next morning. Maxwell felt his headache worsen. He had already decided they would not share a room—he had barely even spoken to the lady, and until he had, he wasn't going to expect her to feel comfortable with any kind of proximity.

"As you say," Hannah murmured. She wasn't looking at him, but staring out of the window. Her expression was miserable, brows lowered, mouth a thin line, eyes sad. Maxwell breathed out slowly.

"We'll stop at the Miller's Rest." It was a spontaneous idea. He liked the inn. He'd made the journey with Father and stopped there, and, though he'd decided he didn't ever want to do the same trip again, with Hannah, it was somehow different. He had another person to care for. The Miller's Rest was considerably better than the Treetops Inn, which was where he'd have stopped if he was making the trip by himself. Perhaps she'd like it.

She just shrugged this time, not even answering, and he shut his eyes. His temper made his head worse, and he didn't want to show it.

"I'm going to sleep," he told her angrily.

"Very well," she murmured.

Maxwell let out a strained breath and sat there with his eyes shut, but with his ears attempting to catch every sound. He wanted to hear what she'd do—whether she'd pretend to sleep or whether, when he was not observing her, she might open her little drawstring purse and take out whatever was in there. A book, maybe. Maybe embroidery. He found that he wanted to know what interested her. She was beautiful, he had to admit that when he saw her in her long white gown with her hair styled so elaborately around her face. He wanted to know if there was anybody behind those blue eyes, or if she was as empty and society-obsessed as her mother appeared to be. She certainly didn't talk much.

He waited.

There was no noise at all from the other side of the coach for a minute, and then he heard something rustle. He fought not to open his eyes, as if he did, she'd instantly stop doing whatever it was.

He heard more rustling, and he breathed deeply. Maybe she was eating something. No smell of food hit his nostrils, but he did detect a slight medicinal odor, like pine.

He could stand the curiosity no longer and he opened one eye, trying to peep at what she was doing.

She was sitting with something clasped between her hands. As he watched, she put whatever it was—a small tin or box—into her purse and then rubbed her hands together, as if she was massaging in some kind of lotion. He breathed in the smell, expecting it was some sort of floral-scented cosmetic, but the strongly medicinal smell of what he'd thought was pine but might be wintergreen hit him again.

Why would she be using wintergreen ointment?

He knew the smell only because the head gardener at the estate used it on his rheumatism. She was far too young to have rheumatism. But why else would she be using it? She certainly didn't work extensively with her hands...they were tiny and petite; but then she herself was tiny. He blushed as he recalled holding her for those few seconds in the stable. She had rested her head on his chest for just a moment, making his heart thump wildly.

Just nerves. I was just anxious about her well-being.

He wouldn't allow that it was because she might attract him. He blushed and opened his eyes, trying to quell the thoughts that chased themselves around his mind.

"You're awake!"

Hannah's voice was surprisingly shrill, and Maxwell tried not to smile. She had clearly thought he was asleep, and she was still busy massaging her fingers, cracking her knuckles as though they hurt. He wished he could ask her about it.

"I just woke up," he said untruthfully, wanting her to think he hadn't been prying. "Coach must have jolted."

"Perhaps," she murmured, her brow lowering skeptically. Maxwell cleared his throat.

"We have about another three hours of travel," he told her, reaching for his pocket-watch. He stared down at the device, recalling when his father had given it to him for his sixteenth birthday. He'd felt strange about accepting it, since Father and he had always had their differences. He'd kept it, though many times during his stay in Spain he'd thought to throw it in the sea, just to purge himself of his anger and resentment towards Father. "Perhaps you'd like to eat something now?"

"I'm not hungry."

He let out a sigh. "Nor am I," he managed to say through the anger that seemed to ball up in his throat every time she gave such a brief, disinterested answer. "But eating is a good idea, since we won't be able to do so until tonight."

"Whatever you say."

Maxwell closed his eyes briefly in annoyance. "I'm going to stop the coach and ask the coachman to bring us the hamper," he decided firmly. "Then, I'm going to eat a sandwich and fall asleep. You can do as you please." He turned away coldly and thumped on the roof to alert the coachman. He turned away before he could see her reaction.

"The picnic hamper, if you please, Mr. Chesterford," he requested through the window.

"Yes, of course, my lord."

The hamper arrived and Maxwell thanked the coachman, then pulled out a sandwich, passing it to Hannah. She took it, holding it in her slender fingers, but didn't unwrap it from the sturdy newsprint paper. Maxwell took one for himself and took a bite and chewed methodically. The coach smelled of ham and cheese. He ignored the delicious smell, eating without much enjoyment—he felt too annoyed even to enjoy his lunch. Hannah was sitting rigidly, the sandwich unopened, and his irritation grew. He didn't want to be unfair, but the young lady seemed either numb with shock or dull in the wits.

Maybe, he thought self-deprecatingly, *marrying me was such a shock she's forgotten how to speak.* It certainly seemed like that. He found his heart softening a little. She was suffering as much as he was. Annoying as she might be, she'd been thrust into this awful situation just as he had, and he had to try.

"There's a flask of lemonade and some glasses too," he stated, trying not to sound unkind. "If you want some, please help yourself. I'm going to sleep now."

He determinedly shut his eyes, leaning back on the chair. There were three whole hours before they reached their destination and he prayed that he'd sleep until then. He was already tired, and his thoughts became slowly more disjointed as he slipped into confused dreams.

"Lord Carronwood?"

Maxwell jerked awake. He blinked, then slowly remembered that he was in the coach, on his way to Carronwood, two days away from seeing Mama and having to explain himself.

"Lord Carronwood?" Hannah repeated.

He glared at Hannah. "Call me Maxwell."

She blinked tearfully and he instantly wished he'd been kinder.

"Maxwell," she said softly.

"Yes. Good," he replied. "Now, let's get out of the coach. That's the inn there, and I suspect the coachman wants to change horses, for which he'll need us out of here." He spoke briskly.

"I know that." Her response was instant and offended, her gaze narrowing to a glare.

The angry expression in her eyes made his lips lift at the corners, real warmth filling his heart for the first time when he looked at her. Her anger was the first emotion he'd seen her display besides shock and fear. When she was angry, her blue eyes blazed.

"Very well," he told her diffidently. "We'll go indoors, and I'll organise our rooms. We can sleep in rooms on the same floor."

That part of the journey had been bothering him since they set out. He was not prepared to share a room with her, since he hardly knew her. Pretty she certainly was, and he was sure he would find her desirable under different circumstances. But until he knew her at least well enough to be able to talk to her, he wasn't going to impose himself on her.

He didn't look to see how she responded to that suggestion, but opened the door and jumped down. He held out a hand to take hers, and she slipped her fingers into his coldly, still glaring at him. He felt almost amused by her defiant air.

"Two rooms, please; your best if they are still available," Maxwell demanded as the innkeeper came out to meet them.

"Very good, my lord."

"That'll be four shillings, my lord."

Maxwell found the money in his pocket and passed it over. As soon as they had paid, Hannah drifted up the stairs, not even looking at him. He felt a stab of pain as he watched her stiff, stately form move up the staircase like a short, slender ghost. He wanted her to be angry with him like earlier. It would be better than ignoring him. He sighed and walked up to her, wishing that she didn't get on his nerves so badly. Too much had happened in the last five days, and he barely understood it.

He needed time to think and to gather strength to tell Mama what he had been persuaded into.

Chapter 8

Maxwell's voice—speaking for the first time in ten miles of travel—interrupted Hannah's silent thoughts.

"Another mile in the coach," Maxwell said, his voice tight as though he tried to be patient and wasn't quite managing. "And then we get to Carronwood Manor."

Hannah leaned back in the seat; her stomach knotted tight with sudden tension. It had been three days of traveling in the coach with him—three days of giving monosyllabic responses to everything he said, knowing she was angering him. It was a kind of game; the only thing she could think of to amuse herself and stop herself going mad with fear when she thought about the situations she was in. She had no idea what awaited her. She hadn't even had the chance to ask if he had any family. Was she going to be met by a stern, silent brace of Carlisles like him? His father had passed away, she knew, or he would not have the earldom now, but whether or not he had siblings or a mother who lived at the manor, she had no idea.

"Where exactly is the manor?" she breathed, hoping that she could try and elicit some more information about it if they could start a conversation.

"It's just around the corner," Maxwell commented. His voice was remote as always, but she recognized another tone in it. It was higher and tighter than usual, almost as though he felt tense, too. Hannah frowned. It was his home, so it made no sense that he was tense. But then, maybe he really was—after all, the only thing she knew about him was that he'd been away from England for three years.

"Good," she murmured, feeling a softening in her heart. The nervousness was the first real emotion she'd seen him display in three days. "I'll be pleased to get out of this coach," she added, trying for a smile.

His eyes widened in surprise, and Hannah realized it was the longest sentence she'd exchanged with him so far. His mouth softened, almost a smile. She felt her own heart lift at the sight. He cleared his throat.

"Me too. It's a long time to sit in one place."

"Yes! It truly is." Hannah nodded in sympathy, delighted to be having a conversation. She'd never liked coach trips. The presence of her mother and Edward made them unpleasant, but it wasn't just that—being trapped in a tight space for hours was exhausting. She was going to comment that she'd much rather be riding, when she heard the coachman let out a shout. They slowed and turned up through a wrought-iron gate. Her heart leapt.

"We're here," Maxwell told her.

Hannah stopped thinking and stared out of the window. She was arriving at her new home.

A long, gravel-paved drive flanked by dark green bushes and a tall building slowly appeared as they rolled up through the gates, and she gazed at the building with fear and fascination. It was large and imposing, built of gray stone, the front of it embellished with carved scrollwork, the upper windows surmounted with arching gables. The place looked more than a hundred years old—the front was at least that old, to judge from the scrollwork and the grand, grim appearance. A shiver of anxiety ran down her spine.

This dark, foreboding house was her home. The coach stopped outside it and her insides twisted with fear and excitement in equal measure.

Maxwell opened the door and jumped down, his boots crunching on the gravel. Hannah sat where she was, trying to feel calm.

"My lady?"

Maxwell stood with his hand out, dark eyes studying her curiously. She realized after a moment that he was waiting to help her down from the coach. She blushed and stood up from the seat.

"Thank you."

She took Maxwell's hand and jumped down, her booted feet jarring on the drive. She smoothed her dress, feeling nervous. It was blue silk, one of her best and the one she had changed into at the inn, a little crushed from traveling. Maxwell strode up the drive, booted feet crunching on the gravel. She followed Maxwell as he strode to the door. He rapped on the door with a bronze doorknocker and she stood on the terrace, heart thudding fearfully, and waited. Her gaze moved around the front garden as she stood there, curiosity making it impossible not to stare.

The front lawn was enormous, extending further than she

could see, the road obscured by the green hedges. The front of the house was softened with a border of white flowers and shrubs. Tall trees flanked the house, a big oak tree spreading its shade over the lawns on the right, where a water-garden or some other ornamental space stood, to judge from the stone paths that led there, winding across the green lawn. The air was cool and fresh, the mood lightened by the sound of birdsong.

The voice of an older man drew her attention.

"My lord! My lady! You're earlier than we expected. Come inside, do! Her ladyship will be delighted."

Maxwell nodded to the man, who had white hair, and a thin-lipped, but friendly face, his dark eyes merry. The man's gaze moved to her.

"Lady Carronwood! Welcome. This is an honour." He bowed low.

Hannah flushed. She hadn't got used to the title yet. She was the Countess of Carronwood. It made no sense to her.

"Have our luggage taken upstairs, Mr. Haddon," Maxwell requested. "I trust the peach suite has been prepared?"

The man had to be the butler because he was wearing a dark jacket and trousers and not any kind of livery. He inclined his head politely. "Yes, my lord," he began respectfully. "I will have the luggage brought up directly. A bath, my lord? My lady?" he bowed to Hannah again.

"Please," Hannah breathed. Her body slumped at the thought. Bathing would be a fine thing after three days of travel.

"Very well," Maxwell said at once, then nodded to the butler, who hurried off to instruct the servants. Maxwell turned to Hannah. "I'll show you to your quarters," he told her distantly. "I am sure you would like to rest for a while."

"I am tired," Hannah admitted. She looked up at him, studying his face for any trace of feeling, for it was all absent from his voice. His brown eyes seemed softer, a little less severe, but his face was unreadable, the same tightness that had been there for the entire journey still etched in the lines about his mouth and eyes. She followed him up the stairs without speaking. He strode ahead, unthinking of her cramped, tired legs, and she struggled to keep up.

They went up the marble-faced stairs into a long hallway,

the space lit with oil-lamps bracketed to the wall.

"You will sleep here," he intoned firmly, gesturing to a door on the left of the marble-faced staircase. "There is a boudoir and a small reading-room attached to the bedroom. I think you will experience no lack." His voice was flat, emotionless.

"Thank you," Hannah breathed. His words struck her speechless. She had never had so much space for just her. Grassdale was vast, and every bit as elaborate as this manor was, but she'd had only her bedroom and the wardrobe-room there. Here, she had three rooms to herself, and the best part of it was that nobody was going to disturb her. She felt her heart lift with relief.

Maxwell inclined his head. "I am going to see my mother now. You may join us in the drawing room when you have bathed and rested."

"Yes, I shall," Hannah murmured, her mind latching on to the fact that Maxwell's mother lived here. Was his mother like her own? That was no pleasant thought. At least Mother was her own mother—that might serve to put some curb on her cruelty. This woman was not her own mother, so Heaven knew how cruel she might be.

She was still thinking about it when she shut the door behind her. The sweet lavender scent of a bath captured her senses instantly, distracting her utterly. She unfastened her dress, undressed and slipped into the bath. The warm, soapy water was heavenly on her skin. She shut her eyes and lay back, her head resting on the raised edge, the blissful warmth easing the cramp in her legs. The water smelled of lavender and she blinked; fighting the urge to fall asleep.

A voice at the door interrupted her—her new maid.

"Wait a moment!" Hannah called. She jumped out of the bath, invigorated by the warm water, and grabbed the towel that someone had left on the bed for her.

Hannah opened the door, her body covered with the long linen towel.

Thank you, milady," a young woman thanked her politely. "I am Miss Staveley. I will unpack your things for you." She was a few years older than herself, Hannah guessed, with strawberry-blonde curls half-hidden under a cloth bonnet and a neat, solemn face.

"Thank you," Hannah murmured. Miss Staveley walked past her to enter, and Hannah watched her go to the wooden box into which some of her clothes had been packed, and take out some things, searching for undergarments. Miss Staveley seemed kind, handing Hannah her shift and waiting for her to dress behind the screen. Hannah's heart twisted. She appreciated the woman's kindness, but she missed Betty already.

Here, there are only strangers.

She tugged on the shift and stood while Miss Staveley searched through the boxes to find her gown.

"Which one, milady?" she asked, holding up three gowns, neatly folded, that she'd found there.

Hannah tilted her head, considering. It was not an easy choice. She was meeting Maxwell's mother and she needed to make a good impression. Married women usually wore bolder colors, while younger, unmarried ones wore pale pastels. Hannah had perhaps three gowns that would do for her new life, and only two of them were with her in this case. The rest were in the bigger wooden box that had yet to be unpacked from the coach.

"The yellow one?" she asked. It was a darker, golden yellow. Perhaps it would be appropriate.

"Very good, milady."

Miss Staveley helped her dress and styled her hair into a simple chignon, then withdrew. Hannah looked around the room, feeling nervous. It was a beautiful room, the walls covered in fine wallpaper, the bed covered with a peach satin coverlet, the windows looking out onto tall trees and a wide lawn. A fire warmed the space, lit in an elaborate fireplace with a marble mantel surmounting it. The floor was fine wood covered with a silky Oriental carpet. It was a beautiful space and she wished she could stay there, but she had to go and meet Maxwell and his mother.

She drew a deep breath, gathering her courage, and walked out into the hallway.

As she rounded the corner, she almost walked into the butler. He bowed low, ignoring her little cry of surprise.

"My lady," he said respectfully. "I regret to inform you that his lordship is currently occupied with estate business. He asked that you wait for an hour. After that, the dowager Countess has requested your presence."

"Oh?" Hannah's heart thudded fearfully. She couldn't face the woman by herself. It would be hard enough to meet a new critic with Maxwell present—without him, she didn't think she could do it. She looked around blindly, seeking any form of escape. "I'll take a walk in the garden. Thank you, Mr. Haddon," she told him swiftly.

She turned in the hallway and hurried down the corridor, and into the garden.

The dew-scented air hit her at once, calming her senses. A light drizzle fell across the lawns, scenting the air with rain. A bird sang somewhere, the song high and fine. Her heart ached for the countryside at Grassdale, and she pushed the thoughts away angrily, not wanting to cry. She didn't want to meet the dowager Countess with a tear-swollen face and red-rimmed eyes. A conifer caught her eye and she swiftly distracted herself thinking about juniper trees.

"They have fine medicinal properties," she murmured to herself, then stopped. Margaret had taught her that, and Margaret was another person at Grassdale, far away. She clenched her fist, fighting her emotions.

I will not cry.

She walked around the lawn, noticing other medicinal herbs in the borders, then stiffened her back and marched up the stairs into the entrance-way. In the hallway, the butler bowed low as she approached him.

"Please show me the way to her ladyship's parlour?" She didn't even know where the drawing room was, never mind anything else. All she had seen of the house was her own bedroom.

"Of course, my lady."

The butler led her up to a third floor, along a short corridor, and to one open door. They paused in the doorway. The heat of a fire almost bowled Hannah over where she stood. The room was searingly warm.

"Ah! Mr. Haddon! Is this the young lady I wanted to meet?" A voice called out.

"She is; my lady. The new countess."

"Come in," the woman's voice called out, addressing Hannah.

Hannah's eyes narrowed to make out the form of a lady seated on a long chair; her knees covered in a white traveling-rug. Her long face was thin but beautiful, the contours of it as elegant as a statue. Her eyes were wide and black, exactly like her son's. She gazed at Hannah and Hannah felt herself start to sweat, the heat and fear flooding her senses, but then the woman's lips lifted in a smile, and a small exclamation broke the silence.

"Why! My dear. Welcome. How lovely to meet you."

Chapter 9

The firelight flickered warmly on the shining porcelain tea-service on the table. Hannah settled down on the comfortable wingback chair opposite the older woman, the tension in her stomach unknotting as she gazed at her. The dowager countess's smile was warm as she waited for Hannah to be comfortable.

"You're the young lady who finally settled Maxwell down," the older woman said in a low, pleasant voice. Her eyes crinkled at the edges with her smile.

"Um, well, I..." Hannah stammered, her cheeks reddening furiously. She was sweltering from the heat in the room, where a blazing fire burned in the grate, but it was shyness that made her cheeks warm. Lady Carronwood clearly knew nothing of how she'd met Maxwell, which was unsurprising, considering how they'd met only a little over a week before. "It isn't really..." she began trying to say, but the older woman just smiled.

"Sorry, my dear. I was so excited to meet you that I forgot I haven't even introduced myself." She smiled. "I am Patricia."

"Good evening," Hannah said, inclining her head formally. "I am Hannah."

"Welcome, Hannah," Patricia said gently. Her voice was so kind that Hannah felt the tears that had threatened to fall all afternoon begin to form in her eyes. She blinked furiously, embarrassed to cry in front of the older woman, but Patricia must have seen, because her smile became even more gentle.

"It's all right," she said softly. "I know. It must all be very strange, being here." Her dark eyes were kind. "It was strange for me, too, moving here. I come from north of here; Yorkshire," she told Hannah kindly. "The entire south of England was mysterious."

Hannah giggled, feeling her heart warm to the woman instantly.

"It was," Patricia told her with a grin. "I'm not jesting. I thought everywhere was like the Dales—vast green fields and rolling hills and mist."

"How lovely," Hannah breathed. She imagined riding on the Dales, which she had heard were exceptionally beautiful. She would feel the wind in her hair, the sun beating down on her arms as she held the reins. The countess interrupted her thoughts.

"There are beautiful things here, too. I came to love it. And I am sure you will too. It is a bit foreboding here, at first...Carronwood is an old house. But I assure you, there are many nice things to see. The gallery, for one. I hope my son has shown it to you—though he might not be a good guide." She chuckled.

"Why would that be?" Hannah felt curious. This was her first glimpse of anything about Maxwell besides his implacable coldness. She was surprised to find that she ached for some information.

"Well, when he was a little boy, just two years old, his nursemaid and I took him up there for the first time. He was terrified!" The older woman giggled, her eyes shining with the memory. "He thought the paintings were real people and he couldn't understand why they were all staring at him so intently."

Hannah laughed, a warm laugh that came from her belly. She imagined him as the small, terrified boy of the story. It was hard to imagine. "Poor little thing," she said, but she was still giggling as she spoke.

"Yes. We had to take him downstairs to his room. He was inconsolable. He kept on murmuring that the pictures were watching him. Poor little thing." Patricia chuckled. "I was glad his papa was not there for that." Her face darkened and Hannah felt her brow knit in a frown.

"Why?" she murmured.

"His father was very strict. Too strict, I thought. Maxwell was a good boy. A fine lad. He didn't need a strict hand. He needed to be nurtured, for his talents to be fostered. His father was not good at that."

Hannah felt her heart twist. She had not guessed that Maxwell had a strict father. She had imagined his Papa would have been like hers; loving and kind.

"I wanted tutors for him, to teach his fine mind. His father wanted him to prepare for the military. Said it would do him good to see action in a few battles before he became earl."

"I see," Hannah replied softly. That explained a lot about Maxwell. The aloof, reserved demeanour was cultivated to conceal his sentiments from all. If his father was the sort who believed the military would do a young man good, he probably also believed boys shouldn't cry. She studied the dowager countess, thinking she looked so kind that nobody would need to hide emotions from her.

"Maxwell and his father had some differences of opinion." The older woman continued. Her voice was delicate. "That was why Maxwell spent so many years in Spain. But now he's back, and he's settled, and I am so glad to have him here. And you, my dear. You're very welcome here." She smiled at Hannah; her gaze warm.

"Thank you," Hannah breathed. Her own family had never said that—that she was welcome. Besides Papa, they all made her feel quite unwelcome. She gazed at the older woman, feeling her heart open to her. With practiced skill, she started to notice small things about her as they spoke. The gaunt face, the eyes lined with wrinkles that suggested constant pain, and hands with swollen and knotted joints. Hannah recalled her friend Margaret telling her the names of herbs to ease that, as well as mentioning that the joints could be affected by disorders of the heart, because the blood did not properly drain from the fingers if the heart did not beat properly. She hadn't meant to study the dowager countess so closely; she just couldn't help noticing.

"Sorry for staring," she murmured.

"Oh, don't worry your head, my dear." Patricia chuckled. "We're very informal here. Not like London. The *Ton* can be a hard set to please. I remember that."

"I am sure," Hannah answered softly. She looked at Patricia thoughtfully. "You didn't like London either?" she guessed.

Patricia chuckled. "My dear, I disliked it intensely. I insisted to Henry that I be allowed to remain in the country during the Season, whether his presence was expected at parliament or not."

"Good," Hannah said with a smile.

Patricia smiled back. "I hated the heat and the crowds, mostly, but the foolery about fashion and etiquette was even harder for me to bear. I mean, manners are manners. But in London they make snide comments if your curtsey is too low or too brief." Her face twisted with distaste.

Hannah nodded vigorously, soul soaring with the relief of meeting someone of a similar opinion. "Well, here at Carronwood we're miles away from that. I'm glad." Carronwood was pleasantly informal—she could wear her hair in a simple loose bun or wear no stays or stockings without criticism.

"Me too," Patricia agreed warmly. "Maxwell doesn't care for London either. Too many people, too hot. Heaven knows why they all want to go there." She sniffed.

Hannah smiled at the news. "I'm glad," she said softly. Maxwell was a strange man—quiet and distant and hard to know. Having even that much in common with him made her feel better about everything.

"I will have to retire to my chamber to rest, soon," Patricia murmured softly, interrupting her thoughts. "I imagine you are tired too. But I thoroughly enjoyed our discussion. I hope you will join me again tomorrow evening for a talk here."

"I would like to, Lady Carronwood," Hannah told her, meaning it sincerely.

Patricia inclined her head in a friendly way. Hannah could see that she was exhausted, and she stood up quietly, bobbing a quick curtsey. The older woman raised her hand in acknowledgement, her exhaustion obvious, and Hannah smiled, then tiptoed silently from the room.

The hallway was already lit with lamplight, the sky blue-tinged with dusk outside. Hannah found her room and pushed open the door and went to sit at her desk. She had barely been there a moment when a knock on the door interrupted her thoughts again. She opened it to find Miss Staveley there

"Milady? May I help you dress for dinner? It's at seven o' clock this evening."

"Oh. Yes," Hannah murmured, recalling that she'd heard the church clock chime half-past six quite a few minutes ago. They would have to hurry if she wanted to be on time. She stifled a yawn and went to the wardrobe, where Miss Staveley had unpacked her clothes. "The green dress, please," she requested.

"Very good, milady."

The green dress was one she knew suited her well—it had a low oval neckline and the long skirt fell like water from the fashionably high waist. The color was a pale sage and it made her eyes seem even bluer than usual. She glanced at herself in the mirror, feeling more confident. She looked very elegant.

The butler led her down to the dining-room and she paused in the doorway, heart thudding. There was a long table on which candles burned brightly, spreading light through the room which was also lit with lamps bracketed to the walls. Maxwell was already there, seated at the head of the table. Patricia was on his right. Hannah swallowed hard. It all looked so imposing. She went across to the table, her soft-soled indoor shoes silent on the wooden floor. The place opposite Maxwell was hers according to custom. She sat down in it awkwardly. Patricia sat on her left. The place opposite Patricia, on Hannah's right, was also set and she glanced at Maxwell.

"Gavin is staying with us," he told her, guessing what she wanted to ask. "He's still out. He'll join us in a moment. We'll begin eating before he arrives...he's used to it."

Hannah glanced at the clock, but she couldn't see it properly and so she looked down at her plate. Her stomach was twisting painfully with hunger.

Maxwell gestured to the butler to come forward and serve the first course. Hannah's stomach lurched with longing as a big spoonful of pale green pea soup was poured into her bowl. The smell was fragrant and delicious. Her mouth watered. She waited for the other guests to begin eating and then hastily joined them.

"I'll go up to Aldgate Woods tomorrow," Maxwell told his mother, swallowing some soup. "It's a short ride. Just an hour there and back; mayhap one and a half hours if I take the long route."

Patricia nodded, but Hannah only noticed one word in that sentence.

Riding.

"You have a stable?" she asked, and Maxwell looked blankly at her.

"We have one of the best stables in England," he told her flatly. Patricia smiled.

"She can't know that, Maxwell, dear," she said to her son gently. "She's only just arrived. We need to introduce her to Carronwood gradually." She cast a friendly glance at Hannah, who slumped with relief. She was grateful the older woman seemed to know how she felt.

"Mm. Quite so," Maxwell murmured. His voice was mild and disinterested. "You like horses?" The question was meant for Hannah, though he barely glanced at her.

"I love horses," Hannah replied, her voice warm with feeling.

She wondered if he remembered that she'd been talking to his horse when he first saw her, but he cleared his throat.

"We don't have much in our stables suitable for a lady. You could ride on Buttercup, maybe...she's our only horse old enough and mild enough for someone with little experience."

Hannah's blood boiled at his dismissive tone. "I have been riding since I was four," she snapped, furious at the insult. "I reckon that ensures that I have as much *experience* as is needed." She glared at Maxwell defiantly.

His eyes held hers. She saw them widen in shock, and a shuttered look descended there, but his mother chuckled.

"That's an honest answer. And no less than what you asked for." Patricia chided warmly.

"Well, I suppose," Maxwell said a little peevishly, his gaze hard when he looked at his mother, then at Hannah. "I suppose you might like to go for a ride, then?" he asked casually.

Hannah nodded. "More than anything in this world." She could feel her heart straining at the mere thought.

"Well, then," Maxwell replied coldly. "I suppose you can join me on my morning ride, then."

Hannah felt her heart soar even as she gazed at him nervously. "I would like to."

He looked down at the plate with evident frustration, and she wanted to laugh. She had surprised him. She felt a twist of excitement in her stomach, and she pressed her lips together to hide her smile lest he think she mocked him. She would soon be riding.

Chapter 10

The stable was dark, the scent of hay and horses as welcoming as it always was. All the same, it did nothing to still Maxwell's irritated mood. He grunted in annoyance as he hauled the saddle over to where Nightfire stood in the stall, placidly eating hay. It wasn't the tacking up that annoyed him; it was the presence of Hannah, humming as she saddled Crimson in the stall next door.

"Damn her," he whispered under his breath.

She'd made a fool of him in front of his mother, but it wasn't just that—Mama wasn't exactly judgmental, and certainly not of him, so that was not a bother. It was the fact that she'd made him feel stupid.

He lifted the bridle, feeling his irritation growing as Nightfire did what he always did, which was to lift his head out of Maxwell's when he tried to put it on. That trick, along with breathing in for the girth so that it was too loose, were the pranks that Nightfire always played and normally Maxwell thought it amusing.

"Come on, you silly," he told Nightfire gently as he raised the bridle. The bit was the softest bit available—Maxwell would have ridden without one, and often did, but he didn't want to risk looking foolish today. Nightfire let him fasten it, and then Maxwell led him out of the stall.

The sound of hoofs on the ground made him turn. He tried not to swear as Hannah followed just seconds behind, leading Crimson, who trotted after her cheerily as though Hannah had lived here always. Crimson was not the fiercest horse in the stables—that was Gavin's horse—but she wasn't the easiest either. Seeing how instantly Hannah and the thoroughbred liked each other annoyed him.

She really is experienced.

He had hoped that Hannah's boast had been empty, that she was going to look a bit silly today, but so far, he had to admit she was not lying to them.

"So," Maxwell intoned, leading Nightfire to the gate. "If you want to mount up, you may go there." He indicated the block in the center of the yard, feeling magnanimous. He could use the fence to mount up; she could use the proper mounting-block. She would need it.

She grinned. "She's a bit taller than I expected, so I might need it," she replied. "I don't always."

Maxwell stifled the sound of annoyance that rose within him. She didn't have to try to make him feel sillier. He waited for her to move, and then stepped up using the fence, cheeks flushing as he made the perfect mount-up. He looked to see if she was watching, but she was stepping up onto the block. He forgot about her watching him and stared at her instead.

She swung her leg up and over and Maxwell felt his heart stop. He hadn't asked if there were any saddles suitable for ladies on the property, and apparently, she hadn't looked. She was using Gavin's, riding astride, and a flash of her muscled calf in the morning light made him feel shocked and confused.

She's beautiful, and unafraid of society.

He couldn't help it. He felt impressed.

He watched as she circled towards the gate, her grin shining like the sunshine that reflected blindingly off the pond. He felt his head spin. Part of him was furious at how foolish he must look, while another cheered her silently.

She's an expert horsewoman.

"We go up that path towards the woods, yes?" she asked. She was still grinning and, much as her teasing smile annoyed him, he fought his own grin that threatened to blossom on his face. She was clearly delighted to be riding, and her joy affected him. That, and her evident defiance of social rules. He had to admire it. He had fought with his father but hated doing it. She flouted expectations every day, it seemed. He couldn't help the sudden admiration that blossomed in his heart.

"Yes," he muttered, trying to keep up the annoyance he'd felt earlier. "The ride is about five miles. It might tire you," he warned.

She flashed a smile. "We do five miles often, my horse and I at home."

He was too surprised to be annoyed and he wanted to ask her about her horse, but she leaned forward suddenly and shot ahead, starting at a trot, and then speeding to a canter.

"Go, Crimson! Go!" She called excitedly.

She was racing him. Maxwell swore and leaned forward,

putting gentle pressure on his horse's flanks that indicated he wanted to speed up. They moved to a canter.

Hannah was riding ahead, her blue bonnet covering her long hair, her blue riding-mantle billowing behind her on the breeze. She was leaning forward, her profile close to the horse, her hands firm on the reins. She looked entirely at ease, and he had to appreciate how lovely she looked, even while feeling annoyed with her for sparking an unplanned-for contest. He leaned forward, increasing speed, and he drew up alongside her in a few minutes.

"You don't know the way," he reminded her as she slowed down. "I should go ahead."

"Please do," she said, her smile glowing.

Maxwell bit back his irritation. He rode in front of her.

He leaned back, settling into a slow and relaxing trot. Nightfire had just made a long sea crossing, to say nothing of weeks of travel beforehand, and he wanted to look after him. Pushing him to a canter or a gallop would be cruel now.

He heard Hannah's horse trotting behind, just close enough to make him feel irritable again. She was leaving just a few yards between them, and that annoyed him. It might upset the horses. Luckily, it didn't seem to bother Nightfire, who was only a little restless, occasionally lifting his head and tossing it like a fly was bothering him. Maxwell guessed his own mood was affecting his horse and he breathed in slowly, trying to find calm.

He found himself still in a state vexation and contemplation. She really is as good as she says; but does she have to make it so clear?

"Are we going to ride uphill a lot?" she asked him from where she rode behind him. He shrugged.

"A bit of the way," he commented. They'd been riding for about ten minutes already, and the path was sloping upward. The woods he'd intended to ride to were atop a slight incline. "Why?"

"Because I think Crimson has a loose shoe."

"What?" Maxwell heard the word burst out of him with more force than he intended. He bit his lip. "Sorry to shout. But that's not possible. The farrier was here last week." He felt angrier than before. The comment suggested he didn't look after his horses, and that was ridiculous. He took the best care that he knew how, and that had been learned over three years on a famous horse farm. He bit back an angry answer.

"Well, she's limping," Hannah said insistently. "It's not much, just a slight shift where she's favoring her left back foot. But in a mile or so, it's going to get worse. We should stop and walk her back to the stables so we can have her seen to."

"I don't believe this," Maxwell challenged. Then he felt himself smile. She wasn't serious, he was sure. She was tired and she didn't want to go on and she was using a lie to make sure they went back. He felt justified in his disbelief of earlier. She knew she wasn't as good a horse-rider as she had boasted, and she was trying to save face. He turned his horse, unsure of what to do.

Part of him wanted to wait, patronizingly, for her, and another part wanted to carry on, forcing her to tell him she was tired. He hesitated, not wanting to be cruel. She had boasted, but she didn't deserve to suffer for it

"Let's turn back now, then," he suggested mildly.

"I'm going to dismount," Hannah flashed back. "If you like, you can ride to the wood you mentioned. I'm going back."

"You can't do that!" Maxwell exclaimed angrily. "You're in the middle of unknown woods. What about finding your way back? And what if there are bandits about?" He cursed himself inwardly—the woods were quite safe; but somehow the thought of her walking back alone worried him, making him imagine dangers that he'd not even consider if it was himself riding on his own.

"I can," she told him firmly. "If you refuse to listen, I'm going to walk back now. I know when a horse is having trouble walking. If you don't believe me, see for yourself."

She stopped the horse, and, before he could guess what she was about to do, she slid out of the saddle, dismounting neatly as a jockey with no need for a mounting-post. He swore inwardly. If he didn't know that she wasn't, he could have sworn she was showing off.

He tried to contain his annoyance and slipped down from the horse, walking over to Crimson. Instantly, he could tell that she was right about something—the horse wasn't happy. As he approached, Crimson snorted and stamped her foot, as if she was annoyed or scared.

"It's this one," Hannah told him. She was pointing to the left back leg and Maxwell walked around to it, murmuring to Crimson as he did so. He had checked horses' hoofs and helped with cleaning them countless times. He knew something about shoeing horses and how to check a horse's feet. He went around to where Hannah had indicated, lifting her big hoof gently in both his hands. He touched the shoe, which was silvery and new. As his finger connected with it, the shoe moved.

"Damn me, you're right," he swore. He reddened. "Sorry, Hannah."He'd meant to apologize for swearing, but if she took it as an apology for his rudeness, that was just as well. "You're right. The shoe is loose. We should walk back."

"Good." To her credit, she didn't crow, as he'd feared, just accepted his answer as fact.

"Let's go back the way we came," Maxwell commented. "It's quicker."

"As you wish." She nodded. "It's important we get her back fast, and it's not too steep this way."

Her tone was calm, and Maxwell found himself feeling impressed. She cared about horses, more than about her pride or his, and that motivated her comments. She was concerned about her horse. All that mattered to her was that they cared for her needs. His heart softened.

"You must have quite a lot of experience with horses," he murmured as they walked back. He found himself wondering about her hands, and if she used the balm in the coach because they hurt from riding. His own often hurt when he'd been out for hours in the cold. He suddenly burned with curiosity to know more about her.

"All my life," she answered lightly. "My earliest memories are with horses." Her voice was quiet but warm.

"Mine, too," Maxwell told her softly.

"That's remarkable," she murmured.

He grinned. "Not sure about that," he said, though his heart was suddenly flooded with warmth. She was the only person who had ever greeted his love of horses with such joy.

She smiled at him, and he smiled back, holding her soft blue gaze. It felt as though he was drowning, falling into the blue lakes of her eyes. His heart was still glowing as he took Nightfire's reins. They walked, slowly and side-by-side, back to the house. It was a strange feeling, this new closeness, and he shook his head as if to clear it, then looked down at the ground and focused on getting them back to the safety of the garden as quickly as possible.

Chapter 11

The pain in her head made the room seem darker than it was. Exhausted but elated after the ride, Hannah sat at the table. Her stomach was growling with hunger again, and she looked at her hands awkwardly, hoping that nobody would hear it. The butler came in with the trolley, serving the soup, and she looked around to distract herself while she waited. The wallpaper was creamy yellow, a design of acanthus worked into the silk. There were paintings of woodlands on the walls, ones that she guessed might be around the estate. Maxwell's gaze caught hers across the table and her heart raced.

That's the second time I've caught him staring at me.

Her cheeks warmed and a small, confused frown wrinkled her brow. He had been staring at her intermittently since she came into the dining room, and it was confusing her.

On their walk—which had been a ride before she'd found the missing horse-shoe—they had talked a little and the mocking, patronizing way he'd spoken to her had annoyed her a great deal. But on the way back, he hadn't talked like that anymore. He'd laughed and smiled and, if the conversation was limited or stilted, it hadn't felt like it was because he was angry or impatient.

And his eyes, staring into mine; it feels so odd.

Maxwell had gazed at her as he did now, and she found the strength of the feelings it evoked in her at once delightful and a bit annoying, if she was honest. He had the power to make her feel shy and elated at once, and that seemed unfair. Whenever she caught his gaze on her she'd look away, wanting to ignore him, but feeling a delicious tingle that made her look again to see if he was watching.

"A warm day," Gavin commented, grinning at her. She blinked in surprise, her thoughts miles away so that it took her a second to discern what the words meant.

"Yes," she replied, still feeling a little vague. "Very warm."

"How was your outing?" Gavin asked.

"We had a fine ride today," Maxwell told the assembled guests, Gavin and Patricia. His voice was warm and content, surprising Hannah. She'd thought at least that he'd be grumpy because Crimson's shoe had, in fact, been loose and she'd been right, but he sounded like he'd had as fine an afternoon as she did. Her eyes widened.

"Grand. I'm so pleased." Patricia's voice was warm, but something about it made Hannah tense. She looked again at the older woman, seeing her brow was damp with sweat. She looked distinctly unwell.

"You went riding, and I stayed in and made my eyes hurt squinting at charts," Gavin teased.

"Nobody said you had to find the route for our ride next week," Maxwell told him lightly. Gavin grinned.

"No, but if I let you decide, you'll make it an adventure. I'm not sure I want to get lost somewhere on the moors."

"Lost on the moors," Maxwell chuckled. "In Kent?"

"I fully expect to get lost even in Kent with you."

Maxwell roared with laughter and Hannah grinned, feeling a tingle in her chest. He had a lovely laugh, and seemed to enjoy it if his friends teased him. It was a pleasant quality, one that made it clear he was not stuck-up and arrogant.

"I got us lost once, when we were in Spain," Maxwell told him, shaking his finger playfully. "Twice. All right."

"Twice!" His friend laughed. "And the first time was worse."

"I learn. See, Mama?" Maxwell grinned, turning to his mother. "I always improve."

"Of course, you do, Maxwell."Patricia's voice was gentle.

Hanah felt her body tense. Patricia's voice sounded strained. The sweat was still there, though she was far away from the fireplace, and only a faint warmth met them. It was a warm evening, but the windows were open, admitting a cool breeze.

Hannah looked over at Maxwell, but he was pouring lemonade for his mother and then for himself, relaxed and happy. She didn't want to trouble him. If Patricia hadn't mentioned it, perhaps she didn't want any fuss.

If she doesn't manage to eat tonight, I'm going to have to say something.

"Pass Hannah the lemonade, please, Gavin?" Maxwell instructed his friend, interrupting her thoughts. "She must be thirsty."

"Thank you," Hannah murmured, cheeks flushing as Gavin

reached for her glass and poured lemonade into it. It was cloudy yellow, the glass cool with condensation. She sipped, gasping at the relief...she must have been far thirstier than she'd thought. She smiled her thanks at Maxwell. He beamed at her, then turned away shyly. She felt her toes tingle at the sudden, stunning smile.

"Bring the first course, please," Maxwell instructed the butler briskly, still not meeting Hannah's gaze. "And another jug of lemonade. Some of us are thirsty after today's sunshine." His gaze moved to Hannah fondly.

"Very good, my lord."

Hannah flushed. His eyes held hers and she felt her cheeks start to burn and looked down at the table. She was wearing her blue dress, and she could see the appreciation in his stare. It made her tingle with delicious shyness.

"Soup of creamed spinach, my lord," the butler announced, and, starting with Maxwell, he went around the table, serving them all in succession. Hannah breathed in as he filled the bowl in front of her. The soup was pale green and looked appetizing, and the savory smell was delicious, making her mouth water. She put her napkin daintily on her knee then lifted her spoon, taking a big mouthful. It was only after she'd done it that she felt embarrassed—she hadn't waited for the others to start but was spooning it in like a soldier after a day's riding. She gazed across the table to find Maxwell smiling at her.

Heat tingled through her that had nothing to do with the heat of the bowl of soup and she looked down, embarrassed and delighted at once.

"I say! This is a fine soup for a hungry fellow." Gavin reached for a piece of bread from the basket in the center of the table. Hannah smiled warmly. He seemed funny and open-hearted. Nothing like the earl, who was reserved and cold.

Or is he not?, she thought.

She took a deep breath, feeling a surge of heat through her body as she remembered his admiring gaze, his friendliness during their ride. She reached for her glass of lemonade, distracting herself from her lovely memories for fear that she'd sit grinning dazedly at nothing.

"Mama!" Maxwell shouted. Hannah shot upright; instantly seeing the source of alarm.

Patricia was falling forward in her chair.

Hannah ran to her, just as she slipped sideways and fell to the floor.

"Mama," Maxwell was whispering, already beside his mother, where Hannah knelt. He reached for his mother's hand, feeling it. "She's warm," he said to Hannah. "What's happened?"

His eyes were wide with confusion and fear and Hannah felt a twist of empathy in her heart.

"She's lost consciousness," she said, feeling for a pulse at Patricia's neck, the way Margaret had shown her. "Her pulse feels normal, just a bit slow. And she's breathing," she added, bending down to listen at Patricia's mouth and nose. She could detect a faint, occasional intake of breath.

"Thank God," Maxwell murmured. He looked at Hannah, his gaze desperate. "What can we do?"

"We should put her on a bed or a chair where she can rest lying down," Hannah said, working partly by instinct and partly from the knowledge she'd gleaned talking with Margaret. "And has somebody any volatile salts?"

"Smelling salts?" Gavin asked. He'd come to join them, kneeling with them where they knelt with Patricia.

"Yes. Exactly," Hannah replied briskly. "We should try reviving her with those."

"Of course!" Maxwell stood up and strode to the hallway, his loud footsteps quietening as he retreated at a run. Hannah stroked Patricia's brow. It didn't feel particularly warm, so it wasn't because of a fever that she'd collapsed. That was good. Once she was conscious, Hannah would try to figure out why.

Maxwell strode back into the room again. "The butler is fetching the salts. Should he not send for the physician?" he asked Hannah. Hannah tilted her head uncertainly.

"Let's try with the salts now," she replied slowly. It was more important to try and revive Patricia as quickly as possible than to get the physician. All the same, Hannah felt her brow crinkle in a frown, pulse thudding with nerves, as she saw how pale and clammy the woman's skin was.

"My lord?" a voice called from the hallway. "Smelling salts."

"Good! Bring them here," Maxwell replied briskly. He took the small glass vial from the butler and passed it to Hannah. "You administer them," he said firmly. "We might need you to send for the physician," he added to Mr. Haddon, who stayed.

Hannah tensed. Maxwell adored his mother. This was a huge responsibility. When she'd run to Patricia, she'd followed her instincts without thinking about it. She wasn't about to stop believing in herself now. Holding the little glass vial under the dowager countess' nose, she waited for a second or two, heart racing. The woman breathed in, and tension tightened around Hannah's body like a band as she waited to see what would happen.

Patricia coughed.

Hannah shut her eyes, sending up a silent prayer of thanks. It worked.

She waited while the older woman coughed convulsively, then sat up.

"My head..." Patricia whispered; her hand pressed to the side of her skull as if in pain.

"Shh. It's all right," Hannah said gently, her hand on Patricia's shoulder, heart thudding in joy and relief. "It's all right. You passed out. Maxwell is going to carry you to somewhere you can lie down properly."

She looked up at Maxwell, who didn't need any telling, but bent down and enfolded his mother lovingly in his arms, cradling her against his chest. Hannah felt her own heart tighten with emotion at the tender way he held her. Love was written in every line of his body, every movement as he lifted her and carried her to the door. That was what love between a mother and son could look like.

Hannah followed them, Gavin walking with her.

"That was swift thinking," he told Hannah, his hazel eyes wide with surprised admiration. Hannah smiled at the compliment, looking down at her toes modestly.

"I'm just glad I knew enough to be able to act promptly," she said instantly. Thoughts swarmed in her mind as they walked upstairs. Just like swollen joints, the fainting could result from a heart that didn't pump well. She recalled seeing digitalis plants growing in the garden—they could make tea to help her. She felt relieved, then nervous. Maxwell had let her assist his mother, but would he trust her with more than that?

70

"You were most professional," Gavin murmured, walking with her to the landing.

"Thank you," Hannah said softly. "I hope I can do more to help."

They had reached the upstairs hallway opposite the dowager countess' apartment. She looked in through the parlor door, where Maxwell had already put Patricia lovingly on the divan. Hannah felt her heart soften as she watched him stroke his mother's brow.

"I'll go downstairs and wait for the physician," Gavin said softly, diffidently withdrawing from the private space.

Hannah stood awkwardly in the doorway. Her throat tightened. Now was the moment to tell Maxwell she could help his mother. She had to be brave and ask him.

"Easy, Mama," Maxwell was saying gently to Patricia. "Don't overburden your strength. Just lie down and rest now. The physician will be along soon."

"I could make a tea for her," Hannah whispered from behind him. "It could help her heart. I know what herbs to put in it."

He ignored her at first and Hannah thought maybe he hadn't heard, but then he stood up to face her. She tensed, thinking he was going to reprimand her for interfering with his mother. His expression was serious, his thin mouth a hard line, eyes even darker than normal. She waited, ignoring the urge to run, and he cleared his throat.

"Thank you," he said.

Hannah stared at him. She could barely believe that he'd thanked her. It was not her expectation. She coughed and stammered a reply, some polite words she didn't even consciously choose.

"Thank you," he repeated more gently. "You have done a great thing. I would be pleased if you would make her a tea. I am sure it would help."

Hannah felt her jaw drop and she managed not to gape at him. She stammered a reply. "Thank you. I'll go and prepare it."

He nodded. "Please do."

She inclined her head to his nod of permission and hurried from the room. She could think only of his dark-eyed gaze and the soft line of his mouth. It was so different to the stern, cold way he'd been with her just the day before, and her soul was soaring as she hurried to pick the herbs to make the tea.

Chapter 12

The sunlight streamed in through the long windows in the drawing room, painting bars of rich golden sunshine on the carpet. Maxwell could feel a strange knot in his stomach—it was excitement, but it was only as he strode to the window that he allowed himself to admit that he was excited to see Hannah.

It was a week since his mother had collapsed, and he felt his lips lift at the sound of laughter drifting up from the lawns. Hannah was there chatting to his mother as they walked slowly around the lawn, and his heart filled with warmth and relief. He strained to hear their conversation.

"...and the roses are going to be covered in blooms this year," Hannah commented, gazing at the bushes around them.

"It's been a good springtime—warm and mild. Enough rain for the garden to flourish," Mama answered contentedly.

Hannah smiled. "I'm pleased to be here in the countryside and not in London."

"I hate London in springtime!" his mother agreed feelingly. "Hot and sticky and no fun at all with all those people crowding in for the Season." She smiled.

Maxwell's heart filled with warmth. He hadn't seen his mother talk so freely with someone in years, possibly ever. She was naturally private and reserved, like himself, but Hannah had reached her heart like no-one else.

Besides the friendship, he had noticed his mother's health seemed a little improved. Her paleness was less, and she seemed as though she had more energy. When he visited her in her parlor she chatted about the garden and the horses, her eyes sparkling, skin glowing with fresh brightness.

A sound in the hallway made him turn and he looked up to see Hannah and Mama coming into the room. His heart jumped. Hannah was wearing a white gown with a pattern of flowers in striking blue worked into the fabric. Her face flushed, a few strands of hair falling loose about her face, and her blue eyes seemed even bluer in the lovely dress. He grinned, her shy smile making his heart thud steadily.

Mama was smiling warmly. "I trust you had a pleasant

morning?" she asked.

"Good enough," Maxwell commented lightly. "I had time for a ride, but only to the village." He saw Hannah's eyes widen and he felt a little guilty that he hadn't asked her to come. "The smith needs to come up to the stable and I thought I might as well ride there myself." He explained, then bit his lip. He'd not yet discussed his passion for horses with Hannah, and she doubtless would wonder at an earl riding to visit a blacksmith. Any normal person would have sent the groom to do it.

"He's going to re-shoe Crimson, I trust?" she asked lightly.

He chuckled, relieved she hadn't even noticed his unconventional ways. "Exactly."

She held his gaze, playfully, and his heartbeat thudded in his chest. "The same smith as before?"

"He usually does a good job," Maxwell said defensively, but she was smiling at him.

"You're as fussy as I am," she teased. "I insisted on the smith from Oakwood village, even though the butler was sweating in annoyance because the smith from Readingfield is cheaper."

Maxwell inclined his head. "Very wise," he told her.

She grinned back and he held his breath. When she smiled, she was distractingly lovely. He turned to his mother, feeling self-conscious that he was staring. "I trust you had a good walk?"

"We did. I managed to reach the stables today," Mama told him, her lips lifting in the corners with evident pleasure. "You have made some good improvements there, son. Your idea about the windows seems to have improved the ventilation a great deal."

"Thank you, Mama," Maxwell said, distracted. Hannah was going to think him very odd indeed. While most earls spent money looking after their horses, very few put the personal effort into it that he did. He shot a look at her, but she was listening in fascination.

"You had trouble with lung complaints?" she guessed.

"Yes." Maxwell nodded briskly. "Two horses had congested lungs. With the new windows we put in, their health has improved considerably."

"Good, good." Hannah inclined her head. "You could try adding sage and other herbs to the feed. They can fight infection."

"Good idea." Maxwell looked at her admiringly. "That's a

very intelligent suggestion."

Hannah smiled.

"Would you like to settle down to tea, now? It looks delicious." Mama commented archly.

Maxwell blushed shyly, his gaze moving to the table where the butler had laid out the tea-service, a loaf-cake and some little tartlets. His stomach growled. The ride had made him hungry. He looked over at Hannah, thinking in some surprise that he had never spoken so at length with her—and he'd never had such in-depth conversations with any apart from Gavin. His heart skipped.

She's a very bright, learned woman.

He went to the table, his eyes lingering on Hannah as he did so. Mama settled on his left, Hannah on his right. He drew in a sharp breath as her hand brushed his when she reached for the teapot.

"May I pass you a plate?" he asked his mother, trying to ignore the heat that raced up his arm.

"I do believe I would like something to eat," his mother murmured, sounding interested as she looked at the food. "I feel as though I could fancy one of those tartlets."

Maxwell felt his heart twist. He hadn't realized until this moment that Mama's diminished appetite bothered him immensely. She picked at her dinner, usually too tired to eat more than a few forkfuls of anything before retiring to bed. Her redoubled appetite was as much a delight as her bright eyes and the red blush in her cheeks.

"Good morning, everyone," Gavin greeted them as he drifted in. He was dressed rather formally, but his hair was wild, and Maxwell guessed he'd been riding about the countryside.

"Good morning," Maxwell said mildly.

"Had to have a fine ride before the weather changes. Looks as though there's going to be a wind later." Gavin gestured to the window. "I'm as thirsty as a desert traveler," he murmured, pouring tea and gulping it down.

Maxwell grinned. "A wind, you say?"

"Mm." Gavin reached for a napkin, dabbing his chin where the tea had wet it. "The barometer indicates a change in the air-pressure, and that portends a wind, you know."

"Ah." Maxwell inclined his head. Gavin had always been

interested in natural philosophy. Maxwell himself had begun law at Cambridge, but his love of horses had taken him elsewhere. Gavin too. "Well, that explains it." He grinned at Gavin, hoping it was clear that it explained nothing.

"Now, it's quite simple," Gavin began, turning to Mama and Hannah, including them in the conversation. He gave a brief, succinct explanation of why the change in air pressure might indicate a coming wind. Maxwell grinned.

"Thank you, Gavin," he told him. "My brain will boil like the tea if you carry on."

Mama chuckled. "It was very interesting." Maxwell felt his heart fill with gladness as he glanced at Hannah. This was her tea that had done the trick, he was quite sure of it. That, and her presence. Mama had not looked so well in years. His mother reached for her purse, and the thought slipped his mind as she produced a small, sealed letter, making his brow furrow with curiosity.

"What is that?" Hannah asked before he had the chance.

"An invitation," Mama told her, beaming at everyone. "I must ask that I have acted sensibly. We received an invitation to the Duke of Larenmont's spring ball, and, since Larenmont House is not too far from us, I thought to accept. I trust I did the right thing?" She glanced at Hannah, who shrieked happily.

"A *ball*?" Her face glowed. "Here in the countryside?"

"Yes," Mama replied smilingly. "Not the same as the crowded, horrid London balls, I think." Her eyes sparkled.

"Why, no!" Hannah beamed. "And how diverting!"

Maxwell swallowed hard. He hadn't thought about how isolated the countryside must seem to Hannah, who was used to the diversions of the city. But he wished his mother had asked him. The Duke of Larenmont had a terrible reputation, his infamy spreading even before Maxwell went to Spain. He was five years older than Maxwell, or thereabouts, but had been a notorious rake for the last five years at least. Maxwell frowned.

"I used to try and avoid balls in London," Hannah confided to his mother smilingly. "But here in the countryside, I think it might be entertaining." Her cheeks were flushed, eyes glowing.

"I imagine it will be quite diverting, especially after the gloom of Carronwood," Mama said firmly. Her dark-eyed gaze, so like his own, speared Maxwell. He swallowed again.

He had been about to ask Mama to write back contradicting her previous answer, but that firm gaze made him hesitate, as did Hannah's blue-eyed wonderment at the idea. Both Mama's and her cheeks were flushed. An outing would do them good. Carronwood, he realized, must be no fun for a young woman who, unlike himself, was largely confined to the house. And for Mama, who was confined to her room or to the small area in the garden, it must be even more stifling. A ball would give them both some fresh air. He hesitated, glancing at Gavin.

His friend shrugged. "Why not?"

"Well, then," he said simply. "We're going to the ball."

"Hurrah!" Hannah whooped. Maxwell chuckled. It made him feel warm inside to see her so delighted. He shot an appreciative glance at Mama. It had been her good idea, not his.

"I wonder if I have suitable clothing," Gavin said thoughtfully. "I've not had a new set of anything made up since we went to Spain, you know." He beamed at Maxwell.

"You're impossible. You have plenty of clothes," Maxwell teased. It was true—Gavin, for all that he was the second son of a minor noble, spent more time and trouble on his wardrobe than most people he knew.

"With London fashions, you could have bought your clothes last week and still be unfashionable," Gavin commented. Hannah shuddered visibly.

"London is like that," she murmured. "People will censure you for having the wrong trim on your bonnet."

Maxwell frowned. He'd imagined Hannah had been happy in London. Her relatives struck him as fashion-obsessed and he'd not given it much thought that she wasn't. Her tone was hard, as though she had experienced more than her share of criticism. He wished he could find out more about that.

"When is the ball?" he asked, hoping to raise Hannah's mood again.

"Next week," Mama replied. "That gives all of us a week to get some clothes made for the ball," she added with a teasing glance at Gavin.

"Thank you, my lady," Gavin told her, inclining his head in mock-thanks. "You save me from an embarrassing evening."

Mama chuckled.

"Next week!" Hannah cried excitedly. "Why! How wonderful. I think I know which gown I shall wear. I will need your advice, Patricia." She turned to Mama, who smiled fondly, squeezing her hand where it lay beside her own on the table.

"Of course, my dear. I'd be glad to assist."

Maxwell smiled to himself. Her smile was infectious, and Mama looked happy, too. He gazed over at Hannah, feeling his heart flood with warmth. She had done this; had brought the smile back to his mother's heart. There was such happiness in the drawing room; and it was her doing—Mama and her. It was a good feeling.

"I shall tell the butler we'll be needing the coach," he commented. He grinned, finding that, despite his lack of enthusiasm at first, he looked forward to the ball after all.

Chapter 13

The Carronwood coach was large and fine, black-lacquered and heavy, made of lancewood. It was dark inside, lit only by the lamp that swung from the front near the driver's seat. Hannah, ensconced inside and surrounded by her warm evening mantle, breathed in, smelling the scent of pomade and perfume and the familiar mustiness of the coach. Her stomach knotted up as she gazed down at the silk gown she was wearing. In a few minutes, they'd be at Larenmont Estate.

They had set out at sunset, but it was now almost night, the sky inky blue, not quite black yet. Hannah stared out, watching the dark forms of bushes and trees race past against the velvet-blue sky. Her chest tightened with excitement, and she glanced at Patricia, who was grinning as if she felt an equal joy.

"Almost there," Patricia murmured.

Hannah glanced down at her hands and tried to calm down, but a warm, excited grin lifted her lips, refusing her attempt to quell it. She was surprised by her excitement. She had hated balls with Mama, Edward and Philipa. They'd harangued her so thoroughly about how she must behave that she'd barely been able to step through the door without fear.

She looked over at her companions in the coach. Patricia was wearing a silk gown in an inky color, as befitted her status in mourning. A brief veil covered her white hair. Dark gems gleamed at her throat, and she looked poised and regal. Gavin, seated beside Patricia, was wearing a charcoal velvet jacket and trousers, a frothy cravat tied elaborately. He looked remarkably serious. She grinned. He grinned back.

"This thing is so hot. My neck sweats terribly in it."

Hannah had to laugh. She glanced at Maxwell, who chuckled. He was sitting beside her, and she'd tried not to stare all through the trip. In a black velvet jacket with a high-collared shirt, he looked remarkably handsome. Her stomach knotted with delicious excitement as she glanced sideways at him.

Since when do I find him so stunning?

She smiled inwardly. She should stop fooling herself. She had always seen how good-looking he was, but had been too angry to allow herself to admit that, even to herself.

Her hands smoothed over her gown—fortunately, they had stopped perspiring with her excited anticipation. She was wearing midnight-blue silk, a gown Patricia had insisted she wore despite her own protests that it was much too elegant. The dress was low-cut, the high waist banded with a dark blue ribbon, and the sleeves were puffs of the same blue figured silk. She wore a silver chain about her neck, one that had been Patricia's, and Patricia's pearl-ended hairclips decorated her hair. She breathed in deeply, feeling the knot of excitement tighten unbearably about her chest, making her breath shallow.

"Halt, there," the coachman was calling. "Whoa! Slow down."

The coach slowed, and Hannah stared out of the window, gaping at the big house on their left. It was lit up in front, pine torches held in their brackets casting bright light on the front stairway. She swallowed, awed. It was no bigger than Grassdale or Carronwood, but, rising from in the dark woodland around it, it seemed like a palace in one of the enchanting tales her nursemaid told her. She breathed in deeply, her hands smoothing her dress again as they did when she was nervous.

"Here we are, then," Maxwell said lightly. His voice was higher than usual, and Hannah swore he was nervous. He jumped lithely from the coach as the coachman opened the door, and she dismissed the thought. He had no reason to be nervous. He had surely attended these balls when he was in the country before—the Larenmont estate was a neighbor to the Carronwood estate after all.

She went to the coach door. Maxwell took her hand, his fingers warm and tight on her own. Her heart pounded. She looked into his eyes and that dark gaze drew her in, his bright stare lit with admiration. She was sure of it.

"There." Maxwell told her gently. "Now, we just need to get in without being crushed by the other guests."

Hannah giggled. She'd never heard Maxwell joke before. He stepped back, helping his mother, Patricia, from the coach, then Patricia took Gavin's arm and they all walked slowly to the doors.

The guests were thronging the way to the doors, the drive lit with the same pine torches to help them see their way. The sound of chatter was loud in the crowd of people, laughter mingling with it like the sound of a waterfall. She felt her head spin as they neared the doors, the bright lights in the ballroom making her senses swim.

Lord Larenmont stood in the doorway. He was remarkably tall, possibly as tall as Maxwell, his black hair thick and lustrous, his face long and saturnine and his smile amused. Hooded eyes regarded her appraisingly. She tensed, nervous.

"Why! Carronwood. This is a surprise. I heard about your, um...retreat from eligible bachelorhood. The papers always tell whoppers, but this time there's truth in them. What a stunning lady." He bowed low, taking Hannah's hand. She tensed as his lips pressed to it. The touch burned. He looked up at her, those dark eyes bright as if he was teasing her. Her stomach knotted, but not in the pleasant way it did with Maxwell.

"Thank you for your congratulations." Maxwell's voice was cold as ice. "Now, if you'll forgive me, we must hurry in. The crowd behind is eager to push their way forward."

Lord Larenmont laughed. "No need to rush. They'll get in before midnight." He gazed after them, his eyes lingering on Hannah. Hannah felt Maxwell's fingers tighten on her wrist as he steered her downstairs.

"That fellow's got a bad reputation," he whispered.

"I can believe it."

Maxwell grinned."Good."

Hannah felt her face light up. She had seen him grin often, the smile fleeting and radiant like sunlight on the moors, but each and every smile lit her up inside. She felt her heart race.

"Maxwell?" a soft voice spoke behind them. It was Patricia. Gavin had her arm, helping her to navigate the crowded entrance-way. "Can you see a quiet corner?" she asked him.

"There are some chairs arranged over there." Maxwell pointed to the left-hand corner of the ballroom. The crowd seemed thicker here than it was outside, people standing so tight-packed that the heat and noise pressed in around them. Beside the stairs the crowd was particularly thick, and they had to navigate carefully to find their way through to the corner Maxwell had indicated.

Hannah walked with Maxwell, her hand in his, her heart thudding. She was pleased to be holding onto him—by herself she was sure she would not have been able to get through the tight press of people by the stairs. They reached the corner, where it was much quieter, the crowd thinning so that groups of people were interspersed a few feet apart, and there they found a chair for Patricia to sit in. Maxwell stood beside her chair protectively.

"It's crowded in here," he murmured.

"I remember Larenmont always had a long guest-list." Patricia chuckled. "And the size of the ballroom doesn't merit one."

Hannah giggled. She looked around, Patricia's amusing comment setting her at ease. The ballroom was small, certainly, compared to Grassdale. There the room could fit fifty comfortably. Here, she guessed there were only about thirty guests, but the room felt crowded. It was, however, beautiful. A high, molded ceiling soared on tall arches, the walls decorated with molding, here and there, of pillars and acanthus forms. The floor was highly polished, the gleam of the dozen chandeliers radiant, where over a hundred candles shed their bright light over the guests.

"I'm parched," Gavin complained. "It's this suit, you see. Too hot." He looked around. "Would you ladies care for cordial?"

"Please," Hannah murmured.

"I shall fetch you some," he offered. "Would you like some lemonade?" This was addressed to Patricia, his aunt.

"Please, Gavin. You're very kind," she murmured warmly.

The men departed to fetch refreshments, and Hannah waited with Patricia, looking around. The noise in the room made talking difficult and she was content, as, it seemed, was Patricia, to observe the happenings without uttering a word. Men and women drifted in, ostrich-feathers in their headbands making some women stand tall, while the men wore dark colors and most of them had donned knee-breeches for the occasion. Hannah smiled to herself. The fashions were not quite as modish as London—the trend for white figured silk gowns hadn't reached this far, nor had the Oriental fashions like patterned silks and turbans for the women. She glanced at Patricia.

"There are always this many guests, you say?" she asked, curiously.

"Sometimes less, sometimes more," Patricia commented lightly. "Here in the countryside it's usually the same families. Ourselves, the Almhursts, the Coveleys and Larenmonts." She smiled, her gaze moving over the room as if looking for old friends.

"Do you come each year?" Hannah asked. It was hard to imagine Maxwell attending a yearly event—he seemed uncomfortable enough to think that he hated balls of all description.

"Not every year," Patricia replied. "We came often when Maxwell was younger. I thought he enjoyed balls, rather. Maxwell likes music," she told her.

"He does?" Hannah gaped.

"Yes." Patricia chuckled. "Always did. His tutor said he'd do well to learn to sing, but Maxwell hated the idea. A pity...he has a fine ear for music."

"Really?" Hannah grinned at her, amazed. She hadn't guessed at a love of music in Maxwell, who was always so formal, so closed off that it was impossible to imagine him dancing, and singing was unthinkable.

"Here, my lady." Maxwell spoke from behind her, startling her from her musings. He returned with a glass of cordial, bowing low. It was dark pinkish-red, and she guessed it was redcurrant—one of her favorite ones. She looked up at him in surprise.

"Thank you."

She sipped it, her mouth puckering at the taste. It was delicious—a little bitter and most refreshing. He smiled.

"I thought you'd prefer it to plum cordial. It was never a favourite with me."

"Me, neither!" She chuckled, amused at even that agreement between them. He smiled and she smiled back, a little breathless.

"Dash it; it's sweltering." Gavin complained, his fingers loosening the fastenings at his collar. "I'm going to breathe some fresh air in a moment. Anyone coming?"

"If there's somewhere to sit outside, I'll join you gladly." Patricia shifted in her seat, a glass of lemonade in one hand. "I can barely think with all the shouting going on in here." Maxwell glanced at her.

"It's cold outdoors," he murmured.

"I'll fetch my cloak if I need one," Patricia promised, grinning at Hannah as if they shared a secret.

Hannah grinned back. Gavin chatted to Patricia about the

83

garden as they walked to the door together, and Maxwell and she followed; then her attention drifted across the ballroom. Musicians were setting up in the corner. The dancing was about to start.

Maxwell sipped his lemonade, not saying anything.

Hannah watched him, longing to dance but wondering if he wished to. Patricia was watching him too, and she gestured to him, requesting that he bend closer to talk to her. Part of her wanted to ask what the matter was, but then someone appeared at her elbow.

"My lady," the duke murmured. His dark eyes, that had gazed at her in the entrance-way so uncomfortably, held her gaze. "If I might be so bold, it would do me real honour if you were to dance with me. May I secure a cotillion?" His smile was bright and insistent, his eyes piercing.

"I..." Hannah stammered. She looked around, wanting someone to help her.

Maxwell was animatedly discussing something with Gavin, and she didn't know if he'd heard. Patricia was watching them, but then the music started up, and, before Hannah refused to, the duke grabbed her hand and whisked her onto the dance floor.

"Your grace. I must protest. I..." she began

"Don't worry, my lady. It will be fine." He interrupted confidently.

Hannah glared at him, but she was on the dance-floor now and she couldn't escape...not without creating a scene. She had been taught each day that it was unseemly and shameful to make a scene, and those censorious words felt like shackles, holding her feet in place. She stayed there, his hand on her shoulder, her other hand gripped in his over-tight fingers. She shivered at the touch of his hand on her back. It felt wrong.

"Your grace," she began again, trying to protest.

"Relax, my sweet countess," he breathed. "We're at a ball."

Hannah tensed, feeling her stomach twist with nausea. Her glance moved across the guests.

Maxwell was standing with his mother. His gaze met hers and she stared into it, asking him silently for help. His eyes were wide, smoldering with rage at the duke. She felt her heart twist.

"Please, my lord," she murmured as the music slowed. "I must protest. I wish to return to my chair." She twisted her hand,

84

sliding it out of his grasp.

He looked at her in surprise. The cadence was just shifting to a close, but she turned abruptly, slithering out of his grasp, and marched across the ballroom. She heard someone gasp, but in that moment, she didn't care. She was wild with anger. She was not a lady, not a noblewoman—just plain Hannah, who loved the countryside and Sapphire.

And for once in her life that was no bad thing.

She stalked across the ballroom, heading to where Patricia sat, her eyes wide and shining. She wasn't smiling, but her expression showed plainly that she admired Hannah's escape. Beside her, Maxwell gaped in surprise. Hannah shuddered at the feeling of the duke's hands on her, her back carrying the feeling of his touch as if his palm burned the skin. She felt safe as she hurried towards Maxwell, Patricia and Gavin—the only family she had here, and the only family she knew. She went to stand with them, shivering, and looked out across the ballroom as the musicians began to play another tune.

Chapter 14

Maxwell's jaw was tight with anger as he stood at the back of the crowd around the dance-floor. Mama's words echoed around his mind, exhorting him to do something he wasn't sure he felt ready to try.

Just ask her to dance, she said. *No good standing about being so enraged because someone was bold and rude enough to do it.*

Watching the duke whirl about the floor with her made his stomach sour with rage. Hannah was so beautiful, the light on her porcelain skin making her seem to glow where she moved in the dance, the exquisite blue of her eyes brought out by the dark blue of her gown. Her hair was fluffed about her face, the golden curls bright in the glow of the room. Her gaze on him implored him for assistance.

He had wanted to walk up and shake the fellow until his teeth chattered.

He looked at Hannah where she stood before him. She was flushed, but not in a happy way. Her eyes were wide, and there was a tense, frightened expression in them. He felt his hand clench. If the fellow had appeared in front of him, he'd have strangled him then and there.

"Hannah. I...think..." He paused, feeling foolish. His first words would have been to tell her he wanted to hit the duke, but that was a ludicrous thing to say, so he swallowed hard and said what he ought to have sooner. "I think the next dance is a waltz. Will we...?"

Hannah blinked at him and her lips made a small "O" shape. He grinned, relief flushing through him as she inclined her head swiftly.

"As you wish."

Maxwell bowed, and, without having to think about it, he took her hand in his and strode to the dance-floor. The waltz was just starting, and he swiftly rested a hand on her shoulder-blade, swallowing hard. He'd never danced with her before, and the feeling of her warm, firm shoulder through the gossamer-soft silk of her gown, the thin fabric doing nothing to stop the warmth of her skin, was overwhelming. She smelled floral and he breathed deeply. His heart thumped as if in fear.

She's too stunning.

He looked across at the musicians to distract himself. It wasn't merely her blue eyes and that sweet face. It was the brightness of her smile and the firm character he knew underlay those lovely looks. He recalled that she had whirled round from the duke, tearing herself from his grasp, and striding off across the ballroom, her steps determined and strong—it was in that moment that he had felt his heartbeat quicken, soul filled with admiration for her spirited strength.

She's easily as strong-willed as Nightfire.

Comparing her to a particularly wild horse was maybe unfair, but there was truth in it, and for a man who admired horses far more than he admired people, it was complimentary.

"There are a lot of people here," Hannah said softly. She sounded quiet and scared now and his desire to hit the duke, hard and purposely, grew and doubled within him.

"It is crowded," he murmured in agreement. He didn't think that she was listening, not really: the noise was so loud, and it was making it impossible to banter. He couldn't really think of anything to say, and it didn't feel important. As they glided forward, he lost consciousness of everything except Hannah, the gentle music and the swaying, sweet motion of the dance they shared.

He shut his eyes for a moment. It felt like he was dancing in a dream. It was effortless, floating and lovely. They stepped across the dance floor gracefully, their steps in unison. They whirled in time with the music, her soft skirt flaring slightly, their motions seamless.

It was impossible to talk as they danced. He didn't mind in the slightest. His mind was too full of amazement to speak, the dance so beautiful that he wanted to appreciate it without having to talk.

She looked up at him, that blue gaze like two cornflower pools, and it felt as though the ballroom melted away and all that was in it was her.

He gazed at her in silent admiration. Her hair was coming loose in one place from its elaborate style, and he wished he could reach up to tuck it behind her ear. He ached to feel the softness of it. Her skin looked like silk and he felt himself lean closer. He had kissed her once, but he could barely remember doing so, the occasion so formal that his mind had been utterly blank. Now, he felt warmth rush through him, and he longed to draw her close, to press his lips to those soft, damp ones.

"Hannah," he whispered.

The music was slowing, and she gazed up at him, her eyes locked with his, and it was only when he heard the sound of talking become louder that he blinked and realized that the rest of the dancers had stopped around them. He hastily moved his hand from her shoulder, bowing briskly.

"My lady," he murmured.

"Maxwell." She curtseyed and he felt his heart thud so swiftly he was sure the entire hall would turn and stare. Her voice was like a breeze, soft and lovely. He stepped back, unable to take his eyes off her.

"Should we fetch some refreshment?" he asked, hastily speaking before he no longer had courage. He didn't mind what they did—all he wanted was that she stayed by his side. He saw her eyes widen.

"Yes please. I'd like some more lemonade. It's so hot in here."

"Of course." He gazed around, glad that he was tall enough to spot the nearest table despite the crowd in the way. He blushed as he rested a hand on her shoulder to steer her through the thronging ball guests. "There's one there."

They reached the table.

"Some lemonade, please. And a glass of cordial." He directed his request at a man in dark red livery working behind the table. They only had plum cordial left, he noticed, but he took it anyway. He could have had wine or brandy, but he wanted to have a clear head. He passed Hannah the lemonade and she smiled up at him. His heart skipped.

"Thank you," she said softly.

"Of course, my lady."

By the table, there was less noise, and they could talk more. Maxwell racked his brain to think of a topic.

"You like dancing?" she asked him curiously. He grinned, relieved she seemed to want to stay and talk as well rather than go back to Gavin and Mama straight away.

"That's a difficult question," Maxwell answered, laughing. "I was apparently quite good at it, but I didn't ever like it. I didn't like anything to do with being an earl. Not until now." He hadn't meant to say it, but the truth found its way to his lips, and she stared up at him.

"That...that's nice." She sounded a little confused. He felt his body heat up and he looked away shyly. He'd never really spoken to her about his past, about his relationship with his father and how difficult it was. He wished he could confide more, but it was the wrong place for talking about something so serious and besides, he still felt unsure of how she'd respond if he let her see his inmost feelings.

"I am glad Mama suggested we come," he mumbled, changing the topic.

"Me, too." She gazed up at him, those beautiful blue eyes like lakes he could drown in.

He looked away, feeling dreadfully shy. It was a lovely shyness, but it was nevertheless challenging to talk. He caught sight of his mother, who found her way through the crowd towards them, beaming at Hannah.

"There she is. Are you enjoying the evening?"

"I am. Thank you," Hannah said smilingly.

"Where is Gavin?" Mama added, looking around the room.

"Over at the refreshments table," Maxwell commented. Gavin was tall enough to spot in the crowd. His chestnut hair stood out too, his tall, lanky form leaning near a pillar. Maxwell grinned, seeing the small group around Gavin. He could guess they were all hanging on his words. Gavin was a terrific speaker. Maxwell had sometimes wished he had his easy way with people.

"Will you let him know I'm going outside again?" Mama asked. "I must get out of doors...the heat and noise are making it hard to think in here."

"Of course." Maxwell answered. "We'll come with you." It would be a relief to get outside.

Maxwell gestured to Gavin, then pointed to the doors when his friend spotted him. Gavin nodded, clearly understanding. Maxwell held his mother's arm on his left, and Hannah's hand on his right, and they walked slowly towards the doors.

The sound of chatter low and steady, met Maxwell as they slipped out. He breathed in, smelling the wild, damp scent of dew-soaked lawns. He smiled to himself. He already felt better. There was a small group there, no more than six or seven people. It was much more relaxed outdoors.

"Look. There's Lady Albury. Excuse me a moment," Mama murmured.

Maxwell breathed out, nervously. Hannah and he were by themselves in a corner of the terrace together. He felt terribly shy. Talking to her while they rode was one thing—here, she was a silk-clad stranger, lovely as midnight flowers, and he felt utterly at a loss.

"It's a beautiful evening," she murmured. She was leaning on the railing, her bare arms pale against the stone. Her skin was like satin, the lamplight from indoors outlining her profile in gold, her face still and mysterious. He found it difficult, suddenly, to breathe.

"It is," he agreed. He could smell the sweet scent of her perfumed skin and he felt as though he was drowning. He leaned on the rail, fighting the urge to take her in his arms.

"You came back to England to become an earl," she began, her tone rising in inquiry. "Why were you in Spain?"

"I spent three years abroad," he smiled, "learning to follow my dream."

"Which was?"

"Horse farmer."

"What!" Her exclamation was loud, and she covered her lips. "Sorry. It's just such a surprise. You wanted to *farm horses*? That's simply remarkable!"

"Yes," he told her, grinning. He hadn't expected such a delighted response. He glowed. His father had made him feel such shame about it that he had not expected someone would be delighted. "I spent three years there, learning that trade."

"No!" Hannah was giggling, her cheeks flushed. "How wonderful. I wish I could do that."

He laughed. "Believe me. You'd make the best horse-farmer there is."

"No." She laughed too, but her eyes were glowing. "Thank you, but I don't believe it. You'd be better."

"No." He smiled and, without thinking, he reached up and

tucked the stray strand of hair behind her ear. Her skin was as soft as satin. His body caught fire as his fingertips touched it. "You would."

She gazed up at him and he gazed back, and he forgot, for a moment, to draw breath. He leaned closer, and the smell of her perfume reminded him of something. He smiled and she frowned, brow wrinkling in an inquiry.

"I noticed you used a particular ointment on your hands once," he told her shyly. "In the coach. It was wintergreen. Why were you using that?"

"Oh!" She giggled; eyes widening as she stared up in shock. "You noticed?"

"Yes. It smells strong," he said, hoping she didn't feel odd or think he'd been spying on her.

"It does." She looked down at her hands, stretching them out before her. "I hurt my hands when I fell from my horse. She spooked in the forest." She looked up at him, her gaze hard as if she expected him to scoff at her for falling.

"You hurt yourself?" he asked. He felt instantly concerned.

"I did," she replied. "Not much—just bruises really, and two scratches on my hands and face. The scratches were shallow, and they healed nicely. But they ache sometimes," she added, flexing her fingers as if they were sore.

"I'm sorry," he said gently. "Riding accidents can be bad. Was it frightening?"

She shrugged. Her gaze softened but she looked more unhappy. "A bit. I was more worried about my hands. And the scratch on my face."

"You thought you'd done some bad damage?"

"No." Her voice was tight. "Mother would have been angry if I'd had scratches in London. She'd have said ladies don't have scrapes and cuts on their hands and faces."

Maxwell felt a flush of anger. "I beg to argue. Ladies can have scratches like anyone else."

Before he could think about it, he lifted her hand and pressed it to his lips. Her skin was soft and floral-scented, and he felt dizzy as his senses overloaded. Her fingers were narrow and delicate, as beautiful as they seemed, and she gasped.

He let go of her hand, thinking he'd frightened her. She

looked up at him and he couldn't see fear in that stare, only confusion and surprise. He couldn't look away. Her eyes were drawing him in, making him want to lean closer, to embrace her.

"Maxwell! There you are. I say, old fellow! What fine music, eh?"

Maxwell spun around, a scowl on his features as Gavin strode through the doors. His friend was smiling, and he couldn't help but smile back, his annoyance shriveling in the face of so much evident joy.

"It's a fine ball," Hannah agreed, her voice soft. Maxwell glowed.

"Indeed it is," Gavin said, holding Maxwell's eye. "Indeed."

He raised a brow at Maxwell, and Maxwell knew he had seen the look the two of them had shared, but found he was not shy. His friend should know how he felt.

Gavin turned towards Lord and Lady Albury and the group who stood by the railing. "Is the dowager countess there?" Gavin asked. "I brought her shawl, if she needs it." He wandered over to the group. "I might as well listen in...Lord Albury's got fine stables." He grinned at Maxwell and blended into the group with Mama. Maxwell chuckled.

He is trying to give us some time to talk.

He shot an appreciative look at his friend. He turned to Hannah, who looked relieved too.

"I'd love to hear about your experiences with horses," he told her shyly. Anything to talk more.

"I'd be pleased to tell you."

Her speech was lively and swift as she described the stable at her home, and he felt his soul soar. He'd wanted for ever so long to be able to talk with her. He just hadn't known how. He was only too grateful, now, that, despite all his confusion and his doubts, he'd come to the ball.

He never would have imagined that such closeness would blossom with Hannah and he knew he'd never forget standing on the terrace with her in the moonlight.

Chapter 15

The light from the candles was a soft golden glow, the shadows growing long. The candles were burning low, and Hannah blinked dazedly in the gathering dark, guessing it was almost time to return to the coach. She felt her head spin and she looked around for a chair, the heat and the noise making her feel ill.

"Hannah?" Maxwell's voice was gentle behind her. She could not forget the way he'd lifted her hand so tenderly to his lips. Her hand still tingled where they had touched the back of it, her mind returning again and again to the tender look in his eyes. "Are you all right?"

"I'm well," Hannah murmured. She struggled to stay on her feet. "Just a little tired."

"You're about to pass out, is probably truer," Maxwell murmured back. There was just a hint of amusement in his tone. "You don't need to hide it. I'll find a chair for you. Or even better—mayhap you'd like to sit with the ladies in the parlour for a while? Mama is retiring to the parlour before we go back. Perhaps you can go with her for a moment."

"Please," Hannah agreed. She could barely see for dizziness, and her head spun. It was the heat and the noise in the room, wearing on her.

"Well, then," Maxwell said gently. "I'll escort you there. Stay until you feel better. You have to promise."

"I'll stay sitting until I feel better," she promised.

"Good."

He held her arm gently, letting her support her weight on him as they walked to the doors. They walked up the hallway and Hannah tensed at the sound of laughter and feminine voices. One of them sounded like Philipa, harsh and mocking, and she felt her stomach twist in fear. She looked up at Maxwell and his eyes widened in surprise.

"Are you all right?" he asked.

"I'm all right," she replied quietly. She had never told him about her family; not really. Mayhap he assumed that they were kind and good—a little overbearing, that he must have already noticed, but basically friendly and kindhearted. She didn't have time to explain how Mother had scared her, how she'd felt belittled by Philipa all the time. The women's voices reminded her of them and she felt suddenly scared to enter, holding tight to his hand.

"I'll let you go in and be seated. I'll return to the ballroom. Someone has to keep an eye on Gavin." He grinned, but she could see he was worried about her.

"Good." She chuckled. "I think you'll have a harder task than me."

He laughed, then gave her a small bow and turned in the hallway.

Hannah hesitated at the door. The scent of perfume drifted to her, subtle and dangerous. She had learned that women were not her friends, but then Patricia was. And she was in there too. Maybe she was being foolish, hiding here in the hallway? She took a breath and walked in.

"Good evening," a woman greeted her as she walked slowly up to the refreshments table. She was a little taller than Hannah, with a squarish face, large dark eyes and brown curls. She was very pretty. Her eyes had big lids and long lashes and she had a haughty look that reminded Hannah of an Arab horse. "I think you are new to this circle?"

Hannah swallowed. It was impossible to tell if the words were friendly or a challenge. "Um, yes." She tried to smile. "I am."

"Ah. I am Lady Laurentia."

"Oh." Hannah frowned. She didn't know if she'd been introduced before during the evening. She didn't think so. She'd surely have remembered that face. It would have been beautiful but for the hard, arrogant look in the eyes. "Pleased to meet you," she added politely. She gave a slight curtsey, hastily remembering the proper manners.

"Charmed," the woman murmured.

"I am Lady Carronwood," Hannah told her, feeling shy. It felt odd to say that.

"I see." The woman's eyes widened. "Carronwood?"

"Yes." Hannah blinked in confusion. Patricia had suggested Maxwell and she were acquainted with most of the guests, but the woman talked as though she didn't know them. "Perhaps you know Lord Carronwood, whose home is about five miles from here...?"

"I know where Carronwood is." Her tone sounded annoyed.

"Sorry," Hannah murmured, instantly apologetic. Her guts twisted with shame, and she suddenly felt as inadequate as if Mother was here with her. She'd forgotten ever feeling that way and she flinched, remembering how small and stupid she was accustomed to feeling.

"No need," Lady Laurentia said quietly, and the earlier sweetness was in her tone. "I was only surprised."

"Surprised?" Hannah felt more curious than ashamed at those words.

"Yes. Lord Carronwood is so unreliable. I had thought he'd rush off to Spain and leave his mother here to take on the former Earl's legacy herself. Oh, I am silly." The woman giggled. "But he's very flighty, you see."

"*What*?" Hannah said softly. She flushed. "Sorry," she said again. She kept on doing unladylike things. "I beg your pardon. But he seems...not flighty." She felt her brow wrinkle concernedly. The word sat ill with Maxwell. He was so reliable, so trustworthy. But then, he had run off to Spain, as Laurentia put it. And his mother had truly seemed surprised he was back.

"Oh, don't believe your first impressions," the woman purred. "He's as mercurial as a windflower. But maybe that's unfair. Maybe I exaggerated. I just find he always hares off after the next diversion." Her voice sounded light, but her words bit like iron.

"Diversion?"

"Horses, mostly." She laughed. "But he's not the sort to take seriously. He's always chasing the next new fashion. Horse farms one day, East India the next." She giggled and her lovely eyes flicked across the room like a horse's might. "Insincere, people might say. But only if they were being unfair. And I don't want to bother you. I mustn't be judgmental." She smiled.

"Is he...is he decent?" she stammered.

"Decent!" Laurentia laughed. "Is Lord Larenmont decent?"

"Is he..." Hannah wanted to ask if he was insincere like the duke. This woman's words seemed to imply that the two were not dissimilar to one another. Laurentia was already turning away, another lady coming up towards her.

"I must excuse myself," Laurentia murmured. "I told Lady Rothmure I'd help her decide on new shades for summer dresses."

"Oh. Excuse me," Hannah replied softly. She curtseyed and stepped away. Her head whirled. Patricia must be here. Perhaps she could ask her about what Laurentia had said.

Thoughts chased themselves around her head, growing wilder at every second. Maxwell was untrustworthy. Maxwell was insincere.

The thought took hold. His coldness, his disinterest. Had that really dissolved? Or had he merely chosen to show her a fresh pretense? Maybe he had his reasons for showing a passing interest.

"Where is Patricia?" she murmured under her breath. She needed her help. She couldn't spot her over the heads of the growing crowd. A small group of women were sitting on chairs near a low table, and she went there, but Patricia wasn't there. She spotted a woman she recognized dimly from the terrace earlier.

"Lady Albury?" she said softly, but the lady was talking, and she stood silently and waited. She could see the diamond on her necklace, and the pearls the woman beside her wore. Everyone here was moneyed, but then, Hannah had also been raised in a rich household. The difference between her home and here was that everyone was titled. Maybe she didn't understand any of them. Maybe Maxwell could trick her so easily because their backgrounds were so different that she could be fooled by him.

"I was saying," Lady Albury continued as Hannah listened in again, "that this new fashion for silk will not last. All those imported goods are going to get expensive soon."

"Ah. Ah," the woman opposite her murmured. "I see." She seemed to catch sight of Hannah, her gaze sliding mildly across her. Hannah looked down at her toes, feeling shamed. "My dear Juliana," she addressed Lady Albury. "I think this young lady here wishes to speak with you."

Lady Albury looked at Hannah and her eyes seemed kind, sparkling as she smiled. "Welcome, young lady. I think I spotted you earlier?"

Hannah began introducing herself, but the other woman interrupted her.

"Ah, yes. I recall. You were with Lady Carronwood. Not so?

Dear Patricia! I'm delighted that she's so well."

"I will pass on the compliment," Hannah stuttered. "Is she not here?"

"No, she went out to the garden. She said it's too hot in here." Lady Albury gazed around, then back to Hannah, her gaze narrowing with care. "Would you like to sit down, dear? You look quite green."

"No. Thank you, my lady. But I think I will look for Lady Carronwood. Mayhap I also need to find somewhere cooler to stand." She fanned herself, pretending she was hot.

Lady Albury smiled. "Well, please do pass my regards to her."

"I'll do so," Hannah said swiftly. She shut the door behind her as though she needed to escape. The woman's words from earlier were like insects, buzzing in her mind. She could not let the thoughts rest. She strode outside to Patricia.

"I say! Hannah! There you are." Gavin greeted her, his voice loud enough to hear over the press of loud people around them. He gestured to the door. "It's getting late."

Hannah looked around. He was right. The candles were flickering, the musicians packing their things. "It is."

"We thought perhaps we'd try to get the coach out before the stampeding people all do the same thing." Gavin grinned. "Maxwell's at the door. He has your cloak."

She nodded, and then Gavin was opening the doors, and they were hurrying to the entrance-way, Patricia walking slowly beside them, her arm in Gavin's own. Hannah felt safe, seeing the older woman's kindly, careworn features. They walked to the doors together, Gavin chattering cheerily as they pushed through the throng. Maxwell waited with her cloak. She felt her heart skip, relieved to see him, but then those confusing, frightening words pressed in and she prayed inwardly that she would learn more about him and about that woman's words that somehow made her feel so small and ashamed and lost once again.

Chapter 16

The distant murmur of voices woke Maxwell, and he blinked at the light that poured onto his face. He rolled over, the bedclothes soft and heavy over him, and opened his eyes. The sunlight was streaming in through a gap in the curtains of his bedroom.

It's late, he thought to himself in surprise. Very late.

Even the fact that he'd slept so long could not dampen his joy and he slid out of bed swiftly and rinsed his face, still smiling. He could not get thoughts of Hannah at the ball out of his head. That moment on the balcony played through his thoughts repeatedly. He recalled the feeling of kissing Hannah's hand. Her soft skin and that surprised gasp had overwhelmed him, and he smiled, thinking of it again. She was so beautiful; so enchanting that it made his heart flip and a grin stretch across his face each time he thought about it.

"My blue jacket, if you please," he asked his manservant, Mr. Wainwright. "And my brown riding trousers."

His manservant went to fetch the items and Maxwell went behind a screen to change into them hastily.

"A fine day, eh, Wainwright?" he asked the fellow as he helped Maxwell tie his cravat. He'd chosen the lace-edged one that was similar to the one he wore for the ball—it seemed to make the right impression. For the first time in as long as he could remember, he cared about how he looked, and he wanted to look good.

"It is, my lord. Very fine." Wainwright murmured. He was at least twenty years Maxwell's senior, with a strong face and solemn dark eyes that focused on the knot as he tied it.

"A fine day for a ride. I reckon I might take a jaunt later."

"Very good, my lord."

Maxwell strode from the room, catching sight of himself in the looking-glass on the way. The navy blue of the jacket definitely did suit him, emphasizing his high cheekbones and soft dark hair. He felt his stomach twist in anticipation of seeing Hannah.

He paused in the doorway. She was there at the table, her blue-and-white dress on, her hair in a simple chignon. He felt his heart thump and it was hard to breathe. The sunshine poured in through the window, highlighting her hair and flushing her cheeks. She looked beautiful.

"Good morning," he greeted, trying for a casual tone.

"Good morning," she murmured. Her eyes lit up and his own soul soared, but then she looked down at her toast almost nervously and he frowned.

Maybe she's just tired.

He ignored the discomfort and confusion and sat down opposite Hannah. Gavin, on his left, beamed at them.

"Good morning," he said, dabbing his lips with a napkin. "My! I was starving. I don't know about you two. That's the trouble with balls...one must either eat early, before one departs, or be content to eat only tartlets and sausages all evening."

Maxwell laughed. "You have a good point." He reached for a slice of toast, buttering it amply. "I intend to go for a jaunt later, so I shall need a large breakfast to make up for that lack. Would you care to ride with me?" He directed the question at Hannah.

She looked back, terrified. "I...I told Patricia I'd stay here and do some mending and sewing with her," she replied. The reply was hasty.

"Well, there's still enough daylight left to ride and then do mending, surely?" he asked.

Hannah just looked down at her plate. "I don't know," she said awkwardly. "I'm also tired after yesterday."

"Of course," Maxwell said gently. "I understand."

That explained her strange look earlier—she really was just tired. He glanced at Gavin. "You'll have to come with me, then. I fancied riding to Almhurst's farm to check if his price for that stallion has changed for the season."

Gavin raised a shoulder, stifling a yawn. "Happy to, old chap," he said sleepily. "Don't know if I'll be of much use to you, but I'm more than happy to accompany you on the ride."

"Good, good," Maxwell murmured.

He sat listening to Gavin talk about the local farms, trying to be interested while his mind was full of Hannah. He glanced at her, longing for her to stare at him as she had the night before. She stared at her plate, listless.

She's just not interested in the conversation, he told himself firmly. *She likes horses, but would any young lady be interested in breeding them?*

He ate another three pieces of toast and pushed back his chair.

"Shall we go and get ready?" he asked Gavin. "Hannah? Have you seen Mama this morning?"

"She was eating breakfast when I came in," Hannah replied, her eyes moving to his briefly and then darting away. "She was weary. I'll go and visit her in a moment."

"That would be grand," Maxwell told her thankfully. He smiled at her, and her eyes lit up for an instant, but then she looked back at the table, reaching for her tea.

Odd, he thought. She hasn't been so shy for at least a week.

Something was wrong.

Gavin was pushing back his chair, talking cheerily. He didn't seem to have noticed Hannah's unusual quietness and he decided not to worry about it.

"We'll be back for luncheon," Maxwell told Hannah as he strode to the door.

"I'll tell Patricia where you are riding to." Hannah barely turned around and Maxwell felt just a little hurt. He had hoped they could talk this morning.

He pushed away the feeling and strode down the hallway to his room to get his riding-coat and change his boots. He hurried to the stables, feeling driven to get out of the house and away from his gloomy thoughts.

"I say, old chap," Gavin murmured as they led their horses to the gate. "That was a fine waltz you had last night."

"Mm." Maxwell looked at Gavin flatly. His friend laughed.

"It was. And I'm sure that's no news to you," Gavin continued. "It's grand," he added, mounting up and riding to the gate.

"What is?" Maxwell demanded.

"Grand to see you happy."

"Mama managed well," Maxwell said, changing the subject. Gavin looked at him, his eyes sparkling.

"Yes. And it's not surprising, given the knowledge the current Lady Carronwood displays. She's a fine young lady." Gavin grinned at him. "And a true beauty, too, if I may say that myself."

"Yes. She is," Maxwell said firmly. He felt a blush heat his cheeks. A curse on Gavin! Did he have to try and make him talk about her? It was unfair to try and coax the secrets from him.

Not that I mind, Maxwell thought as he rode out of the gate behind him. *I don't care if the whole world knows my heart.*

He leaned back, their horses setting off at a trot. The Almhurst stables were quite far, and he wanted to keep the horses' strength up. Nightfire was trotting briskly—he was in need of a long ride. Maxwell looked around, his gaze moving over the green grass and the darker green woodland. Hannah would have loved it. He wished she had ridden with them.

She's tired, he reminded himself crossly. He leaned forward a little, catching up with Gavin. They rode on towards the farm.

Lord Almhurst was in his garden when they arrived, his hunting-dog walking with him around the estate. An older man and a baronet, Almhurst was known for his fine stables and Maxwell was glad to know him.

"Good morning," he called out, lifting his hat. "I wonder if you have a moment? I'd like to discuss the upcoming horse-breeding season?"

Almhurst grinned. "My chief groom's out, exercising the stallions," he told him. He shrugged. "If you two fellows want to come in, you're welcome. We can negotiate."

Maxwell swallowed hard. Almhurst was no fool, but he was also incredibly miserly. He had plenty of money to spare, but the price would still have to be reasonable, or he'd not feel able to justify the spending. Father's words about a "silly pastime" still rang in his ears and it felt wrong to squander the estate's wealth on what he still thought of as a hobby. He glanced at Gavin.

"Let's negotiate."

The negotiation lasted two hours.

"Whew," Maxwell murmured as he and Gavin strode back to their horses. "That was quite a morning."

"It was," Gavin agreed. "But your decision was right—I'm sure of it."

"Well, it should be," Maxwell said with a crooked smile. "I just spent two hundred pounds."

Gavin roared with laughter. "I'm sure it will be clear in future how very wise it was," he told him with amusement.

Maxwell shrugged modestly. In truth his heart glowed with pride.

This was his first venture at his own stables. He was a horse-farmer.

He smiled to himself. It was Hannah's lovely reaction that had given him the courage to try this morning. His father's belittling, shaming words had receded a little in his mind, for long enough for him to try something new.

He was smiling as he rode onto the estate.

As he got there, the senior groom, Mr. Goodman, ran up.

"My lord! My lord! It's Butterfly."

"What is it?" Maxwell demanded, his heart thudding as he threw himself off his horse. Butterfly was one of his favorite mares and she had been carrying a foal through the winter. She was older than most of the mares in the stables, and his heart twisted in fear for her.

"She's delivered a healthy foal."

"*What?*" Maxwell beamed, his heart soaring. "Where is she? Where is the foal? How are they?" "She's in here, my lord," Mr. Goodman murmured, indicating a stall. "She's well. The foal's well. She's just nursing him now."

Maxwell followed him into the stable, then stood where he was, heart twisting in awe. Butterfly, a dark chestnut thoroughbred, was one of his favorite mares. His joy was huge as he stared over the fence. In the stall, lying on the straw, the chestnut thoroughbred nudged her foal. The foal was dark brown, but that might change as he grew; his foal-coat molting out to show his adult colors later. He was tiny and long-legged and delicate, his fur like wet velvet. He was pure brown. His eyes were open, and he was trying to get up, his long, slender legs wobbly as he staggered forward. The blaze on the mother horse's brow was bright in the gloom of the stall. She nudged the baby. Maxwell's heart melted.

He watched, awed, as the big, delicate-boned mare nudged the little foal again. He took a few uncertain steps, moving around to begin to feed. It was a young stallion—the first of the bloodline he was going to establish. His heart soared with pride.

It's really happening.

He beamed and, after watching for a minute or two more,

he turned to Gavin, who had followed them in and stood silently beside him, as silent and awed as he was.

"I'm going to fetch Hannah," he said softly. "She'd be so happy to see this."

"Of course, old boy. I'm going inside about now anyway. Wretched head. Must be a change in the weather coming on."

Maxwell strode indoors and paused in the hallway, hearing voices and laughter. Mama and Hannah were busy sewing in the parlor. He smiled to himself. They sounded happy and he felt relieved.

"Maxwell! You're back earlier than I expected," Mama greeted him warmly, looking up from her sewing.

"I just saw Butterfly. She's given birth to a healthy male foal." He told Mama smilingly, then he looked at Hannah. "Would you like to see him?"

Hannah's eyes lit up, but then, just as they had at breakfast, moved to her sewing. "I don't know...I said I'd stay and mend this sleeve on this gown..."

"Oh, Hannah! Go and see. I know you'd be glad to. And I can sit and mend alone for just a few minutes," Mama told her gently. Maxwell smiled gratefully at her.

"Very well," Hannah murmured, though for someone who had expressed reluctance, she put her sewing into the basket remarkably swiftly and hurried to the door. Maxwell felt his delight that she was coming down to the stables swiftly displacing his concern.

They hurried into the garden together.

"Isn't he beautiful?" Maxwell said softly, leaning on the rail in the stables. Hannah was staring at the foal and his mother with an expression of awe.

She turned; her face lit with a big, dreamy-eyed smile. "He is. So beautiful. I think he'll be black, like Sapphire," she murmured.

"Sapphire?" Maxwell inquired softly, walking away from the rail to give the horse and her foal some peace as they talked.

"Yes," Hannah told him quietly, stepping back to join him in giving the horses a quiet space. "She is my horse. My mare. I..."

He felt his heart twist as she blinked, tears bright in her eyes. "What is it, Hannah?" he asked gently.

"She's at Grassdale, the country estate. I miss her so much," she whispered. She was crying now, silent tears moving over her cheeks slowly.

Maxwell felt a stab of pain in his heart. He hadn't even thought to ask her if she had a special horse. He imagined Nighfire, left on some estate somewhere, where he couldn't go for long rides with his favorite horse. He shook his head. It would drive him mad. "That's horrible," he said softly.

"It is," Hannah replied, sniffing. "Sorry. I didn't mean to raise something so sad at a time when rejoicing is in order." She sniffed again, and he pulled out his handkerchief, passing it to her.

"I understand," he said gently. "And I truly am sorry."

"No need," she said quietly. She took his handkerchief and blew her nose. "Thank you," she added. Her gaze moved to his swiftly, hopefully, and then moved to her feet once more.

"No trouble," he said lightly. He was already thinking of a plan. She wasn't herself since the ball—she seemed sad and frightened. Her words had given him an idea of how to cheer her up.

"Sorry," she murmured again, looking up at him sadly. "I think I will return to the parlour. Your mother will wonder where I am."

"Of course," Maxwell replied. He inclined his head in a polite gesture, and they walked up the path to the manor together. She was silent again. She was sad about her horse, and he had a plan. He walked slowly indoors, then turned down the hallway to his study, to write a letter to put his idea in motion.

Chapter 17

The sky was overcast with clouds, clearly visible from where Hannah sat on the divan in the drawing room. A fresh spring wind blew, refreshing and revitalizing, through the open window, but she had no interest in going outdoors; not even to visit the baby foal. Only one thought occupied her, chasing itself around her troubled mind.

How can I be sure of Maxwell?

She bit her lip, discomforted and distressed. Lady Laurentia had put ideas into her head and when she saw Maxwell, she saw a flighty, unreliable, unpredictable man, just like Lady Laurentia had described. She couldn't shake the notion, since she didn't know Maxwell at all, not really—she'd just met him a few weeks ago and there was evidence for what the lady had said. He had run off to Spain for three years despite his mother's evident illness, had only returned when his father passed away, and even now he spent most of his time riding. Was his return simply to take up the earldom, to inherit his father's wealth? Was he shallow, as well as untrustworthy?

"Stop it," she said aloud, her voice harsh in the warm silence of the drawing room. She looked around her, trying to calm down. A teapot and teacup stood on the table before her, the porcelain decorated with designs of pink roses. The chintz on the wingback opposite was likewise pretty and pink. Everything around her was genteel and pleasant, but her thoughts were like crawling ants, biting at her and denying her rest.

"Hannah? Are you busy?" A voice interrupted her discomforting thoughts.

"Patricia. Good morning," Hannah greeted, voice lifting with pleasant surprise. She stood up respectfully as the older woman walked slowly into the room. It felt good to see a friendly face at Carronwood; all the more so now that she felt she could not trust Maxwell anymore. "How nice to see you. No, I'm not busy." She settled back into the chair again.

"Good," Patricia replied briskly. "I thought I'd bring my embroidery in here. It's much more pleasant to work with good company. Perhaps you can tell me something while I work? A story about your home in Kent, perhaps?" Her gaze was eager.

Hannah swallowed hard. "Mayhap," she agreed. "Shall I send for tea?"

Patricia nodded. "That would be very nice. Thank you."

Hannah stood to ring the bell and searched in her mind for something to tell Patricia. All of her happy childhood stories featured Papa, and she wasn't sure she could talk about him without shedding tears. Patricia was not as ill as she had been, but she didn't want to burden her with her sorrows.

The butler appeared in the doorway, and she sent him off to fetch tea, then drew a breath, clearing her throat. "I thought mayhap I'd tell the story about my first horse."

"Please do," Patricia agreed. "It's so lovely that you're fond of horses. You'll have noticed Maxwell is too, of course." She beamed at Hannah.

"Yes, I have." She cleared her throat again, discomfort rising at the mention of Maxwell. "My Papa was there for my first riding-lesson, when I was just four years old," she began.

As she told the story, she recalled the events vividly. Papa had watched her from the lawn as Mr. Stuart, her riding instructor, led her about the garden on a small pony. At four, the pony had seemed huge, his girth wide, her little legs barely managing to reach to the stirrups. Mr. Stuart had been caring and had taken her very slowly, and the feeling had been so thrilling that she'd laughed aloud. Papa had caught her eye and smiled. In that moment, they seemed to understand something about each other. Her love of horses clearly made a big impression, because he'd never forgotten and had insisted that she always had instruction in riding, despite Mama's objection.

"Your mother said no?" Patricia sounded surprised.

"Yes," Hannah told her. "She said it was no sport for a lady. Edward, my elder brother, didn't really like riding, so he shared an instructor with me. Mama would have much rather that I didn't join in, but Papa argued that, since he was already paying for that one instructor, we might as well share the lessons."

"Good. Sensible man." Patricia beamed. "And lots of ladies can ride," Patricia murmured. "It might be a little controversial, but many see it as a true accomplishment. Of course, with the right saddle and the proper clothes and everything." She grinned.

Hannah had to laugh. "Well, I didn't always ride side-saddle," she admitted shyly.

Patricia grinned, those dark eyes that were so like Maxwell's sparkling brightly. "Well! That must have surprised London."

"I only did that on the estate at home," Hannah explained quickly. She smiled warmly at the memory. "I think the whole of London would be struck dead at the thought of a woman riding astride."

"Quite so, my dear. Quite so." Patricia laughed. "I'm not fond of the London set, as you know."

"Yes, I know," Hannah murmured. She had been reassured by that similarity between them from the first. She looked at Patricia hopefully, wishing she could confide her worries but not knowing how to start.

"Maxwell always said having to associate with the *Ton* was a punishment for anyone silly enough to go to London for the Season." Patricia giggled. "I do think he's right."

"Me, too," Hannah replied quietly.

Hannah looked away. Thoughts of Maxwell distressed and confused her. Maxwell had indeed avoided the Season, even though they could easily have gone. A flighty, shallow person would surely hurry to the Season. Or did Maxwell linger in the countryside to avoid a scandal, like Lord Larenmont did? Her thoughts were alight with speculation, making her head hurt.

"My dear, are you feeling well?" Patricia asked gently.

"I feel quite well," Hannah replied, not quite truly. Her head was sore, her stomach unsettled.

"You are quite sure?" Patricia said kindly. "Are you sure I can't ask the butler to fetch you something? Some water or lemonade? Or a tea of some sort?"

"No. Thank you," Hannah replied. She looked down at her hands. "I'm quite well. Just tired. The ball must have tired me out."

"Well, I understand that," Patricia replied gently. "I might go upstairs to my apartments and rest."

"Of course," Hannah replied softly. "I think I'll take a walk about the grounds." It would be good to have time to think.

She dressed for outdoors, pulling on her cloak and outdoor boots and walked briskly down the path. The wind tugged at her hair and the cold knifed through the thin muslin of her cream-colored dress, but she didn't mind. She walked briskly down the stone pathway to the stables. Despite all the confusion and pain in her heart, the one thing she wanted to do was visit the little foal.

"Aren't you lovely?" she murmured, looking over the fence in the darkened stable. The foal stood unsteadily beside his mother. He already seemed more certain on his feet and his gaze was not as filmy and unfocused. He could see her where she stood, and he seemed unafraid. The mare, Butterfly, huffed a greeting and Hannah stood still at the gate to the stall. The horse stood where she was, and the little foal watched Hannah. His eyes were dark and serious, and she felt renewed, her heart healed, by that gentle-eyed understanding.

"Nightfire's not here," she noticed aloud. Maxwell's horse was absent, meaning he was out riding again. Where had he ridden off to? She deliberately pushed the thought aside. She wasn't going to spoil her visit to the horses by letting thoughts of him distract her again.

The mare huffed again, and Hannah smiled at her, holding her gaze. She wasn't objecting to Hannah's being near them, and that was an honor in itself. She was about to go back inside when she heard a shout from the lawn.

"Lady Carronwood? You're needed in the upstairs parlour."

Hannah's first thought was that something had happened to Patricia. "What is it?" she demanded swiftly as she ran over to meet the butler, who had shouted. "Is..."

"Guests have arrived," Mr. Haddon told her. "I am sorry, my lady, for interrupting your morning walk. But the dowager Lady Carronwood asked me to fetch you at once."

"Thank you," Hannah answered.

"Good afternoon!" A voice greeted them as Hannah arrived in the drawing room, followed by another voice. It was two women who spoke, the one older, dressed in a cream-colored gown with a brief lacy cap covering her hair. Hannah barely saw her—the person on whom her eyes focused was Lady Laurentia.

What is she doing here?

Hannah's startled gaze moved from them to Patricia, who was sitting on the long chair by the window. Her face was stiff and tight, expressionless.

Patricia greeted the guests as they came in. Hannah hurried

to sit beside her. Patricia looked distressed and tense and Hannah's first thought was to protect her.

"Good afternoon, Lady Carronwood." Lady Laurentia greeted Patricia, bobbing an elegant curtsey.

The look Patricia leveled at her was not welcoming, which surprised Hannah. Lady Laurentia had suggested she knew the family well. Patricia, though, didn't seem to approve of her, and that interested her.

"Hannah," Patricia said, turning to her. "May I introduce Lady Grantham and her daughter, Lady Laurentia? Lord Grantham is a viscount who has his estate close to here."

"Charmed," Hannah managed, dropping a brief curtsey. She felt as if Patricia and she were threatened by these two women.

"Lady Grantham and Lady Laurentia," Patricia continued, her voice stiff and hard. "May I introduce Lady Carronwood?"

"Charmed to meet you!" Lady Grantham murmured. Hannah frowned. Her voice sounded friendly and welcoming, but the expression on her face was not.

"It's so good to see you again," Lady Laurentia murmured, her voice sweet and light. She turned to Patricia again. "The younger Lady Carronwood and I have already become acquainted. Mama spotted you at the ball and it seemed like an age since we called on you. We felt we simply *had* to drop in to check on you."

Hannah stared at her. Her words seemed somewhat callous.

Lady Laurentia turned to Hannah. "It was delightful to become acquainted at the ball two nights ago."

"Yes," Hannah murmured. She looked at her toes where her indoor shoes pressed on the silk rug. "Most charming."

Hannah's mother had been an expert in insincere banter, and Hannah was almost grateful for that now. She could chatter away as meaninglessly as the next person, all the while silently detesting whoever it was that she spoke to.

"Yes!" Lady Grantham agreed, smiling at Patricia and her insincerely. "Most delightful. Do sit down, Lady Carronwood," she added, addressing Patricia. "Best if you stay seated."

Hannah bit her lip. She didn't like how they treated Patricia, as if her illness was the only thing they knew about her. *She's an interesting woman,* Hannah wanted to shout. *She has more worthwhile things to say than either of you do. Treat her respectfully.*

Patricia settled uncomfortably on the divan. Hannah came and sat beside her and fixed Lady Laurentia with a scowl.

"Did you wish to stay for tea?" she demanded.

Lady Laurentia's fine eyebrow lifted at the tone. "Why, we had thought to take a cup of tea with Lady Carronwood, yes," she replied.

Hannah noticed that she hadn't been included in the invitation. She smiled inwardly. She'd known far more insulting people in Mother and Philipa. "Well, then." Hannah said baldly. She stood up, walking to the bell-rope and tugging it. "I'll summon the butler."

"Do, yes," Lady Grantham murmured, clearly shocked by Hannah's tone. Hannah didn't care. They had come in here and invaded Patricia's peace. For that alone, she wasn't disposed to think well of them.

"Have you been outdoors?" Lady Laurentia's mother inquired of Patricia. "Of course, I know it's difficult for you to go out at all."

Hannah scowled. Patricia was getting better every day. "Lady Carronwood and I take a daily walk about the grounds," Hannah interrupted. "She is lovely company."

"Thank you, Hannah." Patricia beamed.

The two visitors gaped at Hannah, but she was already turning to the door. The butler had appeared and Hannah sent him to the kitchen to fetch tea. She returned to the divan, settling beside Patricia, shielding her from the onslaught.

"Lady Carronwood?" Lady Laurentia's mother addressed Hannah. "How do you find the countryside?"

"I find it to my taste," Hannah told her, deciding to be honest. "I enjoy riding and being in the fresh air, and the countryside here lends itself to my pastimes."

"I see." Lady Laurentia sounded amused. "You are a rider?" Her tone was scornful. "A hoyden in our midst!"

"Hannah is a skilled equestrian," Patricia said firmly. She smiled at Hannah. "I find her most impressive."

"Thank you," Hannah murmured. She looked at her hands, her eyes wet. She wasn't sure what was worse—the reminder of Philipa's taunts, or the sweet way Patricia had defended her. She'd been persecuted by women too long to expect care. In its own way, it was more disarming than censure.

"I see," Lady Laurentia replied coolly.

"The countryside seems suited to riding," Lady Grantham replied as Hannah looked up again, trying to hide her hurt. She seemed to be trying for a neutral tone now.

"It is," Hannah answered. "It's fine being a hoyden here." She gave Laurentia a hard look.

The other woman looked back silently. Hannah held her gaze. Laurentia looked away first.

"Do you paint, Lady Carronwood?" Lady Grantham asked Hannah, changing the topic.

"I don't," Hannah admitted gruffly.

"Laurentia can paint very pretty scenes," Lady Grantham told them. "And still-life. Is that not so, Laurentia?"

"Thank you, Mama." It was hard to tell if Laurentia was pleased with this confident answer, or discomforted. Lady Laurentia turned to Patricia.

"Are you sure you're feeling well?" she asked in a manner that sounded condescending. "May I pour some tea?"

"I'm quite well," Patricia said in a hard tone.

Hannah glanced at Patricia, worried about her older friend. She was tired already. She had to try and get the guests to leave as soon as possible.

"I would send for sandwiches, but you'll be wanting to return home for luncheon," she said firmly. It was almost lunchtime.

"Oh." Lady Grantham blinked as if Hannah had slapped her.

"We had planned to return home for luncheon, yes," Lady Laurentia replied tightly. Hannah wanted to chuckle. She had been arguing with women far scarier than Laurentia and her mother for a long time.

"Very fine tea," Lady Grantham managed to say, her voice stiff with anger. "We shall return to the manor for lunch."

Hannah wanted to laugh. They were doing their best to hide the fact that she'd offended them, and she found she didn't mind. Beside her, Patricia looked visibly relaxed. That made Hannah's heart soar.

"We ought to return home speedily," Lady Grantham

111

murmured. "The coach-trip is a good half an hour."

"Of course. Let me walk downstairs with you," Hannah replied, standing, all politesse and affability. Lady Laurentia scowled.

"We will not visit before luncheon again," she said to Hannah, as though Hannah might be offended. "It seems it is not allowed here."

Hannah smiled. "Our butler has a routine," she said as if it was the most natural thing in the world.

Hannah walked down to the door with them, all smiles and good wishes for their trip home, and then went briskly up the stairs to the drawing room.

"The guests are heading off." Hannah looked out of the window, glad that even the coach was not visible anymore on the road outside. She breathed a sigh of relief. She glanced at Patricia.

Patricia smiled. "Thank you," she murmured.

"Truly?" Hannah was surprised. She'd done what she did mainly to defend Patricia, but she'd wondered, as she went upstairs, whether she'd been wrong.

"Yes." Patricia leaned back with her eyes closed. "That pair got what they needed. Their faces!" She chuckled, shoulders shaking with silent amusement. "You did excellently."

Hannah smiled. "Thank you," she answered softly.

"Of course, my dear. Thank you," Patricia answered.

"Were you acquainted with the two of them?" Hannah asked as they both seemed to relax a little. Lady Laurentia had spoken as though she knew the family. "I mean, well acquainted?"

Patricia blinked. "My dear, Maxwell was almost wed to her."

"What?" It was Hannah's turn to gape. She shut her mouth again, eyes wide with surprise as she stared at her friend. "How...what? How did that happen?" She saw Patricia smile and she realized how funny she must sound. She attempted to compose herself, but the shocking news left her utterly stunned.

Patricia shifted in the chair, settling down as she seemed to gaze into the past. "Maxwell's father, Henry, had the idea that Laurentia complemented Maxwell. The fact that she lived nearby probably appealed, too...Henry was in some ways unadventurous, and I think he just didn't look very far to find the solution to who Maxwell might wed when he grew up. Laurentia is three years his junior, a neighbour...I think that's all he saw." She shut her eyes for a moment and when she opened them, she smiled a little sadly at her.

"Maxwell's father arranged it?" Hannah felt her heart almost stop. Perhaps Lady Laurentia hadn't been telling her the truth after all. Perhaps she was speaking out of hurt. Or perhaps it was the way she saw the truth, considering Maxwell must have looked very flighty indeed to her, leaving the country like that with no clear reason. She looked at Patricia, longing to hear the rest of the tale.

"Yes. There were...let me say that they had many topics on which they didn't hold similar views, Maxwell and Laurentia." Patricia's tone was delicate. "And it was Henry's insistence on the match that led Maxwell to flee."

"He fled to Spain?" Hannah stared. He had never said that. He'd said he went to learn his trade.

"Yes. Of course, it wasn't the only reason. There were a lot of reasons. He fled the country to try and curb his father's hold on him, I think. But he chose to flee to Spain to follow his dream. That was another thing on which Henry and he had a...a disagreement." She sniffed.

Hannah felt relieved. "So, he did go to Spain for the horse-farming lessons?"

Patricia laughed. "Well, I don't know if he would say he had lessons, really. But yes. He did go there because of his ambition to become a horse-breeder."

"I understand." Hannah let out a sigh. She hadn't realized how similar they were.

"I wished he hadn't," Patricia said softly. Hannah saw the pain on her face. "I longed to have him return home. But, well, now he has. I shan't cry about something that has healed." She sniffed. Hannah took her hand.

"Of course you were sorrowful, Patricia," she said gently.

"He's my son. My dear son. My only son."

"He's back home," Hannah murmured.

"He is."

They sat quietly for a moment. Hannah's mind reeled.

She tilted her head, thoughtfully. "Do you think Laurentia hated Maxwell very much?"

Patricia chuckled. "Laurentia hates anyone who doesn't do

her wishes. No, that isn't fair." Patricia sighed. "But let me say she's a woman I wouldn't lightly cross. She is a little shallow, but she is very insecure, and such people are the most dangerous. And you heard her today—she has her tongue for a weapon."

"She does," Hannah agreed. "Would you say Maxwell is unreliable?"

"No." The word was coldly sure. Patricia was not a strident person, and hearing the forceful tone in her words surprised her.

"You seem very sure."

"Absolutely." Patricia's voice was firm. "I would trust him with my life."

"And you think he's always trustworthy?" Hannah asked, feeling relief wash through her body.

"I think anyone can rely on him. Maxwell does what he says he will."

"Thank you," Hannah breathed.

"Whatever for, my dear?" Patricia asked.

Hannah shrugged. "Well...for telling me that I can trust Maxwell," she told her simply. There was no real way to explain to her what Laurentia had done. And besides, now that it was remedied, she could simply forget about it, which was much more comfortable than talking about it and trying to explain.

"Of course, my dear," Patricia said, sounding confused. "Of course, you can."

"Thank you," Hannah whispered, heart soaring.

She could barely wait to see him and talk with him as soon as possible.

Chapter 18

Maxwell tied his cravat in a simple knot and ran a comb across his hair. His thoughts were all with Hannah and how withdrawn she had been for the past few days.

At dinner, she seemed better. But I still wonder.

He'd returned back late from visiting another horse-breeding estate, and barely had time to change for dinner before hurrying down. His eyes had focused on her as he settled at the table. She'd been wearing a beautiful green gown, her soft golden hair fluffy and lovely around her face. She'd glanced at him during the meal as if she was thinking about something. He had wished he knew what. Now he hurried downstairs to the breakfast room, hoping she'd be there so he could talk to her.

He tensed in the doorway, hearing someone push in their chair, but then he saw who it was and greeted.

"Gavin! Good morning."

Despite his friendly greeting, Maxwell felt a bit disappointed to find his friend and cousin there. He'd hoped he could speak to Hannah on her own. Gavin was grinning warmly, tucking into a boiled egg and toast.

"Good morning, Maxwell," Gavin greeted him, barely glancing up from his food. "I see you're up early. Fine morning, eh? I plan to get a ride in before it clouds over. The barometer promises a change in the weather soon." He reached for the teapot. His mood seemed cheerful despite his gloomy prediction.

"Does it?" Maxwell glanced at the newspaper, but let it fall to the side-table absently. He didn't want to be depressed, and the news was always depressing. He helped himself to a piece of toast, listening to Gavin as he ate.

"Mm. Should be windy soon, then the clouds will come, and it'll rain this afternoon. Or so I believe. All the barometers said is that the air pressure is high."

"I see." Maxwell bit into his toast, not really paying much attention to his friend's chatter about the weather. He was thinking about the special delivery he was expecting tomorrow, or later in the day, depending on the condition of the roads. A voice from the doorway startled him out of his thoughts.

"Good morning?"

Maxwell turned around hastily. It was Hannah at the doorway.

"Good morning, Hannah."

She was wearing a dress decorated with a pattern of little flowers in a turquoise shade, her lovely hair held in a bun tied back with blue ribbon. Her gaze was warm, and she flushed as he looked at her.

She doesn't seem cross with me anymore.

He smiled to himself, heart glowing. The reason for her quietness and apparent mistrust hadn't been explained, but now that it seemed as though it had lifted, he had no desire to question and find out. He poured himself some tea then gestured to her teacup.

"May I pour some tea?"

"Thank you, Maxwell." She smiled warmly.

"My pleasure."

He watched her select some toast, his thoughts drifting between admiring her pretty hands to focusing on the expected delivery that afternoon and worrying.

I want this settled soon.

The delivery had almost pushed thoughts of his other venture from his mind and it was only when he looked up at Gavin that he remembered the deal he'd made at the Almhurst estate just a few days earlier.

"Any news from Almhurst?" he asked.

"Not yet. I can ride that way today if you like?" Gavin suggested. Maxwell nodded and Hannah's eyes widened.

"A ride?" she asked.

Maxwell laughed. "If you like, we can go riding too. Mayhap we can all set out part of the way together." His mind raced. He had planned to be at home that afternoon just in case the rider in charge of the delivery managed to do as he'd promised. But there was no cause not to go out for a jaunt in the morning.

"I'd be delighted!" Hannah's voice glowed.

Maxwell chuckled. "Well, then. We'd best dress for it and head off soon...Gavin believes it will rain today."

"It's not me! It's the barometer," Gavin argued. "You make me sound like a very gloomy sort."

Maxwell smiled. "I had no intention to, Gavin."

"I know you're not gloomy. Is he?" Hannah smiled at them both. Maxwell almost stopped breathing, her grin hitting him with the force of being thrown from the saddle. Gavin likewise fell silent.

"No," Maxwell said, wanting to chuckle as he noticed the mesmeric effect Hannah could have on anyone, even his friend. "He's not. Not at all. I suppose we should hurry up to change for riding soon."

"In a moment," Hannah agreed.

Maxwell ate his breakfast with an alacrity that amazed him and then hurried upstairs to change. He dressed swiftly and then waited in the hallway. It was only natural, he told himself, that Hannah should take more time to prepare. Her dress had a myriad buttons and ladies seemed to wear so many more clothes than men. His thoughts wandered from Hannah dressing to Hannah undressing. He went bright red and looked out of the window, forcing himself to think about something else. If he let himself think of that, he'd be thinking all day and then he'd not be able to look her in the eye.

He heard hurrying footsteps and looked up to see her on the stairway. Her steps were light, almost a run, her long mantle billowing around her, the soft blue fabric making her eyes seem like blue lakes and taking his breath away. He waited for her to catch up and they hurried down the steps to the stables.

"A beautiful morning," he murmured as they walked.

"Yes." Her voice was soft.

The lawns were growing into a lush green covering, the roses just starting to blossom and the daisies white like little stars all over the flowerbeds. He breathed in, smelling the scent of fresh hay as they neared the stables.

They went into the stables together, chatting, as they collected tack, about the new foal and Butterfly, and how the two would be able to play in the field soon.

Maxwell was ready with Nightfire just before Hannah led Crimson out, and he mounted up and waited for her, wondering again at how the distance between them had grown less again seemingly overnight. He did wish he understood it but didn't want to question his good fortune just yet. She vaulted up lithely which made his heartbeats quicken, and then they rode out down the path towards the field.

"You must have ridden here often as a boy," Hannah commented as they crossed the field. The sun was already warm and beat down on Maxwell's shoulders, making his back sticky with perspiration in the long-sleeved jacket he wore.

"I did," Maxwell agreed. "It was a good place for riding. I wanted to ride all the way to Almhurst's as soon as I was old enough to understand I could ride beyond the boundaries of the estate." He felt himself smile at the recollection.

"I wish I could have seen that," Hannah said warmly.

His soul felt as though it was falling into the blue depths of her eyes, drawn there by some force that Gavin and his barometers couldn't have explained. They had both stopped riding, their horses standing still in the field. His cheeks flamed and he coughed, feeling shy.

"I suppose we should ride on," he murmured.

"Yes. I suppose." She looked down at her hands and Maxwell looked too, noting her delicate fingers clutching the reins strongly. They were beautiful hands, ones that seemed as much at ease riding as they did waltzing on the dance-floor.

He was going to mention the ball and the dance they'd shared, but she looked up, her next words stealing his breath.

"When we reach the flat ground, I'll race you."

"You want to?" He gazed at her in disbelief.

"Yes." Her grin was amused, and he had to laugh.

"As you wish."

They rode uphill, coming to a flat field that stretched perhaps fifty yards ahead, perhaps a little more. She glanced at him.

"And...Go!"

"Hey!" he yelled. "That was sudden!"

He leaned forward, racing after her, laughing as she shot across the field, her posture leaning forward, her bonnet-ribbons flaring out in the wind of her passing.

She won easily.

"Whew." He panted, reining his horse in beside her. It was only ten o' clock in the morning, the church-bells ringing, sounding the hour. He was already covered in sweat; sweltering, exhausted.

She chuckled. "See?"

"Yes," he murmured. "Yes, I see."

She grinned at him and he grinned back, unable to help it. She looked so proud and happy that his soul soared. He gave silent thanks to whatever had happened to make her smile and laugh again.

He looked over towards the hills in the distance.

"We'd best move...Gavin's clouds are actually there at the hills already."

"He can really predict the weather?" Hannah asked, leaning back so that they went ahead at a walk again.

"I don't know. I don't understand all of his apocryphal talk about barometers."

She laughed, a clear, bright sound that made the soul lift, like a babbling brook. "Well, he clearly has an interest."

Maxwell was about to comment that he certainly did, but she set off at a trot again and he had to hurry to keep up.

They rode up to the woods and through the cool green woodland for a few minutes, then turned and went to the road.

"It's too hot out here," Maxwell commented as they turned their horses. "I don't think we should go all the way to Amhurst's estate today."

"No...perhaps not," Hannah agreed.

They turned their horses and rode back to the estate.

At the stable, Maxwell jumped down from the saddle, letting Hannah ride ahead into the yard.

"Maxwell!"

She let out a cry as she hit the ground, one foot shooting out from under her. He was there before she fell, grabbing her and holding her close.

"Are you all right?" he murmured.

"I'm fine," she whispered softly. "Just a patch of mud. My foot slipped. Sorry for making such a fuss." She lowered her gaze, embarrassed.

"No need for apologies," Maxwell replied tenderly. She was in his arms, held very close against his chest. He breathed in, noting the heady floral scent of her hair again. Her eyes gazed into his and he stood there, unable to move or look away with longing pulsing through every inch of his body.

He reached up and stroked her hair back from her face and she stared into his eyes. She hadn't tried to step away and she was still held against him, his left arm drawing her close. He could feel her soft curves and he bit his lip, aching with desire.

She was looking into his eyes as she had in the waltz, and he rested his palm on her cheek.

"My lord!" Mr. Goodman's voice yelled from the path behind them. Maxwell whipped round, cursing the fellow inwardly for interrupting them.

"What is it?" he demanded.

"A delivery for you, my lord. Rider just arrived at the gate."

"Oh. Grand. I'll be there in a moment." Maxwell turned to Hannah. "Will you wait here a moment?" he asked.

"Of course," she murmured, sounding confused.

He strode up the path and across the lawn, marching past the terrace. The front gate was far up the drive, and he headed there at a run. There he stopped, a big grin spreading across his face.

A tall, dark-brown horse stood there, looking at him with wary eyes.

"I'll go and get her," Maxwell promised.

He paid the rider he'd sent to Grassdale a substantial fee, then hurried to where Hannah was waiting at the stable.

"Hannah?" he called as he went briskly over to where she waited. "If you could come to the gate for a moment? There's a visitor for you."

Hannah frowned. "A visitor?" she asked, her voice tight and confused. "For me?"

"Yes." Maxwell wanted to grin but he resisted the urge.

He saw Hannah's eyes widen and he took her hand as she hurried to the drive, then followed her as she raced down. She reached the gate just before he did, turning to face him.

"Maxwell? Who..." Hannah began, then stopped as she stepped closer and saw who was waiting on the lawn, the groom holding a long rein. "Oh, my..."

Maxwell watched as Hannah walked slowly forward. He waited on the lawn, but he saw tears glint where they ran down her face and his heart twisted.

"Sapphire! Sapphire!" Hannah murmured. She reached the

horse and he heard her sob as he walked closer to join them. The stable hand gave the rein to Hannah. She was stroking the horse's head and crying. Sapphire, the mare, closed her big dark eyes and huffed, resting her head on Hannah's shoulder, sniffing her with her soft, whiskery muzzle.

Maxwell choked back tears.

"Sapphire," Hannah murmured again. She turned around. "Maxwell," she murmured, looking into his eyes. "I can't believe it. You...you..." She started crying again, a grin of joy bisecting her face and Maxwell opened his arms and she ran into them.

"Thank you," she said, holding him around the middle in a crushing hug. "Thank you. Thank you!"

She was laughing and the tears were running down her face and Maxwell laughed too, and held her close, and felt his soul soar as if it was a skylark as she held him tight and pressed her head against his chest and cried.

"Oh, Maxwell. Maxwell! It's so wonderful. I'm so happy."

He gazed into her lovely face. "Me too," he said simply.

She hugged him and laughed and then she was hurrying across the lawns, already instructing the groom to take Sapphire to the stables and feed her warm mash and rub her tendons well.

Maxwell followed them at a distance, ready to help out with stabling Sapphire, but knowing that Hannah needed no assistance. She was delighted, as this was her dear friend and she seemed confident and complete in ways she hadn't before.

"And make sure she gets a rub-down. I don't want her getting cold from being wet," she instructed.

Maxwell grinned as he heard the instructions and heard Sapphire neigh softly, walking behind Hannah and nuzzling her neck.

"Yes, my lady." The groom answered meekly.

Maxwell grinned to himself. Sapphire was here and Hannah was happy, and the world felt right.

"Should we go for a ride tomorrow? Just a short one, to celebrate. She shouldn't ride too far for a few days. She needs to settle." Hannah informed him.

"Of course," Maxwell agreed. "We could ride to the river."

"Yes! Let's. We could take a picnic," Hannah agreed.

Maxwell stared. He would never have thought of it, but it

sounded like a wonderful idea. He hadn't had a picnic in years, and he had always liked to.

"Yes, let's."

She beamed in joy and Maxwell smiled back, already planning for tomorrow and what the day would bring.

Chapter 19

Hannah lifted her riding mantle and it settled about her shoulders, the blue color a little paler than her eyes and the blue muslin dress that she'd chosen. Her heart was racing, and she glanced in the looking-glass to check her hair. The hasty dressing had dislodged some stray curls, but, framing her face, they only served to make her look informal, which was no bad thing.

She turned and hurried to the stables.

"You were fast," Maxwell greeted her as she stepped in through the big door at the front. It was dark and she narrowed her gaze, locating him two stalls down in Nightfire's stall. He had his back to her. She could just hear his voice and the snort of Nightfire as Maxwell saddled him.

"I was?" Hannah flushed, but then everything around her faded out as she went to Sapphire's stall. The beautiful mare was watching her with limpid eyes and Hannah ran to her, hugging her around the neck, not minding what that might do to her hair or her dress. Sapphire was here. That was all that mattered.

"Indeed. Most ladies take ages to get ready to go out."

Hannah chuckled, ignoring his words and their lilting playfulness as she settled the saddle on Sapphire. It wasn't her own saddle from home, which fitted Sapphire better, and Hannah felt guilty, but it would have to do.

Once they had both tacked up their horses, Hannah led Sapphire to the mounting-block.

"We'll take the long way," Maxwell told her, riding ahead of her up the path towards the wall around the estate boundary. "The picnic has already been transported there for us."

"I see," Hannah said, grinning. She was no stranger to things like that—their own house had a vast staff who would have likewise organized a picnic. It was his gaze on her that was utterly new, making her blood race. She breathed deeply. He gazed at her a moment longer, making heat flare up in her cheeks, and then turned round.

"We'll ride on for a way uphill. Remember we have a long way to go."

"I'll ride as slowly as we can," Hannah agreed. "Sapphire

must be exhausted after her journey."

They rode slowly uphill, the sun rising steadily, so that by the time they reached the grassy slope near to the river, Hannah could feel perspiration on the back of her neck.

"Not too long now. Just a few minutes—it's down there," Maxwell told her, pointing down the slope. Hannah could just make out a glint of water and felt her spirit soar. She couldn't wait to be sitting in the delicious coolness out of the baking-hot sun.

The sun glinted on the water, making it shimmer and sparkle like a hundred stars were scattered there. Hannah breathed in, absorbing the beauty around them.

"How lovely," she whispered.

"It's one of my favourite places," Maxwell told her. He was standing very close; so close she could feel the heat of his body. He'd taken off his long-sleeved coat and stood in linen shirtsleeves, the wide sleeves giving the outfit a romantic look. She gazed up at him. He was looking back at her, and she felt a twist of longing in her belly. He had kissed her, once, and she felt her cheeks heat as she realized she ached for him to do so again.

He looked at her for a moment and she could see longing in his own eyes and her heart thumped hard.

"My lord?" A voice spoke from behind them.

They whipped round to where the butler appeared, carrying a small wooden stool. Maxwell shot him a look of indignant anger. When he spoke, though, he sounded calm and unperturbed.

"What is it, Mr. Haddon?"

"I just wanted to ask if that's the place I should put everything? Beg your pardon, my lord," he added, inclining his head embarrassedly. Hannah smiled at him, feeling a little guilty. He was preparing the picnic, after all.

"Yes, it is the right place," Maxwell told him.

"Quite so, my lord." The butler carried the stool to the position he'd indicated, and Hannah's heart bubbled with amused delight as she noticed a little table, two little stools and a picnic-basket on the table.

Even at my home, we weren't as formal as that.

The butler went to a cart that waited by the riverside, then clambered up beside the driver and they set off to the estate.

Hannah looked at Maxwell. They were finally by themselves.

124

She grinned at him. She couldn't hide her delight. His mouth was a firm line, but his eyes twinkled with warmth and her heart thudded hard in her chest.

"Well, then. I suppose this is a picnic." He grinned at Hannah and Hannah chuckled.

"A fancy one," she agreed.

"It is, rather." Maxwell was chuckling now too, as they went to the table. He sat down opposite her and opened the picnic-basket, from which he produced two drinking-glasses in elegant crystal and a bottle of lemonade. "Would you fancy something to drink, my lady? There's wine too, but I think we might both like to keep a wise head."

"Yes. I would never ride after drinking wine," Hannah agreed.

Maxwell grinned at her. "I agree completely."

Their eyes held and Hannah felt the knot of tension, that she hadn't known she felt, start to relax in her shoulders. On the riverbank, it was informal, so intimate, more than anywhere they had been together before. She beamed at him. He held her gaze.

"Thank you," she murmured. She meant to thank him for the picnic, but he was pouring her a glass of the cloudy yellow lemonade. He nodded.

"No trouble. There is cold pie in here—I think it's chicken. Would you like some?"

"Pie is my favourite," Hannah agreed. "Especially cold chicken pie."

Maxwell chuckled. "I'm quite fond of it myself." He took a cold pie wrapped in a checkered cloth from the basket, settled it on the table and proceeded to cut a slice from it. Hannah reached into the basket and found some porcelain plates, and she held one out to him so he could lift the pie onto it for her.

"Thank you."

"My pleasure."

Again, their eyes held. This time her heart thudded slowly, and his gaze, warm and dark, seared into her soul.

He bumped the plate against her hand rather than passing it to her and he looked sharply away.

"Sorry. I was distracted," Maxwell murmured, looking hastily down at his hands after they'd been staring at each other for a minute.

"No trouble." Her voice sounded strange. She cleared her throat, feeling as though she'd swallowed honey and the sticky sweetness had lodged there.

They ate in silence. Hannah sneaked glances at him as they ate, and she felt her cheeks burn when she caught him staring back at her. He was so handsome, his dark hair tousled from the ride, his fine, chiseled features peaceful.

They ate sandwiches after the pie, and then slices of cake that Maxwell discovered in the bottom of the basket—a loaf-cake sweetened with honey and dried fruits. Hannah's mouth watered as she tucked into a slice.

"I say," Maxwell murmured as he looked up and over to where the horses grazed. "It's rather cool."

"It is," Hannah agreed. At lunchtime, the sun had blazed onto the little patch of grass, and they'd been glad of the shading boughs that whispered overhead as the breeze moved them. But now, the sky was abruptly darkening with clouds. The barometer had apparently been accurate.

"I think it might rain soon," Maxwell said softly. Hannah nodded.

"Gavin warned us again," she commented, but as she spoke, a raindrop fell onto the table, small and round. They stared at it. Soon others followed.

The rain had started gradually, but now it gained strength and Hannah trembled, feeling the icy touch of it saturating her hair and running down the back of her gown. She stood up and clutched her riding-cloak.

"It's raining too hard to get back," Maxwell yelled, already running for the horses.

Hannah caught up with him in an instant, grabbing Sapphire's reins. Her horse was calm, but if the rain got worse, she might become afraid.

"Where can we shelter?" Hannah demanded, thinking of her horse before herself. She was already soaking wet anyway, the rain falling swift and hard from the cloud-dark sky.

"The woods," Maxwell said at once. "There's a little cottage there. The man who manages my estate forest used to live there. We can let the horses shelter there."

"Good!" Hannah had to shout. The rain was making the leaves rattle, and she could sense Sapphire's confusion and fear. She took the reins and ran, Sapphire barely having to exert herself to keep up. Maxwell ran alongside and Hannah's heart soared as they plunged down the track with their horses, the ground soaking and slippery, the roar of the rain drowning all words.

Maxwell stopped beside her, his sigh of relief loud in her ears. They were in a thick section of trees, the leaves overhead blocking out daylight but also most of the rain. The horses relaxed instantly. The sound of their breath was just audible above the hammering of the rain on the leaves.

Hannah looked around. She could see through the gloomy shadows enough to see a whitewashed cottage. She glanced up at Maxwell.

"Is that it?" she asked him.

He nodded. "We'll go in there. I'll show you where the horses can shelter. It's perfectly safe."

"Good." Hannah shivered. The rain had soaked her dress and she felt ice-cold.

Maxwell walked ahead.

"Here we are," he told her. "We can shelter the horses in this lean-to."

Hannah led Sapphire in, feeling tense herself. Her horse snorted and Hannah was glad when Maxwell stepped forward to lead her. He wasn't nervous, but perfectly calm, and that would calm her horse.

"Thank you."

"No trouble at all," he answered warmly.

"Where do we go?" she asked once the horses were safely stabled, their reins looped around the fence and the roof overhead keeping them warm and dry.

"We can shelter in the cottage," he told her.

Hannah said nothing, but followed him to a wooden door, which he opened with a key he located somewhere in a recess.

"We can light some lamps," he began as they went inside. "I have a flint. You're shivering." His eyes widened in concern, his voice firm as he stared at her. Hannah nodded.

"I'm...I'm cold," she managed to say, her teeth starting to chatter. Her mantle was soaked through and water ran down her back from where it had trickled down the wide neck-opening of her gown.

"You're soaking wet," Maxwell said gently. He looked around. "I'll make a fire. You can have my coat. You can't sit around in that wet cloak."

He waited as she shrugged the mantle off, feeling self-conscious as she stood there in the low-necked gown with the short sleeves. The rain made it cling to her form. Outside in public it had been one thing. Here, in a house where there were only two of them, it felt oddly intimate and she swallowed hard, looking at her toes. She could feel his gaze moving over her and her body flushed with heat.

"Here." Maxwell shrugged out of his jacket and lifted it gently onto her shoulders. It enveloped her. She clutched it around her, the soft cloth lining warm and heating her instantly.

"Thank you," she whispered.

Maxwell looked at her. His gaze was wide, his eyes gentle where they settled on her, filled with tenderness and a look of longing that made her catch fire.

She looked down at the ground. He coughed, turning to the fireplace.

"I'll just light the fire," he murmured.

She watched as he arranged logs in the fireplace and then bent down to strike the flint to its striker. He seemed very practiced at making fires, but then he must have made his own fires in Spain, where he had gone as an apprentice, not as an earl. She reminded herself to ask him where he'd learned to light a fire.

"Maxwell, I..." she began.

He was close, now; closer than he had been and her heart thudded loudly in her ears. He gestured to her.

"You should come and stand where it's warm."

"Yes," she murmured.

She stood beside him. His arm rested against hers. She looked up at him. The flames lit his handsome face from the side and her heart almost stopped at the beauty she saw there. He turned to look at her, his lips twisting into a gentle smile.

"Are you feeling better?"

"Mm." She nodded.

"A fire always helps."

"Yes."

She almost stopped breathing as he leaned towards her, his gaze holding hers. It was a strong, firm gaze, filled with longing that made her forget everything except the heat that flooded through her, making her long for him.

"Hannah," he murmured.

She couldn't reply before he reached for her, and she fell into his arms. He drew her close and his lips were tender on hers; tender and gentle and yet burning with a hunger that matched the fire in her soul. She closed her eyes. His lips were hungry on hers and she lost herself in the feelings that burned through her. She leaned on him, feeling his warm, firm chest pressed to her, feeling his arms draw her closer and hold her against him, his lips hot and passionate on hers.

"Maxwell..."

She gasped as he stepped back, his chest heaving.

"I...sorry. I didn't mean to..." he began but she smiled.

"I'm not offended," she whispered. Her cheeks burned with shy delight. His eyes widened.

"You aren't?" He sounded surprised.

She giggled. "No, I'm not." She felt more heat flood her as she said those words, knowing she meant them. His kiss was the most delightful thing she'd experienced, and it felt deliciously wicked to say so. "I'm not sorry about it at all. It was...rather lovely." Her cheeks flared at the comment, and she tried to keep her voice light.

He smiled. "I'm pleased."

She giggled.

"We should keep an eye on the weather. You need to get back home and out of those wet clothes," he told her gently.

"You, too," Hannah said playfully. She felt warmth tingle through her. She'd never felt so bold with him.

He grinned at her, his eyes kindling. "You're right."

They both laughed and went and stood by the window, so close she could feel the warmth and pressure of his arm on hers.

The rain pelted on the leaves outside, a good roof keeping the window sheltered, and Hannah stood closer to Maxwell, letting herself rest against him. She wasn't shivering anymore, the coat and the fire helping her to warm up, but she felt sleepy from getting so cold.

Maxwell wrapped his arm around her shoulders. She shut her eyes, feeling exhausted and contented. She had stopped shivering and all she wanted was for the rain to carry on so that they could be trapped there even longer. She shut her eyes and lost herself in the joy of the moment.

Chapter 20

The scent of flowers and rain mixed headily in Maxwell's nose as he held Hannah close. He tightened his grip, scared she would fall, as she was close to falling asleep. His heart ached with a feeling of intense love as she leaned against him, her soft, silky hair resting against his shoulder, her fine, curved body leaning on his side. He caught her as she swayed, and she gasped.

"You were asleep," he murmured.

"Mm." She gazed up at him and he felt his heart leap. He could almost kiss her petal-soft lips. He drew in a breath, fighting to ignore his desire to draw her close and cover her with kisses. His recollection of the kiss seared through him. He would have to be careful, or he'd let himself get carried away on the wave of desire that had washed through him as his lips met hers. "Sorry. I'm so tired..."

She swayed again and he drew her into his arms, holding her against his chest. Her muslin skirt rustled against his ankles softly.

"We should try to get you home." He murmured the words into her hair. "You're tired and cold. And the rain's stopped."

"Home..." Hannah whispered. She was so tired, and he wanted to smile, an intense protectiveness flooding his heart.

"Yes. I'm going to ride with you on Nightfire. Your horse can follow us on the long rein." He hadn't thought about it, but as he said it he knew that was the best way to get them home.

"I can ride," Hannah said firmly. She was barely able to stand up, which belied her words.

"I know you're a superb equestrienne," he told her gently. "But you're tired and cold and it's time you got into bed. I'll carry you back on Nightfire. And tomorrow you can beat me irrevocably in a horseback race."

She giggled. He kissed her hair. He couldn't help it. She leaned back, her eyes wide as she stared up at him. He had to remind himself to breathe.

"I'll go and fetch the horses," he said softly. "You stay here."

"Don't get wet," she murmured.

"I won't."

He hurried outside, following the path to the little shelter where the horses were waiting. It was colder outside following the rain, and he shivered in his shirtsleeves and marched to the shelter. Nightfire huffed in greeting. Sapphire rolled her eyes.

"Come on, you two," he said brightly. "We're going to ride back now. Come on, old boy," he greeted Nightfire. "You'll go ahead. We'll fix Sapphire to the pommel of the saddle, like this."

He thanked the man who'd taught him in Spain, Feliz Arcones, as he gently took hold of the rein on Sapphire's bridle. The thoroughbred horse shied and rolled her eyes, lifting her head and blowing through her nose at him. He spoke gently and moved as slowly as he could.

He unfastened the rein on one side, then attached it to Nightfire's saddle and opened the stall. Sapphire tried to pull away, turning in the stall, but he spoke gently to her, and she stopped, then followed Nightfire out.

"Good. Good. Well done, you two," he murmured, leading Nightfire by the rein. They reached the door of the cottage and he opened it, finding Hannah standing there, almost asleep on her feet.

"Sapphire," she murmured, walking towards her horse. Maxwell smiled.

"Yes, Sapphire is here. I'm going to lift you up now." He drew a breath, his heart thudding with nerves and longing as he wrapped an arm around Hannah and lifted her up. Her fine, curvaceous body filled his grasp and warmth flooded through him as he lifted her and sat her on the saddle. Her ankles showed briefly as he tried to arrange her dress and his cheeks burned as he tried to cover them.

"There," he said, fighting for calm. "Now, I'm just going to climb up. Hold on tight," he advised, as he shut the cottage door, locked it and then vaulted up into the saddle behind.

He drew her against him, holding her tight as Nightfire stepped forward. She gasped but clung on.

"Easy, old fellow. We'll go back slowly." He looked down at the path, which was slippery and dangerous.

They rode slowly down the path and Maxwell looked around, alert despite the fact that his senses were swimming in her floral scent, his body fighting to act beyond its desire for her. He held her close and rode and let his mind plan what he had to do when they arrived.

Mama would be worrying; he had no doubt about that. He hoped Gavin was there and had the sense to help her stay calm.

"Almost there," he told Hannah as they rode. He could see the fence around Mr. Northumberland's farm, and he knew that they were close. The hedge rose up next to it and the gate that led into the estate. He jumped down to open the gate, Hannah clinging to the pommel on Nightfire. Sapphire had calmed down and was huffing softly as they walked through the gate and onto the estate grounds.

Maxwell stepped up on the stirrup and took the reins, guiding his horse down the familiar path to the stables. As he got there, the groom ran up.

"Rub them both down, please. Check the tendons and make them warm bran mash too," Maxwell instructed, but before the groom ran to enact his wishes, he paused.

"My lord, there's a coach in the drive. You have visitors."

Maxwell frowned. "What insignia is on the coach?" he demanded. He wondered if old Almhurst had thought of traveling this far, and his brow lowered, thinking that the fellow was coming to argue about the stud price.

"None, my lord. It's a plain lacquered coach. No badge or anything." His voice was level.

"What?" Maxwell frowned, puzzled.

"There isn't any badge on the door, my lord," the groom told him again, then bowed and hurried to the door of the stable. "I'll prepare the mash, my lord. And get the flannel to rub them down."

"Good, good," Maxwell said absently. He unfastened Sapphire's rein so that the groom could lead her into the stable, then reached up to help Hannah down.

"I'll carry you inside," he murmured, but she took his hand and he felt that perhaps she was too shy to let him carry her. He wished she would. They walked slowly but firmly down the garden path, the house just ahead. He walked onward, and the sound of voices hit his ears. He tensed.

"...shocking! How can they think not to let us in! The nerve."

"Very right. You're quite right, of course."

Maxwell's frown deepened. Something about that voice bothered him, some memory he couldn't quite place. He was still worrying about it when they turned at the corner of the house and found the front path. The owners of the voices were around at the front steps, and he stopped smartly.

"You," he said.

"Is that a way to greet your mother-in-law?" the woman said in a sing-song voice. Maxwell shut his eyes for a moment.

"Good afternoon," he managed to say, the words ground out and not sounding particularly polite.

"That's better. Hannah! No...Lady Carronwood! How are you, my dear. Oh!" Mrs. Darlington exclaimed. "Your hair is all wet." Her big, insincere smile changed to an expression of horror.

"We were caught in the rain," Maxwell muttered. He fixed the woman with a sharp look. He had disliked her intensely from the moment he saw her, and he found that a few weeks hadn't affected that first impression. "Hannah," he said gently. Hannah was rooted to the spot, eyes wide in shock. "Go inside and get dry, sweetling. I'll show the guests indoors."

His gaze moved from Hannah towards the ladies on the doorstep. Philipa Darlington stood beside Mrs. Darlington. She was a little taller than Hannah, with honey-colored hair in elaborate curls. Her face was thin and pointy, her eyes wide and hazel-colored and she would have had a certain prettiness if it wasn't for the hardness of her stare.

"Hannah's still riding, then?" she inquired. Her tone scorned the pastime. Maxwell tensed.

"Lady Carronwood has a rich knowledge of equestrian matters; one I appreciate," Maxwell growled. "If you are visiting this estate, I suggest you respect that fact."

"Oh!" The woman exclaimed in shock, but Mrs. Darlington interrupted her before she could complain.

"Philipa is tired," she said swiftly. "If you would let us sit down in the drawing room for a moment, we would recover our goodwill. It's become so cold out here." She smiled; the expression as insincere as the tone of her words.

Maxwell scowled. "You may come in," he said with as little politesse as he could muster.

Hannah was still standing beside him. She was already exhausted, and seeing the two guests seemed to have terrified her. He frowned. Distasteful they were for certain, but didn't seem

134

possible that they could cause such terror in anyone. It must just be that she was tired.

"I'll send for tea," he said softly. "But first, I'll take you to your room. You need to lie down."

"No," Hannah said firmly. "I can't expect you to entertain them by yourself."

"You can," he answered, but she was gripping onto his arm as though she was passing out and he sighed. If she had to come up and sit with them, he couldn't stop her.

They walked to the drawing room.

Mama was sitting on the chaise-longue, her sewing at her side just as Maxwell knew she would be. She always went to the drawing room in the early evening so that she could see better in the brighter light there.

As he walked in, she looked up from her sewing, an expression of relief widening her eyes.

"Maxwell! Hannah! Thank Heavens! I...Oh." Mama was halfway to standing when she saw the guests. She looked at Maxwell with a frown.

"There are guests with us," Maxwell said carefully. "Hannah's mother and sister...sorry, sister-in-law," he corrected, feeling Hannah's urgent gaze on him. "The Mrs. Darlingtons...may I introduce my mother, Patricia, the dowager countess," Maxwell introduced his mother formally.

"Greetings, Lady Carronwood," Mrs. Darlington said slowly, as if she wished the words to sound as grand as they could. "I am Amelia Darlington. This is my son's lovely wife, Philipa."

"Good evening," Mama said unsurely.

Hannah stood without speaking by Maxwell's side. Mama inclined her head politely.

"Please, come and sit. I'll ring the bell for tea," she added, turning to the other side of the room. Maxwell stepped forward.

"Allow me to ring it, Mama. Please, sit down. Hannah? Mayhap you'd like to sit down there," he added, gesturing to the chair where he usually sat, at the end of the table. Her dress was soaking and he wished she'd go and change her clothes—she was going to get terribly ill if she sat about like that. She was just staring at the guests as though she'd seen a snake, a look of transfixed horror on her face. He frowned. She must be very tired.

She should go and rest, not sit here and talk in the drawing room with Mama and himself.

He rang the bell and sat down. Mrs. Darlington settled beside Mama, and Philipa Darlington opposite her. Maxwell winced. Mama didn't need visitors at this time...she was already tired.

"Bring tea for our guests, please," he told the butler, who had appeared at the door almost as soon as he'd rung the bell.

The butler bowed and hurried off. He glanced at the guests, who were perched on their chairs as if they were expecting them to burst into flame. They both seemed so on edge, and he wondered, briefly, if it was his title that was so frightening. He had almost forgotten Hannah was not from the same background as himself—she fitted into the household as though she'd been there always.

"Did you have a good journey?" Mama was addressing Mrs. Darlington. Maxwell shot her a look of gratitude. She was always friendly and considerate.

"Oh, it was fine enough," Mrs. Darlington murmured. "Our coach rattled a little. It's new, you know. Though I suppose you probably have all new coaches." She beamed at Mama and Maxwell felt his stomach twist nauseously. Did she have to be so horribly focused on wealth and status?

Mama looked at her in confusion, clearly trying to think of a polite answer. She was saved from reply by the butler at the doorway.

"Tea, my lord."

"How was the weather? On the trip, I mean," Hannah put in. Maxwell reached for her hand, seeing how tense she was.

"How should it have been?" Mrs. Darlington demanded. "The same as here. Kent is not so huge, you know, that it might differ."

Maxwell felt anger twist inside him. He would have expected her own mother to be pleased to see Hannah, but this woman was almost hostile.

"Your journey took several days," he began, but then he heard footsteps, and someone walked into the room.

"Good afternoon! What's this? Cake?" Gavin demanded as he stepped into the drawing room, strides broad. "Good day. I'm

Gavin Carlisle," he greeted the guests, bowing informally. He was wearing his riding-jacket, his cravat loosened in the heat. His hair must have got wet in the rain and dried as he rode because it was tousled and stiffened by the rainwater. Maxwell saw Mrs. Darlington's face fall into an expression of disapproval, and he wanted to hug his friend and relative in thanks.

"Is this man..." Philipa began, but Maxwell interrupted harshly as Gavin settled himself at the head of the table.

"Gavin is my cousin, and he has just been riding," he said, quelling any comments about Gavin and his unseemly appearance. "I'll ring the bell for another cup," he added to Gavin, who was helping himself to a slice of cake.

"No need to trouble yourself," he murmured, taking a cake-plate to catch the crumbs as he bit into the slice. Maxwell was trying to hide his laughter as he turned towards the bell-rope. Having Gavin here made it bearable. It even made it amusing for him.

Gavin shrugged. "What fellow would refuse to sit down and eat a few slices of cake after a long ride, eh?"

Maxwell was still trying not to laugh. If it hadn't been for Hannah's pale, scared face he would have guffawed aloud to see the shock and disapproval painted on her mother's and Philipa's expressions.

"Have you been introduced to the local lords and ladies?" Mrs. Darlington inquired of Hannah. Hannah glanced at Maxwell, who cleared his throat.

"Society in the countryside is not as varied as London," he said formally. Mrs. Darlington looked at him blankly.

"You haven't been?" she guessed. "Well! I think you should have a ball here, Hannah! Invite our London acquaintances. Show them how you've risen in the world. What a fine estate Carronwood is," she added, beaming at Maxwell. He looked at the loaf-cake, trying to school his features to neutrality.

"Balls are tiresome," Gavin muttered, talking through a second slice of cake. "Everyone just stands around talking polite rubbish, or dancing and trying not to stand on one another's toes." He leaned back in his chair. "A hunting party would be better. What do you say?"

Maxwell tried to keep his face blank as his guests' jaws

dropped. He grinned at Gavin, unable to help himself. Gavin's opinion on balls was controversial enough without mentioning hunting, which was likely to draw some strong reactions, especially in female company. Beside him, he felt Hannah relax. He glanced across at her. She seemed pleased that her mother was focusing on Gavin instead of her.

"I...well..." Mrs. Darlington stammered. Philipa had gone pale and was staring at Gavin as though he was some hideous apparition. Maxwell beamed at his guests.

"That's a plan for you. A hunting party. That's one way to appreciate the landscape to its full extent."

Mrs. Darlington was still sputtering as the butler came in. Maxwell sent him off for another cup for Gavin, but he could sense the guests wanted to find a way to exit as fast as they could.

"It's been a long day," Mrs. Darlington murmured. "I..."

"It was a long trip," Philipa stated. She looked hard at Mrs. Darlington. "I am tired."

"Yes. Exactly! We can't simply ride all the way back to Grassdale today," Mrs. Darlington stated, her smile at Maxwell seeming designed to win his approval. "It's a three-day ride. Of course, you'll let us stay here for a few days, to recover, won't you?"

Maxwell felt his teeth clench. He looked at Hannah, but she wasn't looking at the guests and he drew a deep breath. Mama held his eye, and he knew she was trying to tell him to say what would be polite. "Of course. You may stay for three days." He leveled a firm look at the woman, daring her to contradict or to ask for a longer stay. She inclined her head graciously.

"That is most kind. Is it not, Philipa? What fine, polite relatives we have. These are the true gentlefolk."

Maxwell looked at Gavin, but his friend was still eating cake and glancing at a book and seemed unaware of the tension surrounding him. Maxwell stood to ring the bell.

"Please make the green suite ready for our guests," he told the butler as he appeared almost immediately.

"Very good, my lord."

"Looks like rain later," Gavin murmured as the butler retreated from the room. "Plenty of it blowing over from the coast. Kent's a big place," he added, giving Mrs. Darlington a hard look.

"Plenty of room for all sorts of weather."

Maxwell cheered inwardly as Mrs. Darlington's expression shifted. Gavin must have been outside when Mrs. Darlington was so unkind to Hannah. Mrs. Darlington gaped at Gavin. Maxwell wanted to laugh.

"I...I..." she stammered.

"It's all quite straightforward. You just need a thermometer, a barometer and a hygrometer," Gavin told her.

"I..." Mrs. Darlington began, but Gavin was pushing back his chair and walking to the door.

"I'm on my way to the stables. I'll tell the stableman to stable the coach-horses," he added to Maxwell.

"Thank you, Gavin," he murmured.

Maxwell stood, hoping the ladies would be polite enough to go to their rooms. They both stood and he let out a sigh of relief.

He caught a relieved look on his mother's face, and he glanced at Hannah. She was still sitting silently, shivering with cold, and he felt his heart twist in concern.

"You need to go and rest," he told her firmly. "And get into a warm bed."

He led Hannah to her bedroom and bowed politely, then excused himself and hurried to his study. He was exhausted too, and needed a moment to recover.

He had to think about the Darlington visit and how he could make it bearable for himself, Gavin and for his mother.

Chapter 21

The light from the candles on the dressing-table was patchy. They flickered tall in the bronze candle-holders as Hannah regarded her reflection. She could see her own face, a pale heart shape, staring back at her expressionlessly as Miss Staveley arranged curls and tucked locks. She couldn't even feel sorry for herself.

Mother and Philipa invading her sanctuary felt as shocking as if she'd found a dead body in the woods. They shouldn't be there. They weren't welcome. And yet, there they were, sitting at the tea-table, being rude and silly without any clue that they were being so.

I shouldn't judge them so harshly.

She looked at her reflection miserably. Was it judgement to be aware that Mother and Philipa were dedicated social climbers without regard for anything except status? She could no more hate them for it than she could hate the sun for shining. It did only what was in its own nature. But they shouldn't be here, in her home, doing those things. She turned around as Miss Staveley tucked the last curl under the blue silk ribbon.

"Thank you, Miss Staveley. That's a fine hairstyle." Her voice was empty of emotion. Miss Staveley curtseyed.

"Thank you, milady. Enjoy your dinner."

Hannah swallowed again; her throat tight. "Thank you. I will."

She stood up, aware that she was lying. She would certainly not enjoy the dinner where Mother and Philipa would no doubt be judging and criticizing everything around them. Gavin had drawn their ire at teatime, and she felt truly grateful to him for it. But at the same time, it was uncomfortable to see the poor man under their onslaught. She knew too well how it felt.

She shut her eyes, trying to find courage, and gathered her dark blue silk skirt and walked into the hallway. The dress was one of two that Maxwell had ordered made up for her and she was very proud of it. She had only chosen to wear it and risk their criticism because it was one of the few dresses that she had that was suitable to her new life.

"Such fine candle-sconces," a voice was murmuring from the dining-room. Hannah tensed. Mother was already there, and Philipa, no doubt, also.

She paused in the doorway, heart thudding; then noticed that Maxwell was already there too, dressed in a black velvet jacket, his high cravat showing above the collar. His expression was blank, face neutral. Hannah felt her heart ache. She knew how uncomfortable her mother and Philipa made him. She wished she could do something about it. She felt as though their presence here was her fault, though she had not ever thought to invite them.

"Very fine," Philipa said into the silence that followed. Maxwell looked up at Hannah as she came in.

"Good evening, my lady." He inclined his head. Hannah held his gaze for a moment, then hurried to her chair at the other end of the table and drew it out.

"Good evening," she greeted him and the guests. She glanced at the place-settings, seeing only one other, then looked questioningly at Maxwell.

"Mama is indisposed," Maxwell said, giving the words some emphasis. "She asked to stay in her chambers to eat."

"Of course," Hannah answered, stomach knotting. She could imagine Patricia had been too worn out by their guests and had chosen to hide. Guilt twisted inside and she sat down silently.

"Gavin said he might be late," Maxwell continued, not looking at Hannah as she settled in her place and unfolded her napkin from its silver holder. "He requested that we start the meal and not wait for him."

Hannah's heart gave a nervous leap. Gavin had suffered, too, it seemed, from her family's intrusion. While he was always informal about everything, he was always there for meals. "Is he out riding?" she asked, attempting to make conversation.

Maxwell shrugged. "I expect he's busy in his study."

His answer sounded as though he had no interest in what Gavin might be doing and Hannah felt her heart sink. He was disinterested and cold, just like she'd thought he was when she first met him. She thought for a moment that she'd been mistaken, that she'd imagined the warmth and care of the last few days, but that wasn't possible. That kiss in the cottage was real; as real as the cottage itself. She hadn't imagined any of that. It was Mother's being here that had made him seem so strange.

The butler arrived with the trolley of food. He, too, seemed more formal than usual and Hannah watched as he circled the table with a bottle of white wine. He came back a few seconds later with a delicious-looking pea soup. Hannah tried to contain her urge to start eating immediately. She watched as Mother theatrically sniffed the wine.

"A fine vintage. Very fine."

Hannah shut her eyes for a moment. She was sure that Philipa and she were trying to act as they thought other nobles might, but it just looked peculiar. She gazed down at her soup, glancing sideways at Maxwell, who had loosened his napkin from the silver napkin-ring and was lifting his spoon. Hannah took up one of her own, plunging it into the soup as soon as Maxwell had started.

"Oh! What a fine kitchen you must have," Mother declared upon tasting the soup. Hannah dabbed at her lips with her napkin. "Of course, we have a fine chef too—French, he is—but you probably have a whole staff dedicated to preparing meals."

"Carronwood is a small estate," Maxwell pointed out. He didn't sound cross, just very distant and cool. Hannah took another spoonful of soup, wishing she wasn't too tense to taste it.

Gavin arrived as the butler brought in the second course of roast meat and vegetables.

"Evening, everyone," he said informally, sauntering to his place at the table. He was wearing a very formal blue velvet jacket, his cravat not quite symmetrical and his hair still windswept. Hannah felt her cheeks lift in a grin.

"Why! I do declare! Shocking manners. Arriving in the middle of the meal unannounced," Mother scolded. Hannah looked at the table, forgetting how to breathe.

"Very shocking. Very shocking," Philipa agreed.

Hannah reached for her lemonade, trying to distract herself from Gavin's shock and Maxwell's cold disinterest.

"I said I'd be late," Gavin said coolly, and Hannah wanted to spring to his defense, but Maxwell pushed back his chair.

"My guests are all welcome to arrive and retire as they please." His voice was like winter's cold. "And I suggest that it be remembered that this is my home and my household."

"Oh. Oh! How forceful," Mother said admiringly.

"Most authoritative," Philipa agreed.

Hannah pushed back her own chair, sure that if they continued like this she was going to have to go upstairs. She looked at her plate, where delicious-looking roast chicken was swathed in gravy and accompanied by glazed vegetables and crispy roast potatoes. It looked like a wonderful meal, but she had no appetite.

"My dear lady. Do you feel ill?" Gavin asked her in concern. Hannah nodded.

"A little," she said, which was not untrue. Her mother glanced at her, eyes wide and round.

"We must send for the physician!" she declared. "Lord Carronwood! Surely you have a fine physician at your disposal to care for my daughter's needs?"

Maxwell looked at Hannah, who glanced down at her food again.

"Hannah? Would you like someone to send for the physician?" he asked quietly.

Hannah shook her head. "No. No, I'm well. Just a headache," she said quickly. Her head really was starting to pound, and she shut her eyes for a moment, wincing at the stabbing pain.

"Good. Edward is arriving tomorrow," Mother continued. "It would be miserable to be indisposed for his arrival. You must be well to show him about this fine estate together." She glanced at Maxwell.

Hannah swallowed hard. She hadn't even thought about the fact that Edward would come down with the coach to fetch them. Her stomach twisted nauseously. Must he shatter the peace in her sanctuary as well? She glanced at Maxwell, but he was staring at the table as though fascinating stories were written there. Her heart twisted.

He hadn't been cold like this for weeks.

She looked over at him again, wanting to say something, but Gavin shifted in his seat.

"I had a fine ride today," Gavin began, changing the subject. "Of course, the rain came too early to let me ride all the way to Mr. Webster's farm," he added as an aside to Maxwell. "But a fine ride nonetheless."

"Good, good," Maxwell replied.

"Crimson was flighty today...I think it was the weather. She's always one for having strange moods when the weather changes," Gavin continued. "Mayhap it's the bran mash that didn't agree with her, though."

Hannah wanted to comment, but Mother interrupted.

"*Must* you talk of horses and their digestion at the dinner table? It seems a most unseemly topic for dinnertime."

Maxwell shot her a look that could have withered metal. Hannah, seeing it and knowing Maxwell, tensed in her seat. Mother was unaware.

"Horses are a topic of conversation in this house," Maxwell said tightly. "As such, they are an appropriate topic at dinnertime, or indeed anywhere."

"Oh! Of course. Of course. I suppose an earl must have a fine stable," Mother gushed.

"Undoubtedly. Undoubtedly so," Philipa agreed.

Hannah looked over at Maxwell. For a moment, he didn't look too angry, just as though he had a headache much like herself. His eyes were tight at the corners, and he had wrinkles she hadn't noticed before around his mouth. She looked down.

"I think I will go and take the air," Maxwell declared after they'd sat to eat in silence for a good six or seven minutes. Hannah looked up from her potatoes, meeting his eye.

"I might accompany you," she said in a small voice.

Maxwell held her gaze and she was relieved to see some humor in the look. It wasn't the usual dark sparkle of a gaze to which she'd become accustomed, but she could just make out a faint twinkle in his eye and she felt relief flood her.

"You must stay and eat the dessert," Mother told Hannah firmly as the butler wheeled the trolley in, the top section of it laden with delicious looking creme caramel. Hannah's stomach twisted with longing. She glanced at Maxwell who inclined his head.

"I will sit awhile," he said instantly. Hannah let out a sigh of relief.

The dessert was delicious, and fortunately conversation had turned to London and the Season, which was something about which Mother and Philipa could talk at length. Hannah, Maxwell and Gavin ate their dessert in peaceful tranquility. Maxwell pushed back his chair after a minute or two more.

"I'll go out to the terrace," he said firmly. Hannah swallowed hard, feeling the need to apologize to him. She hastily ate the last spoonful of the dessert and then pushed back her chair, excusing herself in a murmur and hurrying into the hallway.

Maxwell was leaning against the wall on the terrace when she arrived. She glanced up at him with a stab of guilt, feeling too culpable to disturb him. He opened his eyes as she walked to the railing.

"I can manage one more day," he said softly. He was chalk white. He looked impossibly weary. Hannah grinned.

"You're more tolerant than me. I can manage only a few hours more."

Maxwell laughed. He opened his eyes, and they were tired but kind. His mouth stretched in a grin. He shifted where he rested against the wall, making room for Hannah, who came over to lean on it with him. The stars were white against the black velvet sky; pearls cast there by a careless hand, glowing bright in the depths of the dark. She stared up at them, letting her tension ease.

"I'm too tired...but it's just nine o' clock at night," Maxwell murmured. Hannah smiled.

"I know what you mean," she said. "I'm sorry," she added softly. "I know they can be awfully tiresome. I am sorry you have them here in your house."

"I'm sorry that they're bothering you," Maxwell said gently.

"That can't be helped," Hannah shot back, her voice light. Maxwell laughed.

"No. I suppose not. I just hope they'll decide it's intolerable here and Gavin will chase them away to London soon."

Hannah frowned. "I don't know how long they might intend to linger here," she said slowly. She hadn't expected them to visit, or certainly not so soon, but now that they were here, she was sure they would try and get invitations to visit the nobility in Maxwell's circles. They had already been attempting to do so.

"I hope not longer than tomorrow," he said mildly, his eyelids heavy with weariness. "I shall move into the stables if they stay longer."

Hannah felt her heart twist with guilt at how he was suffering, and she tilted her head, an idea coming to her.

"Let's go for a ride tomorrow," she suggested. "A long one. Maybe to an inn somewhere for luncheon? Then we can escape them for a few hours."

Maxwell smiled. "I can't let Mama face them either."

Hannah shrugged. "You're right. That's true."

"No. I agree," Maxwell said slowly. "Mayhap not the whole day, but we should go for a ride. Let's escape them for a few hours. You could do with it."

Hannah smiled a little sadly. She had meant that he needed to escape, not her—she was used to them, but he wasn't. He had agreed to it, though, and that was all that mattered.

"That's grand," she said slowly, feeling some warmth flow back to her heart once more. "I think it's a grand idea."

"Me too," Maxwell agreed slowly.

They leaned on the wall and chatted quietly for a few moments, before Maxwell excused himself to go and lie down, but Hannah's thoughts were elsewhere. Her mind was going through the details for the ride tomorrow and planning what they would need to organize. She could hardly wait to get started. And he was right—it would be good to escape for a while.

Chapter 22

The feeling of a horse galloping never failed to raise Maxwell's spirits. He raced along the winding road on Nightfire's back and laughed aloud in sheer joy, the drizzle splashing cold water into his face. He leaned back, slowing the pace a little, and then turned in the saddle, looking to see if he could spot Hannah. His spirits had lifted the instant they rode down the path, and he'd let Nightfire run freely, carrying him out of sight. He felt guilty, but then he grinned as he spotted Hannah on Sapphire, not more than ten paces behind them, her back straight, head upright.

"You're a proper horsewoman, aren't you?" he chuckled as she trotted up alongside him. Hannah raised a brow.

"What would an improper horsewoman be?"

Maxwell laughed, warmth and delight filling him at her quick-witted comment. "I will spend time thinking about my answer," he told her, and she grinned, her cheeks flushing with warmth.

Maxwell chuckled and turned his horse, riding on ahead. They had elected to spend the morning from breakfast until just after luncheon outdoors. He'd discussed it with Mama, and, though she didn't look happy about it, he felt she might manage. Gavin was there, after all, so she would not be alone in facing the awful pair that had come to take up residence in their home. She looked pale but she was so much stronger since Hannah had been treating her with her special tea. And Hannah needed to get outdoors.

"How much longer before we reach the inn?" Hannah asked.

"It's only ten o' clock!" Maxwell teased. "We had breakfast an hour ago, you know."

"I'm hungry," Hannah countered. "It's the wind. It's cold out here."

Maxwell turned to look at her, heart filled with admiration for her beauty and skill. She sat easily on Sapphire, as comfortable side-saddle as she had been riding astride; and her long blue riding-cloak billowed about her, the color making her eyes even more intense than normal. Her long blonde hair was almost hidden in the tight bonnet that she wore, which shaded her face and yet did

147

nothing to obscure those striking blue eyes. She looked almost lovelier with her hair moved back from her face, the fine bone-structure all the more apparent like that.

"The cold does increase one's appetite, it's true," he agreed, turning back to look along the path before them. "We will reach the inn just before midday, I reckon. I trust you will find it to your liking."

"I'm not fussy," Hannah said instantly. Maxwell chuckled.

"I know. It's one of your dearest characteristics."

He blushed as he said it. He'd never actually told her how much he admired and liked her. He felt sure he must have made it plain in the stares he leveled at her, but he'd never actually said it before. She went pink.

"Thank you," she murmured.

"No trouble," Maxwell said, grinning. He felt in a teasing mood—the release from the tension of the house had lifted his spirits. He felt playful like a young colt let loose in a grassy field to run about.

Hannah laughed. She had a lovely laugh, as bright as lark-song. She turned her horse and rode behind him, and they set off at a canter. Maxwell could feel Nightfire's body bunching under him as he ran and he knew that it was a good idea, even for the horses, to ride. They needed exercise just as much as Hannah and he did.

They rode on.

The countryside changed as they rode, shifting from forested hillsides to green fields of crops and sheep-grazing meadows. Maxwell stared out over the landscape, the fields and grazing areas making a patchwork that stretched out around them. He could see a distant farmstead, the estate behind them but the village didn't yet show through the forested sections.

"Not too long now," Maxwell told Hannah. She nodded and she might have murmured a reply, but he didn't hear it over the sound of the wind.

Hannah was, Maxwell thought, looking happier since Sapphire arrived. He wished he'd thought of asking her about her special horse much earlier. But then, it was better that she had her now than not having it at all. He leaned back and they trotted downhill.

The inn appeared on their left just at the point where Maxwell was starting to think he must have ridden past it. It was a small one, with only two floors of rooms for the guests, made of brick and with a thatched roof. The sign outside displayed three hens in various improbable colors. He turned and smiled at Hannah.

"Here we are. The Cockerel's Rest Inn."

Hannah just smiled, looking up at it in a way he knew meant she was delighted with something. He felt pride surge through him and chuckled at his own arrogance. It wasn't as though he'd built the inn with his two hands—he'd just suggested it as a place to stop. All the same, seeing her appreciate it warmed him.

They dismounted in the yard and strode into the taproom.

"My lord! My lady!" The innkeeper greeted them, sounding distressed. "Allow me to escort you to the inn parlour. It is more appropriate to your status."

Maxwell smiled to himself. He must look a lot more noble now than he did when he arrived from Spain. He glanced at Hannah fondly as they went through to a staircase and followed the innkeeper up the creaking wooden steps to a large, warm room.

"Here, my lord. Allow me to fetch you both some bread and ale. It is a cold day for a ride."

"Thank you," Maxwell said mildly. "And have the stable hand rub the horses down, please? And give them warm mash."

"Of course, my lord! Of course. Straight away."

Hannah smiled at Maxwell as the innkeeper retreated. Her eyes were bright, and Maxwell felt his heart fill with appreciation and admiration. He knew many women who would have objected to such rustic surroundings. Even the inn parlor, which was reserved for the nobility, had plain wooden boards on the floor and the paneling was crooked and old. But Hannah was looking around delightedly, as if the rustic inn parlor was the Brighton Pavilion.

"You look happy," he murmured softly.

She smiled. "I am happy."

"That's remarkable," he answered quietly. Hannah frowned.

"What cause has it to be?" she asked, puzzled.

"You know, there aren't many women of your birth who would deign to come into a place like this one."

149

Hannah raised a brow. "I'm not a noblewoman, you know."

"Even so," he said, grinning at her. "Those who weren't born to wealth are often even more fussy about such things."

Hannah inclined her head. "Quite so."

They shared a smile. The fire crackled in the grate and a lamp on the wall cast a flickering warmth across her features. She'd removed her bonnet and cloak in the entrance-way, and her lovely heart-shaped face was calm in the half-light, the lamps carving hollows in her cheeks and making her seem shifting and mysterious in the glow.

"Bread and ale, my lord," the innkeeper interrupted his thoughts.

Maxwell thanked the fellow, telling him to send the account to the estate, and as he ordered stew and pie for dessert, his thoughts moved to his father. Father would never have stopped at this inn.

"What's the matter?" Hannah asked gently. Maxwell shrugged.

"I was thinking of my father," he said quietly. "We never agreed—not on anything. Not ever."

Hannah looked at him sorrowfully. "I see," she said.

"He was different to me. He had different ideas and he saw different things as having worth. He would never have stopped at this inn. And he thought horse-farming was silly." He reached for the ale and sipped it, then helped himself to a delicious slice of hot, fresh-baked bread. The smell was mouthwatering.

"You are clearly very different to him," Hannah agreed.

Maxwell nodded, chewing his bread thoughtfully. There was a pause while they both sampled it, then the innkeeper appeared with the next course. Maxwell was silent, the only sound in the room the clanking of cutlery and crockery as the innkeeper moved the empty plates. Maxwell shifted in his seat, clearing his throat to continue.

"Father was strict, and cold," Maxwell confided, waiting for Hannah to take some more bread before he reached for some for his stew. "He disapproved of most things."

"That's sad," Hannah murmured. "My own father was so kind."

"I am glad," Maxwell said truthfully. "I am glad not all fathers were strict and dominating like mine was."

"No. My father was gentle and kind."

"Good," Maxwell said gently. He leaned back, thinking. "Father was ambitious. And he didn't understand how someone could not feel and see exactly like he did. He was stubborn, I suppose. And one can take stubbornness too far."

"Yes," Hannah agreed. She looked thoughtful and Maxwell wondered if she knew someone like that.

"Father wanted me to wed," he told her, wondering why he was talking about these things now. He hadn't told her any of this before, but the warmth and the sense of closeness made it possible. "He chose a woman...someone I could not abide."

Hannah stared at him. "You couldn't abide her?"

"She was...well, let's say she was nothing like you," Maxwell said feelingly. "She was fussy, arrogant, cold." He tilted his head. Those were the worst things he could say about her, but they were all true.

"I wouldn't like that either," Hannah said softly.

Maxwell chuckled. "Laurentia was perhaps a good enough sort—she just was so unlike me. I had to refuse. Father was furious. Her father was a great one for business ventures and Father and he had invested heavily together. I know he felt my disobedience made a fool of him."

Hannah shook her head. "You couldn't force yourself to wed someone you couldn't love."

Maxwell smiled. "No. I couldn't," he said softly. Even when Hannah was a stranger, she had been a stranger in the stables, talking to horses with him, and he'd known at once he liked her.

"You couldn't?" Hannah was staring up at him and he knew that she'd noticed his thought. He smiled and leaned over and it was very easy, after all, to stroke her hair back from her face and stare into her eyes. His palm rested against the petal-soft skin of her cheek and he breathed in, the scent of her intoxicating his senses.

She stared up at him, eyes wide and round, and, before he knew what he was thinking or could even think to do anything else, he was leaning forward and his lips were pressing to that petal-soft skin.

"Oh..."

151

Hannah was murmuring, and Maxwell straightened up, to find that her eyes were closed but the expression on her face was not shock or fright but pleasure. He sat back, heart racing. It took him a moment to be able to speak.

"Sorry," he murmured. He felt no remorse for having kissed her, but he felt he ought to say something.

"No need," she whispered. Her eyes were open, and her smile was bright, her pink-touched cheeks lifting with playfulness and joy.

Maxwell grinned back. He was still struggling to breathe and he took a deep gulp of air, then another, and pushed back his chair, reaching for the pitcher of water the innkeeper had brought up along with the stew. He needed to keep a level head.

He drank some water, aware of Hannah's gaze on him. He breathed out, his heart racing. He longed to kiss her again.

They ate their meal in silence, eating the stew and then the sweet fruit pie. Maxwell shut his eyes, the juicy goodness running down his throat and making his stomach clench with fresh hunger.

They sat and rested for a moment or two, relaxing after the big meal, and then went down to the stables to check on their horses.

"We can take a longer route back, if you like," Maxwell told Hannah as they led their brushed, rested horses into the yard.

"If you like," she said softly.

Maxwell looked at her thoughtfully, head tilted to one side. Hannah had clearly enjoyed the morning and she looked much happier since they had taken the morning out of doors.

"Let's take the long way back," he suggested.

"Very well."

Hannah mounted up, then Maxwell, and he laughed as she trotted ahead, seeming as though she was provoking him to have a race. He chuckled, leaning forward to encourage Nightfire to a trot. They would not overburden the horses, who had just eaten, but a trot was not too demanding for their strength.

"You're fast," he called to Hannah teasingly as he rode up.

"You, too."

They rode together in silence, seeming to be content to view the landscape and not have to talk. The afternoon was warmer than the morning, the cloud lifting a little to allow golden sunshine down. Maxwell leaned back, feeling relaxed. It had been difficult to choose to go out for the day, but he was glad he had.

As they rode to the estate, he found himself wondering where Gavin was. The poor fellow must be driven slowly mad. He grinned to himself, wanting to tease him later. He stopped at the stable, waiting for Hannah to ride up. She dismounted and then he did, handing the reins to the groom.

"A good rub-down, please, for both our horses, and liniment on the tendons, if you please."

"Yes, my lord."

Maxwell walked slowly with Hannah up the steps. The sunshine was warm in the garden, and a sharp twinge of guilt twisted Maxwell's guts as they wandered across the sunny terrace to the door. Mama had been locked up in the house all day with two horrid, critical women. She must be going entirely mad.

"My lord," the butler greeted him. Maxwell frowned. He could see from the fellow's drawn, pinched expression that something was wrong. He tugged off his boots and put them by the door.

"What is it?" he asked, heart thudding with growing unease.

"It's her ladyship, my lord," the butler said swiftly. "She's been taken ill."

Chapter 23

Maxwell ran upstairs. The staircase was a blur as he hurried up, long strides carrying him to the top in a minute. He raced up to the upstairs hallway and ran to the drawing room, heart thudding in his chest.

"Mama? Where is my mother?" he demanded of her maid, Mrs. Hall, who had arrived in answer, he guessed, to someone ringing the bell.

"She's in the drawing room, my lord. I was summoned just a minute ago," the woman added, as though she was afraid that he'd blame her. He took a breath and tried to calm down. His face surely looked like a picture of anger.

Mrs. Hall went in first and he hurried in behind her and stopped dead.

Mrs. Darlington was standing in front of his mother, who rested in a chair. Mama was chalk pale, her eyes shut, and Mrs. Darlington was trying to loosen the ribbon that held her collar. Philipa Darlington was fanning her with a copy of the newspaper.

"Oh! My lord! No need to fuss," Mrs. Darlington exclaimed, turning around swiftly as she heard footsteps. "Lady Carronwood just needed some air. No need to worry. It's of no consequence..." Her voice trailed off. It was high and tense. She clearly felt more shocked than her casual words sounded.

"Get away from my mother."

Maxwell's voice was like a whip cracking. These bungling fools had clearly upset her to the point that she had a nervous collapse, and now they were trying to cover up their foolishness. He rounded on them, rage fueling his firm strides.

"But my lord! We're only trying to be of assist..." Mrs. Darlington began.

"Out!" Maxwell yelled. "Get out right now."

Neither woman moved. Philipa dropped the newspaper. They were both staring, and Maxwell took another step towards them.

"My mother was fine until you arrived. She was recovering. Get out of this room right now." He stared at his mother. Her face was unresponsive, her jaw slack. She was lying back against the

154

cushioned wingback, and he felt his heart jump. She looked like she was dying. "Mrs. Hall? Send for the physician immediately." His voice shook.

"At once, milord."

Mrs. Hall turned to go. Mrs. Darlington and Philipa stared at Maxwell. Maxwell strode towards Mrs. Darlington, and she turned and ran for the door. Philipa followed her.

"Mama?" Maxwell whispered. He went to her chair. He was aware of footsteps in the hallway, and he assumed the butler had come in to check on her ladyship. He ignored the sound and reached for his mother's hand. It was cold, a small, bony form resting in his own warm palm. He covered her hand with both his own, wishing that he could send his own body warmth into it. Guilt stabbed his heart. This was his fault. He'd chosen to go with Hannah. He should have stayed with Mama, protecting her. But he'd chosen to protect Hannah instead. He felt a sob rise in his throat and he bit it back, trying not to cry.

"Maxwell?" Maxwell whipped round. "Let me come in and see to her. I am sure I know something that can help..."

"Get out," Maxwell whispered. Hannah, who was standing at the door, went white. Maxwell didn't care. This was her fault. She had said she wanted to go riding. She had insisted they stay out all day. She had acted like she was in need, and she'd distracted him from caring for his mother. This was because of her.

"Maxwell! I..." Hannah began.

"Get out," Maxwell hissed. He stood up from where he knelt. "Your family did this. Your ridiculous, social-climbing harridans of relatives. They did this. They tormented my mother to a place of nervous collapse. Get out! Get them out of my sight."

"Maxwell?"

Hannah didn't move and Maxwell clenched a fist, guilt and grief mixing inside him and making it impossible to do anything except feel terrible rage. Hannah stared at him for a second and then whipped round and ran down the hallway.

"Mama." Maxwell turned instantly back to his mother, who lay, white and gasping, against the chintzy chair-cover. He took her hands again, rubbing them, trying to make them be less cold. When that did nothing, he wrapped his mother in his arms and lifted her, carrying her as gently as he could to the hallway. She should be in bed. She was freezing to the touch.

"My lord?" The butler appeared as Maxwell walked slowly up the hallway towards his mother's apartments. "The physician is on his way. The groom rode to fetch him."

"Thank you," Maxwell said briefly. The butler was staring at him with a confused, sorrowful expression and Maxwell guessed the fellow wanted to tell him something about Hannah, but he strode on.

Hannah was not his problem. He had lavished too much care on her and this was the result. He made his heart hard, striding up the hallway to his mother's room and opening it swiftly.

"Mama, the physician is coming to see you," he promised, lying her on her bed. He had never been in his mother's private rooms, and he tried not to look around at the white flocked-silk wallpaper and the embroidered decorations, the sparse dressing-table, or the half-open curtains of white gauze.

His mother was utterly unmoving, the ragged, tight breath that she drew intermittently the only sign that she still lived. Maxwell knelt by her bedside and held her hand, pressing it to his brow.

"Please, live, Mama," he whispered. He could feel tears gathering in his eyes and he did his best to blink them away. He didn't want anyone to find him in here sobbing. He sniffed and sat up, staring at his mother's face. She had aged so swiftly in the last years, with crow's feet etched about her eyes and wrinkles on her brow and round her mouth. She was his mother, and so beautiful. That face with its fine-boned features and those large dark eyes had been there, comforting him whenever he needed her. He'd run off to Spain without warning her, and lost three years with her.

Forgive me, he thought silently, his heart twisting in pain. Mama, forgive me.

He sat with her, trying to control his tears, until footsteps in the doorway made him turn around. Mrs. Hall was there.

"My lord? The physician will tend to your mother now."

"Thank you," Maxwell whispered. He stood up, running a hand over his face swiftly to wipe away the sign of sobs. Mrs. Hall had been his mother's maid his whole life and he didn't really mind if she saw his tears. It was the rest of the household he didn't wish to see them—they had to see him as the earl, not as a man with emotions like everyone else.

"I'll have some warm tea sent to your room?" Mrs. Hall asked him as he strode to the door. He nodded.

"Thank you, Mrs. Hall. That would be very nice."

He walked briskly down the hallway, his heart utterly numb. Now that the physician was here, shock settled in, replacing the rage. He strode to his room and opened the door, then shut it behind him and sat down heavily on the chair by the desk. He shut his eyes, resting his head back on the wall.

"I don't know what to do," he murmured aloud.

The two harridans would presumably exit the house. Edward, her brother, was supposed to be arriving today and the fellow could take them back to London. They were not welcome here. He stopped thinking, not wanting to consider Hannah and how she might want the situation handled. Her horrible family had possibly killed his mother. And it had been because he was considering Hannah and her feelings that it happened.

He had allowed himself to be weak and a fool. Father was right. He had always been too soft, too inclined to listen to his own wishes and not the demands of his estate. Now he was paying the price.

He stifled a sob and a knock at the door made him straighten up instantly.

"My lord?"

"Who is it?" Maxwell demanded, taking his handkerchief and dabbing his eyes swiftly.

"I brought you some tea," the butler's voice continued. Maxwell nodded to himself and opened the door.

"Thank you," he replied, accepting the cup of tea. The butler handed it to him, a frown creasing his brow. "My lord, Lady Carronwood...the current Lady Carronwood, I mean..."

"She may mind her own business," Maxwell snapped. "I am involved in caring for my mother. I cannot focus on her whims and wiles now."

The butler blinked at him, evidently upset by his words, but Maxwell turned away. He couldn't let Hannah weaken him any more. This was her fault. He'd given in to temptation and ridden away for the day because of her. She made him weak. He couldn't be weak.

157

"I'll be in my chamber all afternoon. Let me know when the physician is done so that he may report to me."

"Of course, my lord."

The butler shut the door and Maxwell went to his seat again, putting the tea down on the table. It was warm and steaming and even the smell of it soothed him somewhat. He felt a stab of guilt in his heart about Hannah. He knew she would be distressed, but that was something he could ill-afford to care about. He'd cared too much already, and it had been the wrong thing to do. Now she must care for her own needs and whims while he focused on someone who was in real distress.

"I can't believe I was worried about her."

He swore under his breath. He'd seen her silence and confusion and he'd taken it as something he needed to focus on. It was nothing. Her family were clearly all full of wiles and fancies and her emotions were likely as superficial as theirs were. He couldn't afford to worry about her.

"When Edward comes, he must take those two back with him."

He had made his decision. Whatever Hannah thought, he had to make a point. He couldn't let those two horrid women be in the house and torment his mother. If Mama lived, she had to be protected from them.

"Please, let Mama live." He shut his eyes. He'd never been particularly religious, but he prayed now, intensely and with all that was in his heart. "Please, let Mama live. And forgive me."

He rested his head on his hands, weariness washing through him. It had been a long day and all he could do now was wait. He waited and prayed and tried to ignore the terrible, gnawing guilt that ate away at him. He had neglected his mother too often, and now he was paying the price.

All he could pray for was that he be given another chance to do right by his mother.

Chapter 24

Hannah's gaze was wide and unseeing, focused on the wall opposite. She knew she was in her bedroom, but none of the features of her surroundings impressed themselves on her mind. She couldn't think. She was in shock, unable to move or see or grasp any thoughts.

Maxwell thought it was her fault. That was the only thought in her mind, so huge it blocked all others.

She felt her hands wringing together but she wasn't aware of their movement. Nothing made sense to her. Maxwell knew her relatives had upset his mother and he thought it was all her fault.

She stared into the fire. Thoughts wove through her mind like the flames weaving together—wild thoughts. She couldn't stay here. Maxwell had ordered them to go, but she couldn't go with Mother and Philipa and Edward. She couldn't do that. She knew now what freedom felt like, what it meant to be cherished and cared for, or at least regarded as an equal. She couldn't go back into that place and have Mother and Philipa belittle and torment her. She couldn't do it.

"I need to ride."

Only one thing made sense. Sapphire was here. Sapphire could carry her away. They could ride to the inn where Maxwell and she had dined. She felt sure they could reach it before nightfall. She could use the last of her allowance to pay for a meal and lodging, and then decide where to go next.

Perhaps that wild plan of disguising myself and riding to London will be useful for now.

She pushed the thought away. Grassdale was closer and, though she didn't want to go near to the estate, she could ride to Margaret's home and stay there. Margaret could secure her some sort of employment—mayhap teaching at the village school. Anything would be better than being in the control of those three again.

The thought settled in her head for less than a second and she made up her mind. She stood and reached into her wardrobe, finding the small traveling-case that had held some of her gowns. She could strap it to her back while she rode. She threw in two

159

gowns and a change of shoes and petticoats, and then tugged on her boots and the beautiful blue riding-mantle that her maid had hung on the door to dry. It was almost a magical cloak; her chance to transform herself and ride away.

Throwing the cloak about her shoulders, she ran to the door with the bag in her hands and then out into the hallway. She tensed, listening for servants or her mother and Philipa. Nobody came out of the doors and she ran down the stairs, going too swiftly to be able to care about any noise she might make. She reached the front door and burst through, then ran down the path to the stables. The butler was in the entrance-way as she passed— she'd heard his footsteps on the stone flooring—but maybe he'd assumed she was just going to visit her horse.

She ran to the stable.

Something on the lawn to her right caught her attention— there was a structure that hadn't been there in the morning and she didn't stop to think about what it was. It was only as she reached up for the saddle and other tack and carried them, staggering, into the stall, that she realized what it was.

The coach. Edward was here.

"Shh, Sapphire. It's all right," Hannah murmured as her horse laid back her ears, tossing her head as Hannah reached to put on her bridle. She was scared, and Hannah was not surprised. Her own urgency and fear must be affecting her.

She reached up and settled the saddle on Sapphire's back instead, feeling her mood ease slightly as the familiar work of tightening the girth and settling the stirrups into place occupied her hands. She'd taken one of the spare saddles, not the side-saddle that had been brought down for her. A man's saddle would be much easier to ride on and she needed speed.

"Easy, now," she murmured, the saddle on. She reached up to put on Sapphire's bridle. Her horse's snort was loud and urgent, and Hannah frowned, then let her gaze move to where Sapphire was looking. She wasn't shying away from Hannah, but from a form that had appeared in the corner of the stable.

"Edward..." Hannah whispered, stepping instinctively back. Her brother was there, his face reddened as if he'd drunk brandy, his eyes wide and gleaming.

"You," he whispered. Rage contorted his features. "You. Of

160

course. It had to be. You're always in my business. Always messing around where I am supposed to be in charge."

"What?" Hannah whispered. She hung the bridle on the railing of the stall, her mind reeling from what Edward had said.

"You know what I mean," he shouted. He was making no attempt to be quiet, and Hannah guessed the brandy had got to him, but she stepped back, terrified by the sound. Sapphire was neighing, snaking her head forward and Hannah knew she was trying to protect her. She stepped forward, trying to prevent Sapphire from doing any damage to Edward—it was damage they would both pay the price for.

"No, Edward," she said quietly. "I think you should go back upstairs. You..." she wanted to say that he needed to rest, but his face darkened with fresh rage.

"Don't try and boss me!" Edward challenged. "You always think you can boss everyone. You think you're the best. Father...It was his fault." Edward's voice rose in rage. "He was the one. He made you think you were in charge and I was just a fool. He favoured you. Everyone saw it. He got you the riding-instructor first. I'm the man! It should have been me, learning to ride. Not you! He got you the instructor and the horse and you got everything I should have. You had Father's approval too. I never did."

"What?" Hannah whispered. She gaped at Edward. He had never even talked to her, or only to tell her to be quiet and put her in her place. He had always been superior, acting as though she was little more than a servant or a nuisance. And this was what he thought? This was how he felt, clearly, because he was not dissembling now.

"Shut your mouth," Edward slurred. "I'm not here to take orders from you. It's time that you took orders from me for a change. Father made you think you were so good. Well, I don't. And I'm here to show you your place."

He raised a fist at her and Hannah screamed. She'd come out of the stable now, trying to keep Sapphire calm. She knew her horse protected Sapphire and her would fly into a rage and kick the stall apart if she knew Edward was frightening her. Hannah stepped back, but Edward was looming over her and she cried out again, trying to scramble away even as Edward pursued her.

"You think you can run away! Well, you can't. I'm going to find you. I'm going to teach you what you should have learned when you were four and Father doted on you. I'm going to give you the hiding you should have got then."

Hannah screamed as Edward loomed up ahead. She'd backed along the narrow space between the stalls, trying to put space between her and Sapphire, knowing her horse could cause deadly damage if she truly felt rage. She'd backed all the way up the corridor-like space and now she stood with her back against a stone wall. The tack-room was on her left, but as she tried to sneak into it, Edward grabbed at her, his fist raised.

"I'll get you," he shouted, but just as he raised his fist to her, a voice rang out.

"You will release her. Right now. Get away from her this instant."

Hannah stopped in shock. She knew that voice. It was Maxwell, and he was standing in the doorway to the stables. He was staring at Edward, dark rage making his face a mask of coldness. His body was rigid and she could sense violence in every line of him. She looked at Edward. He dropped his arm.

She wriggled away as he let go, running wherever she could. She flattened herself against the wall, but from that position she could see Maxwell as he strode up to her brother. He rested a hand on the shorter man's shoulder and stared at him.

"Get out of my stables. Get upstairs. Get yourself cleaned up. Tomorrow you are to depart my estate and take your mother and your wife as well, for none of you are welcome here."

Hannah tensed. His voice flickered with rage and she thought Edward would attack for sure, but to her surprise, her brother slumped forward, seeming to acquiesce that instant.

"Upstairs..." Edward muttered. He was very drunk, Hannah realized, and Maxwell's voice was enough of a threat to reach him even through the mists of brandy that had swallowed his thoughts.

"Get upstairs," Maxwell told him. "And get out of my house as soon as you can."

Edward walked out, pushing past Maxwell, striding blindly to the doors as if on firm instruction. Hannah, hiding in the little room at the end of the corridor, watched him march swiftly to the door. Maxwell stood by the entrance to the tack-room. Hannah pushed

162

herself into the corner, too scared to come out. If he could act so boldly with Edward, she had no idea how his rage might be when directed at herself. Edward was certainly more intimidating and yet Maxwell seemed barely to notice that fact.

She sobbed, trying to press herself into the shelves where the saddles stood, wanting to make herself as small and unnoticeable as possible. Maxwell's rage was more frightening than Edward's had been. She hid there, shivering, waiting for the door to shut and the light from the lantern in the stalls to darken.

"Hannah? Hannah." Maxwell called. His voice was gentle and soft, not at all covered in rage as it had been earlier. "Hannah, sweetling. Will you come out? You're safe...he's in the house."

Hannah stayed where she was. She couldn't believe how his voice had altered. He'd gone from cold rage—the same horrid rage he'd directed at her just an hour before—to calm and gentle in a few seconds. She stayed hidden by the shelving, barely breathing.

"Hannah," Maxwell called again. "Please. You're safe now. Come out of there. It's too cold out here to be wandering around in the stable."

Hannah peered out. Maxwell was visible from here, the light from the stable's lantern flickering warm brightness along his profile. She could see his fine nose, his firm chin. His expression was hidden from her in shadow. She took a step forward.

"There you are," Maxwell said softly. "Come on, now. It's all right. Come inside. You need to get in where it's warm."

He talked to her in the gentle, soothing way he, or she, would talk to a scared horse. She took a deep breath. This was Maxwell. He loved horses. She trusted him. She stepped forward and slipped out of the gap between the shelving and walked towards him.

"Hannah." He reached out a hand. His fingers were warm and strong and firm, and they held hers tightly. She stepped out through the doorway, and he held out his arms and she walked into his embrace. He wrapped his arms around her and held her tight against him, his arms enfolding her tenderly, one around her waist and the other cradling her to his chest. "Hannah. It's all right. It's all well. I'm sorry," he whispered.

She held him tight, and he stroked her hair and she was sure he was weeping, but that had to be her imagination, because why would he? She felt her heart melt and she wanted to weep. She moved her head and he let her step back, looking into his eyes.

"Hannah," he murmured. He was crying, tears blurring the dark surface of his gaze. Hannah gazed up at him confusedly. He had no reason to cry. She was sniffing, close to tears, and he gently stroked her cheek. "Hannah," he said softly. "My dear. I'm so glad I found you. I'm sorry. I'm so sorry. I should have known...should have trusted myself and you."

Hannah frowned and reached up to rest a hand lovingly on his cheek. He was crying and she was crying, and she gazed into his eyes, her brow wrinkling in consternation.

"Maxwell," she said gently. "It's all right." He really was crying.

"I know." He sniffed. "I just...I thought you'd run off somewhere. I came down to find you. I was so worried. It's so cold out here and the countryside isn't safe. I couldn't believe I'd scared you so badly that you'd try to ride off." He shook his head. "I know you. I know you'd try to ride away." He smiled and she chuckled. Then he frowned again. "I'm so sorry, Hannah," he whispered. "I should have known. I should have seen how badly they treated you. I should have realised you were truly frightened and threatened by them. I'm sorry."

Hannah shook her head. "You couldn't know," she said softly. Warmth was filling her heart, filling her up like sap rising in springtime. She couldn't breathe, love and joy flooding her as she looked into his eyes and saw love there. He really cared. "You couldn't know Edward would attack me. I didn't expect it either." She let out a small chuckle.

He shook his head. "That wicked..." he began. Hannah shook her head.

"He hated me because of how Papa loved me." The fact still stunned her. Edward had spent so long hating her—fifteen years, at least. And she had guessed not one bit of it. She shook her head, dazedly.

Maxwell took her into his embrace again. He held her close, kissing her brow. "He had no reason to. There is never any reason to hate or to hurt. Nobody will ever raise a hand to you again." He held her tight. "You're safe here. You're safe. I promise."

Hannah leaned against him and shut her eyes. Tears of relief ran down her face. She had never felt safe, not really. Even though she'd been largely unaware of Edward's hate and violence, she'd known he didn't like her and that he disapproved. And while Mother and Philipa had never been physically violent, their critical, cruel words were worse than their fists. She held Maxwell and closed her eyes and felt truly cherished.

Maxwell kissed her hair. "You're safe. I promise to take care always. You're my dearest. I have never had the courage to tell you, but I will tell you now. I love you." He bent down and rested his hand on her arm, gazing into her eyes. His dark eyes were filled with brightness and his smile was a thing of loveliness. "I love you. I always have. I think from the moment you wandered into that stable and petted my horse."

She chuckled. She was crying now too, tears running down her cheeks. She smiled, joy suffusing her heart and making her feel light inside. She reached up and touched his hair gently, stroking it, looking into his eyes.

"I love you too, Maxwell." She breathed out, chest aching with how forceful and strong the feeling seemed. "I love you too."

He bent forward and pressed his lips to hers.

She shut her eyes, the sweetness of his kiss making her feel as though she was drowning in a lake of warmth and gentleness. She held him close and he held her and love flooded her heart.

"You're shivering," Maxwell said gently, bending down and resting a tender hand on her shoulder. "Come on. Let's get you into the warmth."

"Yes."

Maxwell smiled and Hannah smiled back. She took his hand and together they walked out of the stable and up the path. The joy and warmth suffused her heart as they strode up the damp flagstones together, holding hands, and walked back into the warm and safe house.

Chapter 25

It was warm in the parlor, the fire raging, but Hannah still felt cold. She sat on the chaise-longue, a cup of tea in her hands, blankets wrapped around her warmly. Maxwell had carried her here and insisted that she be given hot tea to drink, and she held the cup with both hands. The blanket that swathed her was of fine, soft wool, smelling of lavender from the wooden box where it had been stored. She put down the tea and clutched the blanket around her and wished she would stop feeling so cold.

"More tea, my lady?" The butler appeared in the doorway behind her. Hannah shook her head, turning to smile at him. He'd been so caring since she'd been brought in from the stables, freezing cold, and she felt appreciation and gratitude for his kindness.

"No. Thank you. Is her ladyship resting?"

"She's still resting. His lordship said you must see to her as soon as she is awake."

"I will certainly do," Hannah agreed. She glanced around the parlor. Maxwell had told her to use his mother's parlor, saying that he couldn't guarantee that she didn't need to see her awful family if she used the drawing room. She had agreed, wanting to be nearby should Patricia need help. She'd sent for Mrs. Hall, Patricia's maid, to describe the symptoms to her. She looked up as the woman walked in. She was older than Patricia, with white hair that curled about her face and a serenity that made Hannah feel at ease.

"My lady? You wished to ask me some questions?" Mrs. Hall asked. She looked very friendly, if a little awkward at being questioned. She smoothed a hand down the white apron on her uniform.

"I did," Hannah replied. She gestured for Mrs. Hall to sit opposite her but understood when the older woman remained standing. It would feel too strange, she guessed, to sit down on her ladyship's furniture. "I wanted to ask you about what happened to Lady Carronwood this morning."

"It was just after luncheon, actually, my lady," Mrs. Hall explained, just inside the doorway. "Her ladyship was taking tea with the guests in the drawing room. A cup of tea to wash the meal down; no cake or sandwiches or the like. They were sitting talking, or so Mrs. Darlington told me, when suddenly her ladyship pressed her hand to her side and cried out like she was in pain, and then collapsed, as if she'd stopped breathing."

Hannah swallowed hard. "I see." She let the information sift through her mind, calling on the things Margaret had discussed with her. Sometimes Margaret would tell Hannah about their work, about villagers who had been helped by creams or tinctures they'd bought at the apothecary's shop. Once, she had mentioned an elderly woman who had fallen down after a searing chest pain. She had said the woman recovered slowly, assisted by a preparation of digitalis and willow bark, as well as eating more fish, fresh meat and citrus fruits. After a month she had no more pain and was able to work in her garden and walk around the village as usual.

"She woke up briefly while you were out," Mrs. Hall said. "She wanted to speak with you. She felt sure you'd know how to help."

Hannah felt warmth flood through her. She had half-thought Patricia would condemn her like Maxwell had seemed to do. But it seemed she'd always seen Hannah as different. She smiled at Mrs. Hall, who beamed, though she still seemed awkward, stepping from side to side as if uncomfortable.

"Is she sleeping now?" Hannah asked Mrs. Hall. The older woman lifted a shoulder.

"She was asleep when I was in there just a moment ago. I'll check on her now." She smiled gently.

"Please do, Mrs. Hall," Hannah answered.

She sat and waited while Mrs. Hall moved into another part of the suite and then, after a few minutes, returned.

"She is awake. She was asking for you, my lady."

"I'll come directly," Hannah replied. Her heart thudded as she hurried to find Patricia. She was shown into the bedroom by Mrs. Hall and when she went in, Patricia was sitting in a chair by the fireplace. Her body was swathed in blankets, but her cheeks were not as pale as they had been and when she saw Hannah her dark eyes focused on her, bright and welcoming.

"Hannah," Patricia whispered. "You came. I'm so pleased."

"Shh, Patricia," Hannah told her gently. "You need your

strength. Of course, I'm here. I came as soon as I could." She took Patricia's hand, which was not cold anymore. She held it tight in her own, feeling the pulse that throbbed at Patricia's wrist. As usual, it was slow. She could feel that strange tugging feeling, an occasional missed beat, that she sometimes felt in the older woman's pulse, and she held her hand, mind racing to decide what she should use to treat the condition of the heart that Patricia seemed to have.

"Maxwell..." Patricia whispered.

"He's fine," Hannah said at once. "He found me in the stable. I'm sorry if I caused you concern."

Patricia smiled. "He found you. Good. He's...silly...sometimes." She could barely speak, her breath still ragged as though her chest hurt. Hannah grinned.

"Yes, he is silly sometimes," she agreed.

Patricia grinned back, but her eyes were closing, and Hannah could see how much effort it took for her to talk. She sat and held her hand, waiting for the older woman to sleep, and, when it seemed she was restful again, she gently placed her hand on the coverlet again and tiptoed from the room.

Maxwell had said he'd wait for her in his study, and she hurried there, her footsteps silent on the hallway floor. She reached it and knocked on the door and Maxwell opened it almost as soon as she got there.

"How is Mama?" he asked immediately.

Hannah looked into his eyes, her own gaze firm and unwavering. "She's better," she said in truth. "She's very weak, but if she is able to sit and talk now, as she can, she will recover. I know it. She needs a daily tea, which I will make her, and she should slowly return to walking about the garden. For now, just walking about her bedchamber would be more than enough."

"Thank God," Maxwell whispered. His eyes were shut, and Hannah felt her heart twist. His mother was central to him, and she was so glad that she could help heal her.

When he opened his eyes again, Hannah looked up at him, feeling a little nervous. She had her own questions, but she was so tired she didn't know where to start. Maxwell took her hand.

"Your mother and sister-in-law are in bed," he said. "Edward too, doubtless. The butler organized the white room...it's upstairs on the other side of the house. You shall not need to encounter any of them. They are going to depart early tomorrow morning. Edward assured me of this before retiring to bed. He might not be able to remember that, but I will remind him if needed."

"Thank you." It was Hannah's turn to feel relief flood through her body. She swayed and Maxwell grabbed her, catching her and steadying her on her feet.

"Easy, there," he said gently. "You're tired. You have had a very long day. Me, too," he added, and she could see how he could also barely stand now, his face drained and lined where he had no lines previously. "I think we ought to retire to bed too."

"Yes," Hannah whispered.

Maxwell looked down at her, his gaze warm. "I would suggest you retire to my quarters," he said, his voice thick with need. "But I think we are both, perhaps, too tired. Tonight, mayhap not. Tomorrow, though."

"Yes," Hannah whispered, her heart thudding in her chest, strong enough to hear. "Yes. We will."

Maxwell smiled and drew her into an embrace. He kissed her lips, but gently and tenderly, without the passion that she could hear in his voice and feel in how he touched her. She shut her eyes, letting herself lean against him, feeling safe in his embrace.

"I will see you tomorrow morning. Sleep well, my dearest."

"Sleep well," Hannah whispered. "My dearest Maxwell."

He turned and looked at her and his gaze held hers and she felt her heart soaring. She walked giddily down the hallway to her bedroom and shut the door behind her, then sat down heavily on the bed. She was exhausted, it was true; but the joy that filled her heart was bright as flame and filled her with energy. She was singing under her breath as she unfastened her day-things and slipped a shift over her head, then clambered, exhausted and drained, into bed.

The next morning, Hannah woke to feel sunlight bright on her face. She rolled over and slipped out of bed, her heart soaring with the memories of the previous evening. She pulled on her nightgown, summoning Miss Staveley to help her dress.

"My blue dress, please, Miss Staveley. And a chignon, if you please."

"At once, milady."

Hannah smoothed her dress as she hurried to the breakfast room. It was her favorite gown; one she knew looked particularly good. She tiptoed into the breakfast room and felt her heart soar with delight. Maxwell was there at the table. There were two places set beside his and she drew back the chair she usually used and smiled at him, flashing her best grin at him.

He smiled back, a smile that lit his eyes, the contact between his gaze and hers lingering a long moment. She drew a deep breath and looked at the table, heart thudding in her chest.

"Good morning," she murmured.

"Good morning."

Hannah leaned back in her chair. Maxwell poured her tea, and she thanked him, looking around the room. Only one other place was set, and she assumed that it was for Gavin, since Patricia likely could not join them yet. That meant Mother, Philipa and Edward had departed. She looked at him, not sure how to ask.

He nodded. "Your mother, Edward and his wife have already breakfasted. The coach rolled out of the gates at a quarter to nine this morning. They must be half an hour on their way by now."

"Thank you," Hannah said in a small voice. Maxwell smiled.

"I think they'll be just as pleased to get out of here as we are to have them departing. Imagine...we talk about horses all day."

Hannah giggled. The twinkle in his eyes made her laugh and she reached for some toast, her joy sparkling inside her.

"Now we can talk about horses all day," she told him, buttering her toast. "Each day. And nobody will ever tire of the topic. Not you or I, certainly."

"Absolutely," Maxwell agreed. He beamed at her. "You know, I think that is a positively lovely thought. I am very glad about that. I'm very lucky, you know."

Hannah blushed. "Me, too," she said, meaning it with all her heart.

Maxwell chuckled. He reached for her hand. "I love you, Hannah Carlisle. I love you with every fiber of my being."

Hannah beamed at him, her heart soaring, soul flaring bright with love. "I love you, too, Maxwell Carlisle. I love you so very much."

He reached for her hand and held it, his fingers tight and warm on her own. She sighed and stared into his eyes, her heart melting in her chest as she gazed at him. He drew her closer, as close as they could get without knocking things off the table and they sat, arms around each other, lost in the beauty of how it felt to be close to one another.

"Hannah," Maxwell said slowly. "There's something I want to ask you. I never had a chance to ask you before, but I've wanted to for a long time now."

"What is it?" Hannah asked softly.

Maxwell held her gaze, his own stare firm and warm. "Will you marry me?"

"What?" Hannah's heart flooded with joy, even as her brow creased in puzzlement. "But Maxwell..." she stammered. "We are already wed."

He grinned. "I know." He paused. "But it didn't feel right. I love you, Hannah. And I want you to know that. I love you and that is why...why I ask you now." His voice was solemn.

"Oh, Maxwell..." she breathed. She held his gaze. She felt her heart race and she leaned forward, taking his hands in hers. "Oh, that would be wonderful. But could we?" She stammered.

Maxwell shrugged. "It cannot be an actual wedding but we could just get a blessing from the paeson. I think anyone would understand our wishes. We didn't really have a chance to say what we meant last time, and really mean it. I'm sure our parson here at Carronwood wouldn't mind giving his blessing."

"You mean it?" Hannah lifted her hand to her lips. That would be the most beautiful thing she could imagine. She truly loved Maxwell, and it would be wonderful to be able to celebrate that, to be able to pledge themselves without the shadow of anything over their love.

"Of course. Why not?" Maxwell laughed.

They decided. They would host this little ceremony at Carronwood, in the private chapel, in two weeks. By then, they both agreed, Patricia would be recovered enough to attend. They spent the rest of the breakfast planning the ceremony. Hannah gazed at Maxwell, joy making her heart soar with the spring breeze. She grinned at him, and he grinned back, both of them full of love. Hannah chuckled, the light in her heart impossible to express in any other way, and Maxwell leaned in and kissed her gently.

They were both content.

The gathering took place on a warm spring morning, the roses all around the estate blooming in riotous profusion of white and yellow and red. The parson waited at the altar with Maxwell, while Hannah walked to him with Gavin, who took the role of bringing Hannah to Maxwell. Patricia was their audience, along with some special guests. Margaret and her father, and Betty, Hannah's maid from Grassdale. They thronged the tiny chapel, and their congratulations were warm and loud and loving.

"Whew," Hannah sighed as they sat on the terrace together. Their guests were in the dining-room, sitting down over cheese and biscuits after a lovely luncheon. She tucked a strand of blonde hair under the simple wreath of flowers that Betty had made for her. "That was a big lunch."

"It was," Maxwell said with a grin. "We'll need a long ride to aid the digestion."

Hannah chuckled. "Sapphire has the day off," she reminded him warmly. Sapphire had been there to greet her after the ceremony, walking across the stable yard and snuffing her own congratulations into her hair. Hannah had wrapped her arms around her beloved horse's neck and wept. The only thing better would have been to have Papa there, too; and she didn't doubt that he was there, where the North Star burned on the other side of daylight, watching her and smiling.

"Well, then," Maxwell said with a grin. "Tomorrow, we can go for a fine ride up to the new pastures."

"Indeed," Hannah agreed.

They shared a smile. Hannah leaned back, feeling exhausted but happy. Maxwell and she had talked a great deal—not just about their life, but about the horse-farm he planned to establish at the estate. The new pastures were part of that. She could not wait for tomorrow to come so she could see them.

"Gavin seemed to be enjoying the lunch," Maxwell commented. "I mean, he always does, but today was different."

"I agree," Hannah murmured. She grinned; eyes closed drowsily in the sweet late spring heat. Gavin had talked non-stop with Margaret, whose knowledge of nature and even the weather seemed considerably impressive, especially to Gavin.

"He never stops about his weather predictions," Maxwell

said with a chuckle.

"Well, Margaret didn't mind," Hannah said smilingly.

"No. That's right." Maxwell laughed.

Hannah sat in the late afternoon sunlight, her hand in Maxwell's, her heart warm and a delicious drowsy feeling filling her from the warmth and good food. She gazed up at Maxwell, her heart full, almost too full of love to speak.

He smiled down at her, tucking a strand of hair behind her one ear. "Well, I suppose we talk about horses a lot," he said with a grin.

"All the time," Hannah answered instantly. She beamed. "It's the best topic."

"It is," he agreed. "And I'm so glad you think so too."

"Of course, I do." She made a wry face. "Horses are the most important thing in the world."

They shared a chuckle.

"I love you, Hannah, my dearest," Maxwell said softly. He drew her close and his lips pressed against hers, warm with desire and longing that made her own body heat up, her heart dancing with love.

"I love you too, Maxwell, dearest." She drew him close, arms wrapped tight around him, and they kissed and her soul soared and she knew that she had never imagined anything like this before. Her heart was full of love and she held Maxwell tight, her soul knowing that the future was bright and that new joys were around every corner—she just had to hold onto the reins a minute to ride into all the brightness she could imagine.

Epilogue

The sound of laughter, high and sweet, filled the drawing room, along with a gust of air from outside.

"Dearest? Have you seen Alexander's shoes?" Hannah called out into the corridor. She was trying her best to catch little Rachel, their daughter, who was rushing around the wide space of the drawing room in childlike delight.

"Horses, Mama! Horses. Outside. I want outside."

"I know, Rachel," Hannah reassured her with a grin, unable to contain her delight in the little three-year-old's joy. "But we have to get prepared...it's still a bit cold outdoors."

"Sunshine!" Rachel retorted, turning around and grinning at her mother, showing fine teeth. Her eyes were blue like Hannah's, her little face, despite its childlike softness, promising the fine bones of her father's countenance. Her hair was a mop of blonde curls.

"Yes, I know," Hannah said with a chuckle, enjoying her daughter's precocious reply. "I know there's sunshine. But it's cold. I promise. Here...if you stand still and let me put your cloak on, we can go outside."

Rachel planted herself firmly on the mat, allowing Hannah to reach down and drop a little blue cloak over her head, tying it around her neck with a blue satiny ribbon. The little cloak reminded Hannah of her own riding mantle and she beamed, seeing the tiny child toddle off with determination across the mat. Her brother, Alexander, was clambering on the chaise-longue, doing his best to see through the window. Hannah ran over swiftly.

"No, sweetling! You'll fall," she said, lifting him promptly before he fell of the end into the fireplace.

"Outside!" Alexander shouted, adding his excitement to Rachel's own demand from earlier. "I want to see the horses."

"I know," Hannah said, laughing. She put him carefully onto his little stubby legs and he ran towards Rachel, who had found a spinning top and was attempting to roll it. "Where's your papa?" she asked, not expecting an answer. She'd called Maxwell a few moments ago, and he'd still not appeared in the drawing room.

"Here. He's here," Maxwell said with a grin, appearing in the room. "And here are some outdoor things for a little man who, I hear, is eager to get outdoors?" Maxwell asked. He kissed Hannah and then bent down to Alexander, who put his little arms up for a hug. Maxwell lifted him up, planting a kiss on the soft silky hair. Alexander was also blonde, but his hair was honey-dark, not the bright, pale curls of Rachel's. His eyes were not as dark as his father's, but Hannah suspected they might become the same almost-black that Maxwell and Patricia shared as he aged.

"They're very happy about the news," Hannah said with a laugh.

"Horses! Papa! Want to see horses!" Alexander informed Maxwell. Hannah felt tenderness fill her heart as Maxwell addressed the little boy.

"You'll see them in a moment. I promise. Papa's just getting his jacket, and then we're off. Ready?" he called to Hannah.

"Absolutely. Horses, Rachel!" she called, striding to where their daughter was still rolling the top determinedly across the floor. She lifted Rachel up as the little girl whooped with delight and carried her to the door. Maxwell was a little ahead, hurrying down the stairs.

"We'll need to ride to the paddock," he was saying, informing Alexander more than Hannah, who knew well how to get there. "And then we'll be able to see the horses."

"Long?" Alexander inquired. "We stay long?"

Hannah laughed. The wistful note in his voice suggested he'd want to stay all day. She glanced out of the front door as Maxwell opened it. The day was sunny, as Rachel had already informed her, but as she suspected, the early summer air was still a little cool. The lawns were bright green, a little overgrown, and roses and daisies bloomed in the flowerbeds. The air smelled of dew and earth and freshness.

"We'll stay until luncheon," she promised. "At least."

"When is luncheon?" Alexander wanted to know.

Hannah and Maxwell shared a glance, his eyes sparkling. The twins both seemed to evidence some of Hannah's stubbornness. Their bright, inquiring minds amazed Hannah and Maxwell daily.

"It's in three hours," Hannah informed him as they strode to the stables, Maxwell and she both carrying one of the children.

Alexander looked at her confusedly. At three years old, he

hadn't much idea about how long an hour was, but she knew that, as soon as they needed to go indoors, he'd declare the time had been too short. The two children loved the outdoors, and Hannah and Maxwell delighted in that fact, sharing their passion for horses and riding with the children whenever they could.

"We'll have plenty of time to play," Maxwell informed Alexander. This notion pleased him, clearly, because he grinned brightly. Maxwell reached the stables, where the groom had saddled both Nightfire and Sapphire. Hannah walked forward first, handing Rachel to Maxwell so that she could mount up. She rode astride, using a special saddle that had been made for her—smaller and lighter than a man's saddle, but designed exactly the same.

"Ready," she called as she arranged her skirts about her. The long blue mantle she wore reached to her ankles despite the unseemly saddle, making sure there was nothing indecent about it. Not that it would have mattered on their estate, but one never knew if a hunting-party from Almhurst's manor might come through the woods and it proved advantageous to to cater to their folly on occasion.

"Here," Maxwell said gently. He lifted Rachel carefully, so that Hannah could settle her on the saddle before her. She wrapped one arm around her daughter, guiding her horse with the reins in her right hand. She turned, glancing sideways to watch as Maxwell mounted up.

As always, she felt a shiver of delight, seeing his lithe, easy movements when riding a horse. He put Alexander on the saddle, holding him with one arm, then swung up swiftly, hugging the child with his left arm and holding the reins with his right. His muscular body was a blur of motion as he swung up, his dark riding jacket and dark trousers matching his fine chocolate-brown hair.

"Off we go," he said simply. Hannah blushed, knowing he knew she'd been watching him and seeing his clearly flattered grin. He never really showed off, but sometimes she had the sense that he did things while riding to impress her.

She leaned back and they rode on.

The morning sunshine was bright and Hannah squinted a little as they set off uphill. The paddock to which they were riding lay at the far end of the estate, where Maxwell had bought some new land. He'd extended the estate's boundaries, purchasing grazing land where they had built a new stable, this time for the fast-growing Carronwood Farm. Already, they had their first three colts and two yearlings, and it was these that they rode to see.

"Almost there," Maxwell assured Alexander, who was raising a question in a bright chirp.

The farm appeared as they rounded the bend of the hill. Hannah stared down. The new stable was a fine example of the art of stable-building, made of grayish, weathered pine wood with thatch on the roof to keep it warm and big windows at the front for good airflow. The insides were packed dirt, the clay for the floors specially selected to be absorbent and stay dry. Every inch of the place, from the wood to the hay they used had been meticulously chosen by them both, after discussions with several experts, including Gavin.

Hannah smiled at the thought of their dear friend. She saw Maxwell vault off his horse, holding Alexander in his arms, and a second later he was raising his hand, waving at a figure who was walking across the bright green field.

"Morning, Gavin!" Maxwell yelled cheerily. "Grand to see you here."

"Morning, Maxwell," Gavin greeted Maxwell warmly, his thin, handsome face lighting up in a grin. He waved to Hannah, his eyes lingering on the little children brightly. "Good morning, young fellow. Good morning, sweet lady," he greeted the children in turn. They both looked up at him wide-eyed. They were a little in awe of Gavin.

"Gavin's going to let the colts out now," Hannah informed Rachel, handing her carefully to Maxwell so she could dismount. Her arms weren't as long as Maxwell's, and nor was she tall enough to dismount easily with Rachel in her arms. She felt her ankles jar as they always did with the impact with the ground, then she reached for Rachel and the five of them walked slowly across the field to the stables.

"I'll let Flame and Sable out first," Gavin told Maxwell and Hannah. "Brightfire was limping a little yesterday...I want to check his tendons before I let him run with the rest."

"Of course," Maxwell agreed. He frowned. "Was it from play-fighting with the others?"

"No," Gavin replied, shaking his head. "Just from running too much, I reckon. I asked my lady to put some balm on the stove for him. Didn't ask what she made," he added to Hannah. "But I reckon it'll have him running like a racehorse."

Hannah laughed. Her heart filled with affection. Just before she could ask him how his lady was, she looked up to see her. Margaret was walking across the field to them, her long, blue-and-white dress covered with an apron. She wore Gavin's coat and she beamed at them both.

"Hannah! Maxwell! And the two beauties. What a surprise," she greeted them all. Hannah ran and hugged her, breathing in the familiar herbal scent of her hair. She never asked Margaret what she used to wash it, but it smelled the same and it was thick and lustrous, her long braid glossy dark brown as always.

"Margaret. How lovely to see you," Hannah murmured, holding her close. Her friend lived on the horse farm with Gavin, whose small but beautifully furnished cottage was perhaps a hundred yards from the stable.

Margaret grinned at Hannah as she stepped back. "It's a pleasure to see you," she said. "If you're staying, you might want to come up to the cottage. I baked some walnut biscuits—the little fellows might like them?"

"Teatime!" Alexander yelled from where he clung onto Maxwell's hand. He beamed up at Margaret winningly. "I like teatime." Teatime was his favorite time of day.

"Horses. Then teatime." Rachel sniffed, reminding the adults around her about their priorities.

Hannah laughed aloud. "Yes, dearest. Horses first. If we let him, I think Gavin will go and let them out now."

"In a moment. In a moment, my impatient ones," Gavin said, beaming at the children playfully.

Alexander and Rachel both chuckled; small, delighted laughs that lifted on the fresh morning air. Hannah felt her heart fill with so much love she thought it might burst. She looked up at Maxwell and he smiled gently back and she knew he was thinking the same thing.

They stood with the children clinging onto their fingers and waited while Gavin went to fetch the horses.

Hannah caught her breath, as she always did, when the two colts appeared. Flame was a roan thoroughbred, and Sable was

Sapphire's baby. She stared at him; her throat tight with so much love she could barely breathe. Behind her, Sapphire let out a loud call to greet him and Hannah led her forward, letting her walk over to her baby.

The graceful mare bent her head on Sable's neck and breathed in and Sable bowed his own head, snorting softly to acknowledge her greeting.

Hannah swallowed around a lump in her throat. Seeing the two together was always beautiful and she stood back to watch. Later, once the colts had exercised a little more, they'd remove the tack from Sapphire and let her run with them.

"So," Gavin interrupted her thoughts, dusting his hands as he came out of the stable. "Brightflame looks just fine. I don't know what was in that balm, my dearest," he said, grinning at Margaret. She tilted her head, a bright, joyful smile full of pride stretching her lips.

"A secret," she said playfully. "I'm sure Hannah could guess." She shot a grin at Hannah, her eyes sparkling in challenge.

"When we come in for teatime, I'll try," Hannah told her. Margaret chuckled.

"I hope the nut biscuits are to your liking. I added a new spice."

"Don't tell me what it is until I taste it," Hannah said teasingly. Margaret chuckled.

Since they purchased the land for the farm, Maxwell had set aside part of the garden at the estate for a conservatory, where Hannah grew many medicinal plants, some that had never been grown there before. Mr. Blackwood and Margaret had advised her on many of them, and she'd accumulated quite a collection. While Margaret extended her knowledge of animals, Hannah had extended her own, first of all tending to Patricia and later, starting to recommend teas and other remedies to their neighbors. Margaret and she were becoming known for their wisdom.

"There he is. See? Leg's grand," Gavin informed them as Brightfire exploded out of the stables. He was a chestnut thoroughbred, the white blaze on his brow like snow against the flame of his coat. His sire was Nightfire, for whom he had been named, and his temperament was even more fiery than Flame's, who was taller and just a little quieter, and his name fitted him

179

perfectly.

"See! Mama. Want see."

Hannah murmured an apology and lifted Rachel up onto the fence so she could watch the horses playing together in the paddock. Maxwell held Alexander just beside her.

"Big. Flame is big," Rachel informed her. Hannah smiled warmly. The children knew all the horses by name and their fascination with them was every bit as big as hers had been at their age.

"Yes," she told Rachel gently. "Flame is big. I think Sable will also be big...he seems to be growing more slowly." Sable's father was a thoroughbred, while Brightfire was a cross with an Arab mare. He would not get as tall as either of the other horses, they thought, but his inner fire more than made up for that fact.

They stood and watched the colts chasing each other around the field, and then Gavin went over to help untack Sapphire while Maxwell and she held the children. They untacked Nightfire too, but kept him in the paddock next door, just in case he chose to fight with the colts.

"Hungry," Alexander declared once the older horses were playing with the colts. "When's teatime?"

Maxwell let out an appreciative chuckle and ruffled the little boy's head playfully.

"Teatime is now, young man. If Margaret would be so kind as to invite us?" he asked.

Hannah smiled as Margaret inclined her head. "Of course. The tea's brewing. It's ordinary tea, not anything special."

They all laughed as they trooped across the field together. Inside, the fire burned warmly, and Hannah looked around appreciatively. The space was beautiful, with chintz wingbacks and fine linen curtains and wood paneling. She breathed in, smelling spices, and her stomach twisted hungrily at the scent.

They settled down at the table for tea.

Conversation was bright and ranged from horses to herbs to the weather and the children. Margaret was expecting a baby, the slight roundness of her stomach just showing beneath the muslin dress she wore.

"Is it midday already?" Maxwell asked as the sound of distant church-bells filtered in. His expression was one of surprise.

180

Margaret smiled. "I think so. I'm sure you'll get back in good time for luncheon," she assured Maxwell, who looked worried.

"It's not far, no," he agreed. "Alexander? Rachel? I believe we have to ride back shortly," he told them formally. Alexander was chewing a biscuit contentedly, while Rachel tried to make a stack out of three of them on the tray. Hannah chuckled to herself at their blissful play.

"I'm sure Patricia will hold luncheon back for us," she reminded Maxwell gently as she lifted Rachel, kissing her daughter who made a small indignant noise as she swung her up out of the chair.

"Biscuits," Rachel informed her crossly. "Playing."

"We'll call on Margaret and Gavin soon," she promised her.

"Margaret visit us," Rachel told her. "My doll's at home."

Hannah chuckled. Margaret beamed at Rachel, fluffing her soft blonde hair lovingly. "I promise I'll visit soon," she told the child fondly. "And bring biscuits and cake."

"Biscuits!" Rachel yelled.

"Cake!" Alexander sounded delighted.

Maxwell chuckled. "They sound hungry. Best get them back for luncheon," he said to Margaret and Gavin warmly. Gavin shook his hand.

"Visit soon," he told Maxwell with a smile. "Always lots to talk about on the farm."

Maxwell nodded. "We'll be back soon," he agreed.

They walked out to the paddock, where Margaret entertained the children while they hastily tacked up and got ready to ride. They waved as they rode off, the children shouting cheerily to Margaret and Gavin, asking them to visit soon, as they headed back.

"I hope Mama isn't too hungry," Maxwell commented as he swung down from the saddle at the stable. Hannah smiled reassuringly. She knew Maxwell was worried about Patricia—his mother was much better, but he'd cared for her for half his life and he still worried.

"I'm sure she'll be all right," Hannah said gently. "Mrs. Hall will bring her soup up to her room if she needs it."

"Yes. Yes, you're right," Maxwell agreed.

They hurried into the house, the butler greeting them

happily as they strode in.

"Let my mother know we're here," Maxwell told him firmly. The butler nodded and hurried off. Hannah put Rachel gently on the floor, unfastening her little outdoor boots and hastily changing her shoes and cloak. Rachel wriggled impatiently.

"Grandmama," she said firmly. "Want see Grandmama."

"She's coming down in a minute," Maxwell informed Rachel warmly, ruffling her hair as he helped Alexander with his shoes and coat. Hannah lifted Rachel so that she could go upstairs, and they all hurried to the drawing room

"Mama," Maxwell greeted Patricia, who was sitting in the chintz wingback by the window, her embroidery on her lap. She looked up, her thin, elegant face lit up with a beaming smile as she saw the children. "I trust you're feeling well?"

"Most well," Patricia said softly. "Ah! My darlings. How was the ride? Did you see lots of horses?" she asked the children, who were both wriggling with impatience.

"Horses!" Alexander yelled delightedly. "Lots of horses."

"We saw Flame," Rachel informed Patricia more calmly. "And Sable, and Brightfire. Flame's big."

"Sable's growing!" Alexander added enthusiastically.

"Well! Well," Patricia answered with a grin, holding out her arms as the children toddled across the rug towards her. "That sounds exciting. Are you tired? Have you eaten anything?"

Hannah smiled to herself. Patricia was a loving grandmother and the children insisted on spending as much time as possible with her. Patricia often walked around the garden with them after tea, her gentle voice answering their excited inquiries as they rushed about the lawn.

"Biscuits," Alexander told her cheerfully.

"Margaret made biscuits," Rachel added.

Patricia beamed at Hannah over the children's heads as she embraced them both. Her dark eyes were bright with warmth and Hannah felt her own heart twist. Where once Patricia had been deathly-pale, her cheeks were now warmed with the faintest hint of pink. Her lips were not almost blue anymore, and when she stood she wasn't breathless.

Hannah felt her heart flood with gratitude and joy as she watched Patricia stand up. She walked slowly but confidently

182

towards the door, smiling at the grandchildren who clamored to follow her.

"Let Grandmama take the stairs slowly," Maxwell told them gently.

"Grandmama! Want to show Grandmama my horse," Rachel called out. The children had wooden rocking-horses, ones Maxwell had ordered specially, made by a master craftsman.

"You can show her soon," Maxwell told the child gently, though Patricia had seen the rocking-horses many times already. "First, we need to have lunch."

Hannah grinned at the children's protesting shouts. They wanted to play first, then have lunch, but Maxwell lifted Alexander onto his shoulders and ran down the hallway, making the little boy shriek with joy and apparently decide luncheon wasn't too bad after all. Rachel had her turn and then they went downstairs together.

Luncheon was, as always, a joyful time. Hannah leaned back, the smell of delicious spinach soup reaching her nose as she watched the children eat, quite daintily, with their own little silver set of cutlery. Most, if not all, noble families they knew of would have sent the children to the nursery to eat, but they decided to have them eat with their parents. Patricia loved having the children there and Hannah was sure it could only be good for all of them. She watched lovingly as Alexander spooned hot soup into his mouth and then let out a small yell, and Rachel stared at him in incredulity and confusion.

"It's hot," Maxwell informed him gently. "Take from the edge."

Patricia chatted with them while they ate, telling them about the local news. She was visited regularly by the local nobility, and she was their main source of information, since neither of them paid much mind to the doings of their neighbors.

"And Lady Larenmont came past for a ride. Little Gerard can walk now, I understand."

Hannah smiled to herself. Lady Larenmont had recently been Lady Laurentia. She had settled down with the ill-reputed duke, and seemed quite happy. She was glad for her. The cruel words she'd poured into Hannah's ears had done no harm, and the only thing she wished from Lady Larenmont was that she kept her

183

distance. She did.

They sat and talked about the local news, and Maxwell discussed his plans for the horse-farm, and then the children were yelling for dessert, which was trifle, and summarily falling asleep at the table after consuming it.

"We'll take them up to the nursery," Maxwell said softly. Patricia chuckled.

"Yes. They need a rest. I'll walk with them about the grounds later."

"Thank you, Mama," Maxwell replied appreciatively. Hannah nodded, smiling her thanks. Patricia was a wonderful help, spending at least an hour a day with the little ones. Betty, who had decided to stay with Hannah, and Mrs. Hall both helped too, along with their nanny, but Patricia was a source of real gentleness and wisdom for the children, and she appreciated that above all.

They carried the children upstairs, settling them into their beds in the nursery. Their nanny, Mrs. Crakehurst, looked up from her sewing, smiling as Hannah and Maxwell settled the children down and tiptoed out once more.

"We'll let them rest for two hours," Maxwell told Mrs. Crakehurst softly.

She nodded. "If they wake up, I'll keep them occupied in here, my lord."

"Thank you," Hannah said gratefully. She tiptoed out with Maxwell and they went up to the drawing room together.

"So," Maxwell said softly as they sat down at the big table. "You think he'll arrive in two days' time?" His tone was casual, but Hannah, who knew him, could see the brightness in his gaze. She nodded.

"I was informed so, yes," she replied. She leaned back, her own heart filling with excitement. Gavin had helped her, and she had been able to organize a birthday gift for Maxwell that she knew he would love. She'd had to tell him, at least the general idea, but the excitement grew every day and she gazed at the window, wondering what the weather would be like on the day they both waited for.

"Good. Good," Maxwell said with a nod. "I'll be sure to be here. Mr. Halley can wait with the confounded accounts." He grinned, his brow crinkled with a frown despite the happy expression. Mr. Halley was their solicitor from London and he traveled down three or four times a year to discuss taxes and incomes with Maxwell. Hannah smiled fondly at him. She knew he hated the duty. He was good at finances and managing the estate, but it was distasteful to him, and she understood that. They would both much rather have as much time as possible to discuss the horse farm.

"Yes. We will need to have a day set aside for that."

Maxwell smiled and took her hand. "You know, you are the dearest person I have ever met. I hope you know that."

Hannah felt her heart twist with so much tenderness it was almost painful. "I don't know that I can be the dearest. That would be you, my sweet."

Maxwell grinned and lifted her hand, pressing his lips to it gently. Hannah felt her pulse race, as it always did when he touched her. She breathed in deeply, trying to find calm.

His eyes met hers and she gazed back, and it was difficult to resist the urge to cover him with kisses. She glanced at the clock.

"We have two hours," Maxwell reminded her playfully.

"Yes, we do."

Her heart thudding in her chest, she stood and they exited the drawing room, heading up to their sleeping quarters.

Extended Epilogue

Two hours later, almost exactly, they woke and dressed hastily. Hannah summoned Betty to arrange her hair and they went down to the drawing room for a cup of tea before the children awoke. The butler brought up the tea-trolley, walking first to Hannah's place by the low table.

"A letter, my lady. Would you care to read it now?"

"Please. Yes," Hannah replied swiftly, taking it from him and gazing at the seal. As she had expected, it was from Mother.

Maxwell glanced over at her lovingly and Hannah slid her finger under the seal, opening it. She let her gaze dart across the page, reading the neat, flowing handwriting swiftly.

My dear daughter, she read. I write to you in better health than I have experienced for many months. I was gratified by our visit and the sight of my dear grandchildren cheered me mightily. Should you need any extra assistance, I can recommend a servant I heard of recently—Lady Epstone said she is a most excellent nanny.

Hannah looked up from the page, a smile tugging her mouth. Her mother had changed in some respects, becoming more respectful and kinder towards Hannah and Maxwell, but in some ways, she was just the same. Social climbing came naturally to her, and the urge to drop names, it seemed, was also very much still there.

She read on.

Rachel and Alexander are most dear to my heart, and I trust that I may call on you again on my return from Brighton in the summer. Edward and Philipa have refurbished the house there and we travel there often to take the beneficent air and water. I find my nerves are quite recovered and I thank you for your agreement that I might visit the little ones. They have quite restored my spirits.

Hannah felt her heart fill with warmth. If anyone could reach into her mother and find the vestiges of a heart and love there, it would be the two little children. They were irresistible, and it seemed they had reminded her mother of what was truly important, more than she or Edward ever could.

Please send greetings to his lordship and to my beloved grandchildren. I enclose herewith the details of our journey, so that you might plan for my visit. Yours sincerely, your mother.

Hannah folded the letter and set it aside. She felt unsure, as she always did, when receiving correspondence from her mother. Her cruelty had harmed her greatly, and it was hard to trust her, but gradually, with time, the trust was building, and she felt it was possible to include her in the little one's lives, if only gradually.

After the confrontation with Maxwell, Mother had suffered a depression, or so Edward had written to inform her some months later. Only because of that had she agreed to write to her, and with time, it seemed, Mother's nerves had improved. Her social climbing ways had become less obsessive, tempered by her own bout of infirmity. Perhaps, Hannah hoped, she would come to realize what really mattered in this world. Status and wealth were certainly not what mattered.

"What did she say?" Maxwell asked gently.

"She'll visit again in summer," Hannah said, taking a breath. Maxwell smiled.

"We have three months to organise it. It'll go wonderfully, I am quite sure of it."

Hannah took his hand, feeling love and gratitude fill her heart. Maxwell was always so calm, so supportive.

They sat in the silence of the drawing room, their love like a blanket around them, sharing warmth and care between them both.

Two days later, as Hannah had been informed, the gift arrived.

"Papa! Papa! Can we come too?" Alexander demanded loudly as Maxwell shrugged on his riding-coat.

"You're going in the cart, with Mrs. Hall," Maxwell told him gently. "You'll come up and see him as soon as he's settled. I promise," he added, patting the little child's head gently.

"Soon?" Rachel asked hopefully.

"Yes. As soon as possible," Maxwell promised.

Hannah kissed the children, thanked Mrs. Hall, and hurried outdoors to the stables, running with Maxwell, both of them laughing with excitement.

They mounted up swiftly and rode as fast as they sensibly

could to the horse-farm.

"He's here," Gavin informed them as they rode up. "I'm just getting him rubbed down now. We'll let him out to run in a moment. He needs all the fresh grass he can get."

"I'm certain." Hannah felt her heart twist with care.

She felt Maxwell's fingers tighten on her hand and they stood at the fence, both barely breathing, as they waited for the stable door to be thrown back.

"He's here," Hannah whispered.

A red foreleg appeared, followed by a fine, graceful head and then, before she realized it, a beautiful Arab stallion was prancing into the paddock, tossing his head and snorting a challenge to whatever dared to be in his vicinity. Hannah drew a breath, her eyes misty.

"He's beautiful," she whispered.

Maxwell chuckled. "He is," he agreed. "Very."

He was also misty-eyed and Hannah watched with delight as the Arab horse slowly explored the field. He saw them and blinked, stopping in his tracks. Maxwell held up a hand.

"Ven aca," he said softly. "Ven aca."

Hannah smiled to herself. She knew Maxwell had learned to speak Spanish while he was living there, and most of the time he spoke it with the horses. She never stopped appreciating the beauty of it. He was calling the stallion, telling him to come over.

The horse heard him and looked almost puzzled. Hannah felt herself stop breathing as he stepped forward slowly, first one hoof and then another, approaching gradually as though uncertain. He reached Maxwell's hand and stopped.

"Shh, beauty," Maxwell whispered. "Hush, there. I won't hurt you."

The horse snorted and then, slowly, sniffed Maxwell's hand. Hannah stared at them, heart full of love for the beauty of it all.

The stallion snorted shyly and stepped back and Maxwell let his hand fall to his side. They would try again in a moment, Hannah knew. The first trust was establishing itself.

Hannah glanced at Maxwell, seeing his gaze full of care and appreciation as he watched the beautiful horse exploring his paddock. She felt her heart fill with love for him. He was a good man, a kind one, and she respected and loved him with every fiber of her soul.

Maxwell smiled at her.

"Thank you, Hannah," he said softly. "He is the best gift I ever had."

Hannah smiled warmly. She had asked for a portion of her dowry to be given to her, and with it she'd purchased the stallion, with Gavin's help. It had not been easy to keep it a secret.

"He's the best gift for you," Hannah murmured.

He chuckled. "And for us," he added. "You're riding him too, I hope you know."

Hannah laughed, joy sparkling bright in her heart at the thought of it. "I'll certainly attempt to."

Maxwell grinned. "I know you. You'll manage very well."

She smiled. They leaned on the rail together and watched the horse for a while, until the sound of yells of joy behind them let them know the cart had arrived. They took the children to see the horse, and then they all rode home again.

"Thank you," Maxwell murmured again as they sat in the drawing room together. "That was a beautiful morning."

"Thank you, Maxwell," Hannah replied gently. "Thank you for loving horses as I do, for sharing your love of them with me."

"That wasn't hard," Maxwell said with a chuckle. "I couldn't very well stop you loving horses, could I?"

"No," Hannah agreed.

They both chuckled. Maxwell took her hand and held it, looping his fingers caringly through hers. "You have beautiful hands," he said, kissing the back of it gently. "I always thought so. You can see you ride—they're strong hands."

Hannah laughed. "Yours, too," she replied, raising a brow at him. He laughed.

"I suppose."

She sat beside him, staring out of the window at the treetops, her heart full of love and contentment. Their life was a joy to them both, circling around the horses, the little ones and the estate, with Patricia and their dear friends close by. She gazed up at Maxwell, heart full of love and warmth.

"I'm so happy," she whispered.

"I am too," Maxwell agreed softly. "I love you so much, my dearest Hannah. So very much."

Her heart twisted, her throat tight with the intensity of it. "I love you too, Maxwell," she whispered. "I love you too."
They kissed.

The End

Made in the USA
Coppell, TX
30 June 2024

34104378R00105